THROUGH
the
SURFACE

THROUGH
the
SURFACE

Above the Rain Collective
2022

Above the Rain Collective
abovetheraincollective@gmail.com
North Georgia, USA

Contributing Editor:

J.A. Sexton

Publisher's note:

ISBN: 978-1-7377970-3-6

julietrose.author@gmail.com
authorjulietrose.com

Cover graphics and interior formatting by J.A. Sexton
Above the Rain logo artwork by Bee Freitag, text by Jack Freitag

To fifteen-year-old me, who thought it was a good idea to read horror novels in a cabin in the woods on an island in Maine.

You awakened the beast...

PROLOGUE

*H*e stared at the picture of his family as the boat jerked and swayed on the ocean. He'd checked the lobster cages and didn't even find enough to feed his own family. Year by year, the hauls had been less, not like when he and his own father came out when he was a kid. Sometimes the cages were so heavy and full then, it was a struggle to get them to the surface. Now, he was lucky if there were a few in each one. The ocean had changed, the world had changed. His family came to the island generations ago and successfully lived off lobster and crab sales. The demand was still there, the creatures were not. He touched his wife's face in the picture. She'd been the love of his life. They'd met when he visited family in Vermont as a teen, and she was more than happy to move to the island after school. They began a family right after, knowing they were starting the perfect life together. It'd been good then. Their boy Ledger was born soon after they married. Six years later, their daughter Duffey came along.

The all-American family.

Life on the island was tough. Being off the coast of Maine, the summers were busy with tourists, and the island shut down to a sleepy few hundred during the winter. The families who stayed year-round were close and relied on each other. The only way on or off the island was by boat. The newer generations didn't want to stay, though, and he couldn't blame them. Life as a fisherman was hard and now a struggle to keep families fed. Little by little, the population was aging. Ledger was fourteen now; he doubted there'd be much for the boy to take over as a business by the time he was an adult.

The fisherman kissed the picture and sighed. He was holding them here, holding them down, when there was a whole world off the island. He slipped the picture into his vest pocket and wiped the tears off of his face, staring back at the coastline. The only home he'd ever known. He'd made sacrifices to stay, things he couldn't undo. Things he wasn't proud of. He could never leave and if he stayed, he'd take them all down. He placed the barrel of the pistol in his mouth, said a small prayer, and squeezed the trigger. Seagulls startled overhead and the boat continued its rhythmic sway with the waves as the fisherman slumped forward into a pool of his own blood.

~

Two months later, in a small town in the mountains of Georgia, a woman sat biting her nails at her sister's kitchen table. She and her thirteen-year-old daughter had made it there the day before and she told her sister everything. About the abuse, the threats. About how Iris had told her that Daddy had forced himself onto her. How she'd begged him to stop and that it hurt, but he told her it was his right as her father.

When the woman heard that, she and Iris ran. The only place she had nearby to go. Her sister's. Her sister was afraid for them, and her own young daughter, but couldn't turn them away. They were just waiting for the sheriff to come around that morning. When they heard the car pull in, she sighed in relief. They could turn him in and stop the nightmare once and for all. Iris would be safe. However, it wasn't the sheriff whose car she'd heard.

A minute later as her sister ran into the kitchen covered in blood, she knew she'd made a terrible mistake. Her sister collapsed and barely got out the word, *"run"* before taking her last breath. The woman jumped out of her chair to escape, but he caught her by the door and stabbed her repeatedly. The man she let into her life, the father of her child. His eyes were set, firm, and determined. She prayed Iris and her cousin Lina had heard and made it to safety.

She was wrong.

The girls heard the screams and ran into the woods, however, having just woken up were still barefoot and he caught up to them. He got to Iris first, grabbing her by the hair, and spun her around. He drove the knife into her chest with a look of satisfaction, revenge for her speaking out. Her head fell back and she gurgled blood as he threw her body down. His own child. He caught Lina and she begged for her life. He didn't respond and slit her throat. She crumpled into a lifeless heap and he nodded satisfied as he wiped the warm blood onto his pants.

He stared around for a moment, then sighed. It was over. He'd won. He headed back to his car and climbed in, pleased with his handiwork. He headed down the road, bopping his head to a song on the radio, and felt nothing. No, not nothing. Power. He snapped his fingers to the beat of the song, then tossed the knife out into the woods about thirty miles down the road. He'd make it home before dark and feign grief when he heard the news about his precious wife and daughter being murdered on a visit to her sister's.

Who could do such a thing?

What he didn't bank on, is right about the time the knife hit a tree and skittered under some leaves, Iris opened her eyes and coughed out blood. Barely alive and her body screaming in pain, she began the slow crawl out of the woods just in time for the sheriff to pull into the driveway.

CHAPTER ONE

*T*he anchor was caught on something and he leaned over the side of the boat to pull it in. The giggles of the drunk women behind him grated on his nerves, so he used that energy to free the anchor and drag it up. As he turned around, one of the women dramatically winked at him out of her husband's sight, and he smiled politely back. She took this as approval and reached out to grab his behind. He deftly sidestepped her and headed to the front of the boat, hoping to avoid the inebriated woman's roving hands. The last passenger climbed on board and shed his scuba gear.

Good. They could get back to shore before dinner time and Ledger could make it home in time to eat with his mother. He made his way to the standing shelter over the steering wheel and fired the engine up. The sooner he got the plastered guests back to shore, the less likely one of them would pitch overboard. Not that they didn't deserve it as irresponsible as they were acting.

"Why the rush?" a very slurred voice said in his ear as she ran her finger down his arm. It came out more like *why za ush* and Ledger had to stop himself from laughing straight in her face.

It wasn't a glamorous life but when the boat was given to him after his father's death, he knew he certainly didn't want to be a fisherman. He'd docked the boat for a year and once he turned sixteen, he began taking passengers out. Mostly tourists on fishing trips and the occasional scuba divers. Sometimes hauling things to the island from the mainland. The ferry ran multiple times a day, but it was always crowded and outside of groceries and packages from day trips, there was no room for anything sizable. The ferry was smaller than his fishing boat, really just a glorified passenger boat.

The lady, not getting the attention she was hoping for, staggered back to her friends and plopped down, eyeing him rudely. It happened a lot. Women came on to him and he'd no interest in getting into a fight with a disgruntled husband. He kept his head down and kept an eye on the boat. Sure, when he first got it, he snuck out with friends and they would find a small island or cove to drop anchor and party. Quickly he realized the gas didn't pay for itself and his mother didn't need anything else to worry about.

It'd been fifteen years since his father was discovered drifting out to sea, birds picking at his dead body. Ledger grew up fast. Since the age of sixteen, he'd been the main supporter of his family. His father's death being ruled a suicide prevented any insurance money from coming to his mother, and the money the other families raised for them went fast with the funeral arrangements. His mother worked the front desk at the four-story hotel where the ferry dropped off, however, nothing paid very much on the island.

He eased the boat up to the dock and helped the passengers off. One of the men slipped him a hundred-dollar bill, nodding toward the stumbling woman. "Thanks, man. They insisted on coming out today with us and we couldn't say no."

Ledger took the money and slipped it into his bag. "No worries. They were fine. I just made them keep their life vests on the whole time."

"Smart man," the guy replied and caught his wife right before she pitched off the dock.

Ledger waited until they left, then cracked a beer as he cleaned up after them. Someone had vomited between the benches and tried to cover it with a towel. He mopped down the boat and hauled the trash out. He looked at his docket and saw he had a pickup from the mainland in the morning. A woman named Iris and her belongings. Looked like she was moving into the old Crowley Lodge on the channel. No one had lived there in decades and from the sound of her name, he pictured a blue-haired, old lady. Great, more old people on the island. That's almost all there was anymore nowadays. He shook his head and closed the docket.

He made it home and smelled fishcakes cooking. He dropped his bag outside the door, slipping off his shoes. Their house wasn't fancy but they tried to keep anything they might pick up on the outside out. Picturing the bright pink vomit he'd just cleaned up, he could understand why. He stepped into the kitchen and gave his mother a hug from behind.

"Wasn't sure if I'd beat you home or not," he said, then washed his hands.

"They cut me early. Slow today. How was your day?" his mother replied and flipped the fish.

"Scuba divers and their drunk wives. Guy slipped me an extra hundred, though."

"Oh! That's good. Grab some plates and put them at the table, this is almost ready." His mother turned off the stove and chopped a quick salad. She still had on her white button-down blouse and black slacks required by the hotel and slipped off the apron she'd been wearing to avoid getting splattered with oil. Her blond hair, streaked with gray, was pinned up off her face and she flashed her green eyes at Ledger. "Can you see if Duff is around?"

Ledger set the plates at the table and went off in search of his sibling Duffey. He rounded the corner, almost running into Duff in the hallway. "Dinner."

"Coming," Duff replied.

Ledger reached out and gave Duff a little playful shove. "Come on then."

Duffey grinned, ducking under Ledger's outstretched arm, then headed for the kitchen. Ledger followed and watched his little sibling disappear through the door. Duff had been born a girl but at around fifteen came to their mother and expressed they weren't sure they identified with being a girl. They cut their hair short and changed the way they dressed, which caused some issues at school. Eventually, they switched to a homeschool program. The island was still isolated, small, and mainly conservative. While the families supported each other, there were some things that were just unfamiliar. Ledger expected Duff to leave after graduation but their family was close and they stuck around after, taking the ferry into the mainland a few days a week for college. Duff wasn't sure they identified as a boy either, so neither Ledger nor his mother pushed the issue.

After dinner, Duffey and Ledger cleaned up and put the food away, insisting their mother get off her feet. Ledger brought her a glass of wine and sat with her on the porch. She watched him and put her hand on his arm.

"Not that I don't love having you here, but is this what you want to do forever?" she asked softly.

He turned his light brown eyes on her and shrugged. "I can't say forever, but it's where I want to be now. See where Duff ends up. I don't want to leave you here all alone."

"Where would you go if you could?"

"Not sure. Sometimes I think about getting on the boat and just going down the coast. But this is my home."

"Ledge, I don't want you staying here for me. You remind me so much of your father. While he loved being here, it drove him insane over time."

"Mom, he loved being here... being poor drove him out of his mind. Worrying all of the time about making ends meet."

"It's only gotten worse."

"Yes and no. For the fishing industry, it has, but anything tourist-based has picked up. I'm booked pretty solid right now and summer hasn't even come yet. Don't worry about me."

"One day you're going to want a family of your own. All the young people here leave right after graduation and your window is closing," his mother reasoned.

Ledger laughed. "First, I'm only twenty-nine, so the window is more than open. Second, I'm not looking for anyone right now. The tourist women and summer girls keep me plenty busy."

"Are you sleeping with them?" his mother asked, surprised.

"Mom, not a conversation I want to have with my mother. I'm not hooking up left and right, but every now and then I do spend time with someone. Can we please drop it now?"

She took a sip of her wine and bobbed her head, not saying anything else. His parents had married young and had him almost immediately, so she was only fifty. She looked younger. Ledger had no desire to be in a serious relationship or have children anytime soon. His father was only six years older than he was now when he ended it all. It was an age Ledger felt he needed to pass before even considering what having a family meant.

Duffey headed out, waving their painted black fingernails at them as they headed down the road. Ledger's mother waved back and sighed.

"I worry about Duff. Sometimes I think it would be better if they'd just move to the mainland where they could find other people like them, and I wouldn't worry so much they weren't coming home because they were beaten up and left in a ditch."

"That can happen anywhere, Mom. Even on the mainland. Duff is on a tough path. One that most people can't understand and some won't accept. They're taking precautions, staying in groups, avoiding certain areas."

"Still." Her voice was tired and small. Ledger reached out and squeezed his mother's hand. She'd lost too much and was always waiting for the other shoe to drop. She squeezed his hand back and stood up. "I'm going to turn in, watch tv in my room. Early morning at the hotel tomorrow."

"Alright, love you, Mom."

She kissed him and went inside.

Ledger looked at the time. It was seven. He knew his mother was depressed and coping the only way she knew how. His father had been her everything. He remembered as a teen hearing her cry night after night, cursing his father for being so selfish. Sometimes he still did. If his father was still around, his mother would be happier, maybe Duff would be less cynical. If his father was still around, maybe Ledger would have someone to talk to.

He watched his mother fade into the darkness of the house and sat by himself on the porch rocking. Year by year, more of the people he knew moved away or died and he wondered if he'd end up like his mother. Alone on an island, going to bed with the tv as it showed a world he'd never experienced.

He waited up until he heard Duff come home and only then allowed himself to go to sleep. It was after midnight and he heard Duff slip into their room. He was glad they still had their lifelong best friend, Kelsey. The kids these days, even being isolated on an island, seemed to have a more open-minded view of the world. Duff would be okay. He was proud they knew who they were and weren't afraid to express it. He rolled over and let sleep come over him, hoping the nightmares wouldn't come.

By the morning, his mother and Duff were already gone, and he shuffled around the house getting ready for his pick up. There was an old dock by the Lodge he hoped was still in decent shape to unload on. If the lady was old, he'd end up dragging all of her stuff up the hill from the dock to the Lodge by himself. The pay was good, so he set his mind to it and packed his bag. The weather was clear when he pulled the boat out of the marina and he played with the idea of going the other direction, away from shore and to freedom, but guided the boat toward the mainland. He was too responsible for that and shoved his wavy, dark blond hair out of his face, letting the sea spray hit his face as he put the engine into full speed. He passed the ferry on its way back to the island and waved at Leo, the ferry operator. Leo had been the operator for as long as he could remember. Some things on the island didn't change. It was a comfort in some ways and a trap in others.

It was a twenty-minute trip and he eased the boat up to the dock on the other side, scanning for an old woman. Not seeing one, he cut the engine and tied the boat off, then headed up the dock. He almost didn't see her because she wasn't what he was expecting and she didn't take up much space. He wondered if he'd been stood up when he heard a voice speak to him.

"Hello, are you Ledger? The fishing boat that was chartered?"

Ledger spun around to see a young woman about his age, sitting on a stack of bags and he cocked his head. Did the woman have a granddaughter with her? He'd been told it was only one passenger and about twenty boxes and bags. He glanced around, then nodded. "I am. Who are you?"

The woman stood up and brushed off her skirt. She was only about five-foot-four and had her long, chestnut hair tied at her neck. She wasn't mousy, but she was easy to miss. He'd passed her and not even noticed her sitting there. Her eyes were a pale blue and she wore no makeup. She looked like she could be fourteen or twenty-five. She had a small pair of glasses perched about mid-nose and smiled genuinely at him, which changed her whole face. All of a sudden, she was captivating. She picked up a couple of her bags and tipped her head at him.

"I'm Iris."

CHAPTER TWO

*T*he rest of her belongings were still in the parking lot and they took multiple trips hauling them to the boat. She was obviously coming to stay. Ledger watched her from his side-eye and tried to unravel what her story was. Young people never moved *to* the island. Not to mention something about her was just off. Like she was there but almost on a different level. A different plane of existence. However, she was still there, sweating and dragging boxes across the dock with him. He couldn't put his finger on it, but he was intrigued by her presence. He almost felt if he reached out, his hand would pass right through her. She accidentally brushed his arm as she was climbing on the boat, sending electricity through him. So, she was physically there.

Once the boxes and bags were loaded, Ledger kicked the engine up and backed the boat away from the dock, careful not to clip the edge. Iris was sitting at the back staring out over the ocean, her face unreadable. He skirted around the island to the channel side. It was still big enough for a large ship to pass through, but a person could stand on one shore and see the other. A world away, yet not.

As he made his way through the channel between the island and the mainland to the Crowley dock, he admired this side of the island. It wasn't one he saw often and still held the wild ruggedness of an undiscovered land. All of the tourists stayed on the other end with the big hotel, restaurant, store, and shops. He seemed to remember the Crowley Lodge had been a place for the elite, a step above the regular tourists or island folk. It even had an inground pool and tennis courts at one point, but those had likely deteriorated over time. As he came closer, he could see the dock was still in decent enough shape to pull up to unload and slid up next to it. Even though it'd been years since anyone had lived or stayed there, someone was clearly paying to keep the repairs up.

The Lodge sat on the hill overlooking the channel, and the only way from the dock was a winding path through juniper and blueberry bushes. There was an old, overgrown road to the beach, but they'd have to take the bags and boxes along the beach from the dock to get it, so the path up seemed the fastest way. He tied the boat off, making sure it was secure and they began unloading everything onto the dock first. He went into the hull of the boat to see if he'd anything which might make hauling the belongings up a little easier. He found an old, flat, rolling dolly and some rope. He made quick work of loading boxes on the dolly and tying them securely. He made a loop to put around his waist and began the steep, slow climb up the trail. Iris followed behind carrying bags, pushing the contraption Ledger was dragging when it got stuck on roots or rocks.

It took the better part of the afternoon before they had everything up to the Lodge and stacked out front. Outside of small talk, they didn't say much, saving their energy for the work. Ledger was impressed by Iris's ability to keep moving, considering she couldn't weigh much. Once the last load was brought up, Iris dug around until she found a cooler.

"Can I offer you lunch, or I guess dinner? I have some sandwiches, fruit salad, and drinks," she offered and opened the cooler.

Knowing they still had to move everything inside, Ledger was grateful for the break and even more grateful for food. He nodded and sat down on one of the sturdiest boxes. Iris handed him a soda and sandwich, then sat down on the ground to eat. He peered around the outside of the Lodge which was both beautiful and kind of creepy.

"You're moving here all alone?" he inquired.

Iris swallowed her bite of food and glanced around at the Lodge. "I am. It's been in my family for a couple of generations and when my grandmother passed recently she left it to me."

"Isn't it sort of big and weird to live in all alone? I heard it has like five cabins and six inside rooms," Ledger said and took a gulp of soda. Even sitting outside gave him the heebie-jeebies. "Like The Shining."

Iris laughed, a delicate melodic sound, then shrugged. "My plan is to get it going again. Open it up to tourists. I think it's kind of quaint."

Ledger couldn't see it and watched her for a moment. "That's a lot to take on, don't you think? All by yourself. Won't you get spooked out here by yourself?"

"I don't spook easily. Besides, I guess there's been a caretaker all these years. Checking on things, doing repairs. A guy they call Bertie?"

"Oh, Bertie! Yeah, I know him well. He takes care of a lot of the summer homes," Ledger replied. Bertie was a character for sure but did good work.

"The what?"

"Summer homes. People who only come and stay for the summer. We call them Summer People."

"Naturally," Iris replied dryly and finished her sandwich. "You want to go inside with me and check things out? My arms are already tired and I'm not in a rush to carry everything in quite yet."

Ledger stood up and stretched. "Sure. I've never been inside there. No one has been a guest here for as long as I can remember. I think there was an old lady who lived here when I was a little kid, but I don't think the place was still in use for guests."

"There was and it wasn't. They stopped using it for guests in the early eighties when my great-great-aunt got too old to keep up with things. She lived her days out here and when she passed it was closed up and hasn't been used since. My grandmother was too busy raising kids to think about it and my mother..." her voice trailed off, then she shrugged. "Anyway, my grandmother told me about it when I was a teen and regaled me with stories about the guests who used to come. She seemed wary of the types of people who came here. The rich and entitled, she said."

She fished a key out of her pocket and went to a small porch between two long dining rooms. One screened in with optional shutters, the other glassed in. Each ran the length of the side of the Lodge they were on. She slid the key and jiggled the handle to force the door open. Ledger followed behind, feeling like he was following a child as he towered over her. The door led to the main room of the Lodge which was two stories high and ran the full length of the building.

On the right, was a stone fireplace that went to the ceiling. To the left, was more seating and a few inside tables and chairs. The middle was left open he assumed for dancing as there was a piano against the wall. Each side had a large driftwood light fixture with so many small lights it was impossible to count. The floors were wooden and while worn, had a sheen to them of decades of foot traffic. Above one side of the Lodge, was an upstairs loft and six doors leading off it to bedrooms. Under the loft on the bottom, was a door that led to bathrooms and a galley-style commercial kitchen. Large windows were set high above the porches so the upstairs rooms could see out from the upper hallway. Wood bookcases flanked the fireplaces and ran to the ceiling. A rolling ladder was pushed to one side and was the only way to access the upper books. It was intimate, yet grand. Ledger whistled and nodded.

"Wow, this place is amazing. No wonder you wanted to come out here."

Iris eyed him and headed up the narrow stairs to the loft. She opened each room to air them out and shoved the sticky windows up. A cool breeze came through and blew the curtains. Each room had a full-sized bed, pair of easy chairs with a table in between, a closet, and a dresser. The decor was very turn-of-the-century and Ledger guessed it hadn't been updated in some time, if ever. The last bedroom would be Iris's, she told him, and already he was dreading what she'd need to bring up that narrow flight of stairs. She opened the door and peered around.

"Don't worry, just a couple of bags and my bedding. Maybe a picture or two. And some knick-knacks," she said, reading his mind.

This room had double windows, being at the end and she opened them, a cross breeze quickly making the room seem fresher. Originally her great-great-aunt had lived in a small house outside of the Lodge, but over the years raccoons had taken up in it and it'd been torn down. They made their way back down and started dragging the boxes and bags in. Sheets covered all of the furniture, making the room seem almost ghostly and Ledger helped take them off, not being able to shake the feeling they weren't alone. Iris didn't seem to mind and folded the sheets as they were removed. Once the sheets were off, Ledger wasn't any more comforted as the furniture looked like it belonged in a haunted house. He shook his head.

"This place needs to be brought into this century," he murmured.

Iris peered around and cocked her head. "Oh, I don't know. Kinda has the castle vibe."

"Or the murder your family vibe," Ledger joked.

Iris turned pale and flinched. Ledger realized he might have scared her by that and mentally kicked himself. After all, she was a young woman out here all alone. He reached out and touched her arm.

"Sorry, that was stupid to say. I was just joking. Everyone on the island is nice and looks out for each other. I know Bertie will be by to check on you."

Iris stared at him, her mouth set in a line. "It's fine. I'll make this place my own and honestly, I don't mind being alone. Thank you for your help."

Ledger got the feeling she was asking him to leave and nodded. "If you need anything else, I'm around. Out on the boat most days, but I have a little truck and can get you around until you have transportation."

"I'm good. Bertie left a bike in the shed and it has a basket. I only need to get enough groceries for myself, so that should do. Plus, I brought in an initial supply. I can take the ferry in for anything I need, and I'll have deliveries scheduled."

Ledger felt like he'd offended her and his cheeks got hot. "Hey. I'm sorry if I did something to make you upset. It's just that there aren't too many young people left on the island and I was kidding around. My mother, sibling and I live about half a mile away if you need anything. You have my number."

Iris smiled, again changing the landscape of her face and her eyes twinkled. "Thanks, Ledger. I need to unpack and am pretty beat. I have your number and I think you have mine. Maybe our paths will cross, it being such a small island."

"They will, it's inevitable. Alright, well I'll leave you to it. Call me for anything."

He walked to the front door and glanced around one more time. There was no way in hell he'd stay in this place alone. Iris had already opened a box and was taking personal items out, looking for places to put them. She waved her hand at him and placed a crystal bird on the mantle. Maybe she could bring some light to the place. Ledger headed down the trail to his boat and paused to look back up. The Lodge was foreboding but it also was built to appreciate nature with its large glass windows and natural elements. He climbed on the boat and felt relief when he heard the engine fire up. He pulled away from the dock and didn't look back. He wished her the best in opening it back up to tourists but wondered if people of this day and age would want to stay in a place that felt like it was stuck in the past century, maybe even had ghosts of previous tenants.

Summer was fast approaching and Ledger put Iris and the Lodge to the back of his mind. He was hauling tourists out to sea six days a week for various activities and on his day off he ran errands and slept. The island came alive and everywhere he went were people upon people. He heard wind about the new lodge on the channel and wondered if Iris had started taking in guests. He ran into Bertie in the grocery store one day and bent his ear about it. Bertie nodded.

"Ayup. She's only using the inside as the cabins need some work, but she's staying full. Hired a cook, too. She's doing the rest. That little thing is a firecracker. Every time I go out there, she's doing something. Planting flowers, washing sheets, fixing things here and there. I knew her grandma, she used to come out as a kid. Up until she married that fella and had them two little girls. I don't think she came back after that but we exchanged Christmas cards. She told me when she took Iris in. Damn shame what happened. They were all glad that girl survived."

Ledger had no clue what Bertie was talking about and wondered if he'd gotten his stories crossed. Bertie sometimes did that. Bertie had to be in his eighties by now and sometimes went off rambling about one thing or another. Ledger listened, even so, waiting politely for a break in the conversation before taking his leave.

"Thanks, Bertie, next time you go out, tell Iris I said hello."

Bertie eyed him, then nodded. "Sure will. Iris. Such a pretty name and she's a lovely girl. Hard to believe he did that to her."

Ledger paused. "Did what to her? Who?"

Bertie shook his head and waved his hand in the air. "Maybe I should stop running my mouth. Not trying to start gossip, you know."

"Bertie," Ledger replied firmly. He couldn't open that door and then walk away.

"Yup." Bertie leaned in close, the smell of stale cigarettes on his breath. "You keep this to yourself, you hear?"

Ledger nodded and acted like he was locking his mouth shut with his hand. Bertie sighed, resigned.

"Her father. He butchered her family when she was just a girl. Left her for dead. She dragged her body out of the woods by her fingernails."

Ledger felt the hair stand up on the back of his neck and took an involuntary step back. For some reason, the image in his head made him less sympathetic to Iris and absolutely terrified of her. Instead of a little girl coming out of the woods, what he envisioned was a horrific creature... dragging itself from the depths of hell.

CHAPTER THREE

*I*t wasn't hard to avoid running across Iris throughout the summer, as Ledger spent most of his time on the ocean. The money was good even though the days were long. People had changed. When he was a kid, the demand was more of what they could have on the island. Fine dining, tours, the best places to stay, and to learn about the history and secrets of the place they were staying. Now, it seemed they just wanted to take pictures of themselves with their phones and didn't care about the true experience. Time and again he was asked to shuttle them around to photographic spots, then after they posed and took pictures to move on to the next. The funniest was the group who dressed to the nines and asked to be taken to some of the smaller islands. When he explained there were no docks and they'd have to swim to get to any of the islands they were aghast and pouted the whole way back.

One evening after a long day, Ledger was sitting on the boat at the marina, drinking a beer before heading home when a familiar figure appeared at the front of the boat. He squinted at her and his stomach turned. She was beautiful with her long brown hair loose, in a pair of rather short white shorts and a pink tank top. Yet something about her made him uneasy.

She shifted from one foot to the other and placed her hand above her sky-blue eyes as she watched him. She bit her bottom lip before she spoke.

"Ledger, right? You helped me transport my stuff to the Crowley Lodge?"

As if he could forget her. "Yup. One and the same. What are you doing all the way down here?" Ledger replied, attempting to sound casual.

"Looking for you. I tried calling but didn't leave a message. I figured I'd just find you."

"That right? What can I do you for?"

"I was wondering if I could charter you to pick up a large amount of lumber from the mainland? They can get it to the dock, but from there it needs to be hand loaded and brought over."

Ledger laughed, despite his unease earlier. "You like making me sweat, don't you?"

Iris blushed. "Yeah, sorry. Some of the cabins have rotten floorboards, so before I can use them for guests I need to replace the boards."

"I think that can be arranged. When is the lumber coming in?"

"I waited to talk to you first before ordering since it is such a large amount, but they said once the order is placed it would be the next day. So, how about tomorrow if you can swing it then?"

Ledger pulled out his docket and saw he had the afternoon free after taking some fishermen out in the morning. "Looks like I'm free in the afternoon. Say two?"

"That works! I can make you dinner this time if you'd like."

The idea made Ledger uncomfortable. "Just you and me? I mean, unloading?"

Iris furrowed her brow and thought. "I could see if Bertie could help. I have a few guests but don't want to ask them. You have anyone?"

Ledger shook his head. "Not really. As I said, there aren't too many of us younger people left here. I doubt Bertie will be much help hauling. Save him for putting the floors in. Sounds just like the two of us again. Should be fun."

Iris watched him, trying to read if he was joking or not. Ledger grinned and took a sip of his beer. She visibly relaxed and smiled back. He couldn't help but find her attractive. He stared out to the ocean and brushed it off. As soon as he'd think about her in that way, her face would contort in his mind and he'd see something much darker. She grew awkward at his silence and cleared her throat.

"Okay, well, I'll see you at two? Should I come here or wait at my dock?"

"Come here. We can leave from the marina, which will be quicker, then drop the lumber at your dock."

"Thanks, Ledger. See you tomorrow."

He watched her walk to her bike and climb on. She glanced back at him as she pedaled away, her face showing she was unsure about his demeanor. He knew he was being cold toward her, but the alternative to get too close wasn't something he was willing to take on. He was drawn to her and wanted to run screaming at the same time. Keep it business and leave it at that. Which was a damn shame, he thought to himself, watching her golden, lean legs peddle away. She was hands down the prettiest woman to set foot on the island. Sure the summer girls and tourists came in with all their glitz, made up to perfection, but something about Iris was different. Without trying, she held the ease of beauty. Almost like a siren from mythology. Ledger reminded himself those had lured sailors to their deaths.

The next day, Iris showed up fifteen minutes early in a large sun hat, blouse tied off at her waist, and pale blue shorts which matched her eyes. Her hair was in two braids and she looked like she stepped out of a magazine spread for a country picnic. Ledger was checking the engine when she came to the boat side.

"Permission to come aboard?" she joked, and he turned to meet her eyes. Damn. This was going to be tough.

He nodded and shut the cover for the engine. She climbed on and sat down next to the driver's seat. She swung her feet back and forth and waited for Ledger to start the boat. He came in next to her and got the engine going. He smiled at her, feeling a desire run through him. Nothing scary this time. She was just a girl, a woman.

A really alluring woman.

They eased out of the marina and when he picked up speed she giggled. It made him laugh and as the salty wind blew over them, he felt the knot in his stomach relax. He didn't know why he was getting so spooked by her. They made small talk about the island and by the time they hit the mainland, Ledger was enjoying his time with her.

The pallet of wood boards was daunting and Ledger hoped it would all fit on the boat. It took over an hour to load it all and both were drenched in sweat by the time they were done. And that was the easy part. On the ride back they were quiet, tired, and dreading getting the wood up the hill. They moved slowly through the channel and parked at the Lodge dock. Somehow the hill looked ever higher and steeper. Ledger sighed, tying the boat off.

"No time like the present."

Iris nodded and began handing him boards. They stacked everything on the dock and then, like before, tied it off to the dolly to move it up. Ledger pulled and Iris pushed. By the time the last board was up the hill Ledger lay in the grass with every muscle aching. He glanced around, impressed by what she'd done. Paths were lined with flowers and suncatchers hung in windows, creating rainbows inside and out. The outside had a fresh coat of stain and seemed more modern.

"Hey, let me get you a beer and whip up something for dinner. Feel free to roam around if you'd like. Check out my handy-work," Iris said and ducked inside. She came back out a minute later with an ice-cold beer.

"Thanks, I'll wander. Looks like you've done a lot with the place."

"I have! Trying to bring it into this century, as you once said," Iris replied with a twinkle in her eyes.

Ledger cracked the beer and slipped the cap into his pocket. He wandered around the back of the Lodge to where the old tennis courts and pool were. The tennis courts were revived through weeding and repainting the lines. New nets were up and lights had been strung above for use at night. The pool had been cleaned out of the junk thrown in it over the years, and a wood deck made from reclaimed wood pieces was placed at the deep end with chairs and tables. Lights were strung over those and potted plants covered the shallow end. The only way in was through the deep end ladder and once in, it created an intimate sanctuary.

"My idea. I felt using a pool was outdated and too much in repairs. So, I made a space where people could go to have drinks or listen to music and feel like they were in their own world," Iris said from behind him.

Ledger turned around and smiled. "It's brilliant."

"I forgot to ask if you have any allergies or foods you don't like?"

Ledger shook his head. "Nope. I'm pretty open."

"Great! I was going to make gnocchi with a pesto sauce. Garlic bread and sauteed asparagus?"

"Oh wow, you don't need to go all out. I was fine with sandwiches."

Iris laughed and shook her head. "No, not for the work you did today. If you want to go down into the pool while you wait, or come inside you'd prefer."

Ledger was intrigued by the pool space and gestured his head toward it. "I'll check that out."

Iris nodded. "I'll bring our food there. You'll have to grab it once I get there 'cause I don't think I can make it down the ladder with two plates. Still working on a pulley system to lower things into the space."

"You got it," Ledger replied and made his way to the ladder. He held his beer in one hand and used his other to hold on. That was the tricky part. Once he was down, he felt like the world outside had been shut out. A mural was painted around the inner walls of trees and birds, giving the feeling of being deep in the forest. He sat on one of the teak wood chairs and looked up at the lights. He didn't know he'd dozed off until he heard Iris calling him from above.

"Ledger, you down there? Come grab these plates."

He sat up and shook off the fog. He felt like he'd been drugged but must've been so exhausted from hauling the wood, his body couldn't help itself. He stood up and came to the bottom of the ladder. He reached up and grabbed a plate Iris was handing down to him and set it on the table. After he grabbed the second one, she scaled down the ladder with a bag strapped around her.

"Drinks," she said and pulled it over her head. She took out silverware, beer, and water.

They ate in silence. Afterward, Ledger leaned back in his chair and gazed at her. "That was super nice. Thank you."

"Of course. It's nice to cook for someone other than myself. Usually, I just go to the kitchen after the guests have eaten and pick at the leftovers."

"You have a lot of guests?"

"For sure. Since I officially opened back up, the rooms have been full. I could make more if I was willing to sleep on the couch and rent my room out," Iris joked.

"Then they'd just want your couch," Ledger replied. Tourists were never satisfied.

"Probably! But it's good. Covering all of the expenses and able to make repairs."

"Not to be nosy, but even when no one was here it looks like repairs were being done? How was that financially possible?"

"My grandmother, on my mother's side, had money. Or guess, now I have money. Since I'm the sole survivor, it passed to me along with the Lodge."

"If you have money, why did you reopen the Lodge? Seems like a lot of unnecessary work?"

"That's fair. Purpose, I guess. I wanted to do something to honor my grandma for taking me in. To keep her family's legacy going. Something like that?"

Ledger nodded. It was like his father's boat. He didn't want to be a fisherman but felt like he should keep the boat in use, keep it running. It was a way to honor his father's memory, his legacy.

"I get that. My boat was my father's."

"Oh, was he a fisherman?"

"Lobster and crab man."

"Did he retire?" Iris asked curiously.

"Of sorts. Not to get dark, but he committed suicide on the boat. When I was fourteen. I guess things weren't going well and he felt like he was hurting our family," Ledger choked out.

"Oh, I'm sorry! I can't imagine that was easy on you. Losing your father so young. My mother died when I was thirteen, as well."

Ledger didn't want to say he'd heard but nodded and met her eyes. "I'm sorry. I guess we were both dealing with a lot of shit at around the same age."

"We were. Your mother? You live with her now?"

"I do. I felt obligated to be there for her. No, not obligated. I *want* to be there for her. She's been so good to me and Duffey, my younger sibling. Losing my dad broke her heart, but she was there for us even so. She made sure we were taken care of, loved, and supported. We never went without and she sacrificed a lot."

"It sounds like your parents were in love and cared for one other."

"They did but my father was wrong to leave like that. He hurt her by doing that. He left her to pick up all of the pieces alone with two children. It was selfish."

"Still," Iris whispered, "maybe he did it out of love. My father murdered my mother. He murdered my aunt and cousin Lina, too."

Ledger touched her hand. "That's horrible, Iris. I'm so sorry."

"He murdered me also. But I came back from the dead."

CHAPTER FOUR

L edger involuntarily drew back and stared at Iris. He felt
his eye twitching and tried to will it to stop. She looked
up from her plate and met his eyes, hers unblinking and
bottomless. Unapologetic. Ledger shook his head and opened his
mouth to speak, but the words got stuck in his throat. What did
she mean she came back from the dead? How? His brain buzzed
around questions, not being able to land on one to ask. Iris sat
back and watched him, apparently used to people being
speechless when she told them.

She cleared her throat and leaned slightly forward, her
words factual but emotionless. "He stabbed me in the chest,
puncturing my lung, lacerating my liver, and I choked on my
own blood. He discarded my body and went on to kill Lina. I
died. I remember. There was no bright light or hallways. But
there were demons and apparitions. Things trying to grab me
and drag me under. I don't think it's like they say, that when you
die you go one place or the other automatically. I think there's a

battle for your soul and you're a part of it. You need to prove yourself. I could feel good and bad trying to get to me, almost tearing me apart. I was confused and lost, fighting to get back to save Lina. I could still see the woods where we were, my body lying off to one side. I saw him grab her and cut her throat. I desperately tried to get to her but couldn't. She passed me on the other side, just like the wind. She was caught by the good apparitions. I don't know why the demons didn't fight so hard for her. Maybe there was something in me they wanted more. She was younger than me by two years."

Iris paused there. Ledger resisted the urge to get up and climb out of the pool away from her. Away from the horrible story she was telling. What did she mean by demons? Like creatures with horns and gnashing teeth? She couldn't seriously believe that. She was bonkers. Her father trying to kill her must have driven her over the edge. He should never have doubted the feeling he got when he was told about what happened to her by Bertie. He should've kept his guard up. He pushed his chair back but felt a strange weight on him.

Iris sighed. "I know. It all sounds crazy, like something supernatural. I suppose it is. I don't know how I got back, but suddenly I was thrust back into my body and vomited up the blood in my airway. I was lying in the woods and Lina was yards away from me, dead. I didn't know if he was coming back, but I needed to get to help. I was hurting so much and felt like my body was dead weight. I dragged myself little by little out of the woods, hoping my mother or aunt had survived. When I got to the edge of the woods, the sheriff pulled in, coming to take a statement from my mother about the abuse and rape."

"Rape?" Ledger barely got out of his tightening throat.

"My father raped me, which is why my mother took me and ran. That's why he came after us and killed us."

"But you survived."

"Barely and he didn't know I did. The sheriff radioed for an ambulance and begged me to stay with him. I kept slipping in and out, back to the darkness, back to the light. Eventually, the ambulance came and took me to the hospital. I was in surgery for six hours and they said I died a couple of times on the table, but they brought me back. They induced a coma and when I awoke finally, my father had been arrested from what I told the sheriff. I don't remember saying anything, but they said I told him, *Daddy did this to us. I died but we came back."*

"We? I thought you were the only survivor," Ledger asked, confused.

"I was. As I said, I don't remember saying anything but it's on the record. I was probably just out of it and not making sense. I don't really know, to be honest. A lot of what happened is a blur."

"Jesus."

Iris ran her finger through the juice left on her plate and nodded. "Anyway, a lot to share when we hardly know each other. You were going to hear about it, anyway. This shit follows me everywhere I go. I went to live with my grandma, and she ended up schooling me at home because the kids at school treated me like crap. Called me a freak. Said I was a zombie and would run screaming when I came down the hall. They thought it was some grand joke. Meanwhile, I was grieving and suffering from PTSD."

"Kids are shit. When my father killed himself, kids around here said all kinds of cruel things about him, about me.

They knew our family, yet the draw to be mean about it was stronger."

"So, in that way we are alike," Iris replied, sounding somewhat defeated. "The club no one wants to be in."

Ledger laughed softly at that. It was the truth. He met her eyes. "Now, you're here. An island off the coast of Maine where the average age of residents I think is now late fifties, early sixties. Why?"

"For the Lodge."

"No, but really? This is where people come to die. To live out their years. It used to not be like this. It was a thriving fishing town and people had a lot of children. I grew up riding my bike with gangs of kids and we pretty much ran this place. They all moved on to bigger and better things. There is nothing left here. Few jobs, no relationship prospects, nothing to do. I should've left, too."

"Okay, to turn it on you. Why didn't you leave?" Iris asked.

Ledger ran his hand through his shaggy hair and shook his head. "I have no fucking idea. I like to think for my mom, but she has pushed me to go for years. My sibling Duff probably will after college."

"You say sibling. Brother or sister?"

"Both, neither. Not sure. Duff was born a girl but doesn't identify as one. Nor do they identify as a boy."

"Between two worlds. I can relate to that," Iris replied.

"On some levels, I can as well. I never feel like I'm here or there," Ledger agreed.

They collected the dishes and climbed out of the pool. It was getting late and Ledger paused to look up at the stars. Iris went inside and put the dishes in the sink. He followed behind, then paused at the door, still reluctant to step foot back in the Lodge.

"I guess I better go. It's dark and I need to get the boat to the marina before they lock the gates." A reasonable excuse to leave.

"You can sleep on the couch if you'd like and leave in the morning. The rooms are full and the cabins unsafe," Iris offered.

"Nah, I like to sleep in my own bed. Besides, my mom might worry." Ledger knew his mother wasn't necessarily expecting him, but it sounded kinder than the truth.

"Fair enough. You want a quick tour to see what I've done with the place?"

"Sure," Ledger agreed out of politeness. He didn't want to go back in there but didn't want to hurt Iris's feelings, either.

They headed through the door from the kitchen into the great room and Ledger peered around. She'd replaced the old, heavy curtains with airy, white ones and added modern pillows to the dense couches and chairs. Light-colored rugs covered much of the floors and fun abstract art had been placed around the room, giving it a more up-to-date feel. Ledger stared around, impressed by her influence on the space.

"Wow, much better. You have a nice touch," Ledger said honestly. He could see people wanting to stay there now.

Iris grinned. "Thank you. Trust me, I found it stuffy and cold before. I want people to feel like they are staying at an upscale bed and breakfast, not an old person's study. Show a bit of modern flair."

"You nailed it for sure. Alright, well, I'd better get going. Thank you for dinner, Iris."

"Thank you for hauling all that wood." Iris smiled brightly and pushed her hair off her shoulder, exposing a slender, pale neck.

Ledger couldn't resolve this petite, open girl with the one who crawled out of the woods after her own father tried to take her life. She seemed weightless, easygoing. He still carried so much weight from losing his father, he didn't know how she didn't go mad. He waved, walking out the front door and down the hill. The moon was bright and full. With the changes in the Lodge and it being full of people, it seemed less daunting. He paused on the dock and gazed back up at it. He saw Iris in the window watching him leave... for a second he thought he saw someone standing with her. Behind her. He blinked, clearing his eyes. She raised her hand and he waved back. No, she was alone. He boarded the boat and fired the engine, letting it throttle for a moment before pulling away from the dock.

The marina was still when he drove in and he cut the engine, considering just sleeping on the boat that night. The draw of his bed swayed him, so he walked to his truck. His mind went back to her story and he shuddered. Had she truly seen demons and apparitions? Things trying to drag her under? Even the thought made him hold his breath, and he was relieved to slide into the truck seat and shut the door. Maybe they were delusions from loss of blood and injury. Her mind reeling from being attacked by her father. It was likely. Trauma could cause all kinds of odd responses. Hallucinations of different sorts. That had to be it.

He thought about his own father and how kind and loving he'd been. Overly sensitive, honestly. He'd get emotional on holidays and it wasn't rare for the kids to see him cry. Ledger was grateful to have a father who raised him with such nurturing and openness. Sometimes he felt the same way, like things in the world were too heavy at times. When they'd told Ledger his father had died, he didn't believe them. He'd convinced himself his father had just taken the boat and gone out to sea, that he needed time to work things out. Then Ledger saw the boat and he knew. His father would never leave the boat behind. It'd been cleaned and stored by the time he saw it, but Ledger always wondered what they'd discovered when they found the boat. The boat had drifted overnight and a search had gone out when his father hadn't come home. He was discovered miles from shore just floating away. He'd left his body long before they'd found it.

Ledger drove out of the parking lot and headed for home. The island was quiet at night, all the businesses closed by eight. Except for the hotel bar. That stayed open until two in the morning, but the locals tended to stay away unless they were looking for a quick hookup. His mother had left a light on for him and a soft glow was coming from Duff's room. Home. The one place he felt like himself. He crept in and shut the door softly behind him. His mother was already in bed. The floorboards creaked under his weight and he shifted to the side to silence them. Duff stuck their head out of their room at the noise and raised their hand.

"Hey, Ledge."

"Hey, Duff."

Duff's door closed and Ledger went to his room. He lay in bed and replayed the events of the day. He enjoyed spending time with Iris. She wasn't overly chatty but made easy conversation. She was very open about herself, almost oddly so. He'd wanted to lean in and hug her before he left but was afraid it would seem forward. He pictured her light blue eyes and how they were so set when she spoke about what happened to her. She didn't peer away when being honest. She met his eyes and watched. It was disconcerting, yet comforting at the same time. Maybe she did die and come back; in doing so didn't feel things like other people. She seemed very sure of herself and what she was doing. Ledger felt like he was just floating along, wherever the tide took him. He yawned and closed his eyes, letting sleep sedate him.

He woke up and was on the boat. But it was daylight and he could see the island in the distance. He was holding a picture in his hands. His wife and two children. Grief surrounded him, making it hard to breathe. He'd failed them. He should've never asked her to move to the island. They should've stayed in Vermont near her family. He touched her face in the picture. Her blond hair and green eyes. He'd fallen for her the moment he saw her. He stared at his son smiling back from the paper. He was no fisherman. He was bright and funny. If he stayed on the island, his life would be over. But he'd stay and become a fisherman like his father and his father's father before. It was almost predetermined. An almost impossible cycle to break. They should've stayed in Vermont.

His eyes shifted over to his daughter. She was so fierce and determined. There was something different about her, but he couldn't put his finger on it. Her eyes seemed to bore out of the photo, she was going places. She had a confidence he'd never seen in one so young. His son looked just like him with light brown eyes and blond hair, his daughter her own person. Green eyes like her mother but almost black hair which neither of them had. They traced it back to previous generations but she always looked like she'd been placed into the wrong family in pictures. He slipped the picture into his vest pocket and looked back to the island. This place had too many secrets. He was the only thing keeping them all there and it would end them. He drew out the pistol and placed it in his mouth.

Ledger sat up in bed stifling a scream and shook uncontrollably. He glanced around his room and tried to get his heart under control. The dream was too real and he couldn't stop feeling he was still in it. He'd never had a dream like that and realized talking to Iris had brought up things he didn't typically deal with. He didn't talk about his father's suicide and the dream had put him dead in the center of it. He'd been his father and felt the things his father had been feeling that day. Or what Ledger's brain told him was so. There was no way for him to know what his father had gone through.

He laid back and wondered if he should cut off ties with Iris. Talking to her had dug up old feelings, terrible memories he'd packed away in his mind. After the initial grieving for his father, Ledger had learned to keep things under wraps. To stay in the present moment and not let the past overcome him. Telling Iris about his father had unpacked at least some of that. But he liked her and he couldn't blame her for his past. He let his mind drift to her and thought about seeing her in the window when he was leaving.

Her waving and smiling at him from the window when he was on the dock, getting ready to leave. His chest tightened in fear as he remembered.

There had definitely been someone, or *something,* standing behind her.

CHAPTER FIVE

*T*he end of the summer came with much cooler nights and the tourist season starting to wrap. While they still had tourists through the holidays, the bulk of them were gone after Labor Day. Ledger made his money in hauling supplies between the mainland and the island and had a few offers on the boat, which he turned down. The offers were good, but he couldn't bear the thought of selling the boat. It was part of him. Duff moved to the mainland to attend school full-time which brought a sadness to the home. Duff brought spirit to the house, just by being themselves. With just Ledger and his mother rolling around the halls, it seemed like a weight neither could shake. Ledger was happy for Duff, who'd shine in a world where they were accepted for who they were. Duff came back some weekends but Ledger could see the gap growing. Old life and new life. Part of him was envious because he felt he was stuck in the old life. Like his father.

Not able to bring the two together.

Iris called him one day and asked if he was looking for any work. He was but didn't want her to know that. His mother's hours had been cut at the hotel and making ends meet was becoming harder. He secured work a few times a week but since it was for other locals, he only asked what they could pay, which often wasn't much. They were beginning to cut necessities and couldn't trim too much more. He skirted around the question.

"Oh, you know, keeping busy with the boat. Whatcha got going on?" he asked, his voice light and non-committal.

"Bertie was supposed to help me with the cabin floors and walls, but he had a medical issue which laid him up. I wanted to try to get them done before it got too cold," Iris explained. "I pay well and am kind of in a bind. You'd be doing me a huge favor."

That was his in. He would be doing her a favor. "Sure, I can shift something around and come out tomorrow if that works. I have a haul later in the afternoon but can come over in the morning."

"That would be great!" Her voice was relieved and excited. "I'm usually up by six."

"Six? In the morning? How about eight?"

She laughed lightly. "Eight it is."

Ledger hung up the phone and took a deep breath. The money would come at the right time. They had bills due and were going to have to choose between groceries or paying those. He was grateful Duff had a full scholarship and was one less mouth to feed. He scrounged the kitchen and decided to use up some vegetables that were on their last days. At least in summer, vegetables were abundant from neighbors' gardens, and Ledger traded services for those. He made a stew and had it ready for when his mother came home. Her eyes were tired and she smiled at him with gratitude as she set her apron and bag on the table.

"Thank you. Otherwise, I think I would've ended up eating saltines and gone to bed."

"You would've been out of luck, I ate those for lunch," Ledger teased.

"Ledge, we may need to talk about selling this place. With Duff gone, I should consider moving to something smaller. It's getting to be too much."

"This is our home, Mom. Besides, what would you get? There is nothing on the island."

"I didn't mean the island, hon."

Ledger set his spoon down and stared at her. If they sold the house and she moved to the mainland, it would all be over. Five generations of his family had succeeded on the island. "So, what? You'd live in some shithole apartment and work some shit job there?"

"Ledger, it's how life is. Things come to an end. Times have changed. Honestly, do you think you could raise children here? There are less than a quarter of the children than were here when you were in school. If it weren't for the tourists, this place would dry up. Duff won't be back. They'll finish school and find a life somewhere else. I say good for them! There is no life left here. You can't get blood from a stone."

"Mom, this is our history. I don't know if I'll ever have children but if I did, I'd want them to know this. To see what we've built."

"It's a grand idea, but the reality is life here isn't sustainable. Maybe in the summer, but then we struggle all winter. I'm getting too old for this. When I moved here as a young woman, this island thrived year-round. The community, the children. Now we're getting older and the kids, they just leave. You wouldn't want to do that to your children. I regret doing it to you and Duff."

"If they built the damn bridge they've talked about for years, things would change," Ledger reasoned.

The town had talked about having a bridge put in at the narrowest part of the channel, connecting the island with the mainland, but that'd been in talks since he was a kid. They were never going to do it. It was expensive and would make the island part of the mainland, which those old-school residents wanted no part of. They liked their isolation.

His mother placed her hand over his. "If they do that, how would it be different from me just moving to the mainland?"

Ledger felt heat rise in his cheeks and shrugged. "I just don't want it all to go away, Mom. I want something left to hold on to."

"I know, sweetie. Sometimes we need to let go of those dreams."

Ledger got up and washed the dishes, trying to ignore the pain in his heart. His father had felt it and couldn't go on. They might make it through the winter and another couple of summers, but his mother was right. Eventually, it would suck them under. He and his mother were the last of the family left on the island. Anyone else had either moved or passed on. He didn't see children in his future and asking his mother to stay for his own fantasy was unfair. He turned to say something to her, but her chair was empty and he heard the tv going in her room. He caught his reflection in the windowpane and paused. He looked like his father.

He didn't want to end up like him.

The next morning, he woke up early and checked on his mother. She was sleeping peacefully, so he wrote her a note and slipped out. He passed a small group of children heading for the ferry. There had been schools on the island at one point but with the drop in enrollments, they were closed and the remaining children were shuttled to the mainland for school. He drove toward the Lodge and wondered if one day the only purpose of the island would be rich people's getaways. Iris was pulling weeds when he eased in. She wiped her brow and gave a small wave.

"I wasn't sure if you were coming by water or by road."

"Road. Gas for the boat can get super expensive if I'm not making money on using it," Ledger explained.

Iris nodded and stood up, brushing dirt off of her knees. "Coffee?"

"Sure, that sounds great."

She went in and came out with two cups, spirals of steam rising from each. She handed him one of the mugs. "Wasn't sure how you took it?"

"Black is fine," Ledger replied and took a sip. "So, what's on the docket for today?"

"We got flooring in two of the cabins but still need to do the other three. Just yanking up rotten boards and replacing them. Then sanding and treating."

"You still have guests?" Ledger asked, peering around the area.

"A few. Three of the rooms are full."

"Nice. Alright, ready when you are."

Iris laughed, her eyes sparkling. "Okay, then. Forget the small talk. Let's do it."

Ledger dropped his head, realizing he sounded impatient. "Sorry, a lifetime of conditioning. I was raised to work hard and fast."

"Fair enough. I'd prefer getting it done earlier anyhow, so I can go to the beach later."

"To swim?"

"Swim, collect rocks, just be."

Ledger couldn't think of the last time he just went to the beach. Not since he was in his early twenties and still had friends to hang out with. Life just got in the way, even though the island was surrounded by beaches. "Sounds like fun. When I was a kid we went to the beach every day until it got too cold. Now, not so much."

"You should come."

"I have a haul this afternoon but maybe sometime," Ledger answered, trying to not sound like he was brushing her off.

Iris eyed him, reading the moment. Recognizing he wasn't attempting to get out of anything, she bobbed her head. "I go almost every day. It's my moment of peace."

"I can see that. Okay, where do you want me to start?"

"You can take the far cabin. I'll take the one next to it. It's tight for us to work in the same one, so we can double-team it," Iris replied and pointed out the farthest cabins in the woods.

The walk to the cabin was cool and Ledger felt like he was in a fairytale where children got eaten by some terrible creature or another. Yet he also felt safe, covered by the trees. Lumber had been stacked by each cabin and he brought his own tools. The cabins were musty and dark but he could tell at one point they'd been very nice. Each one had a set of bunk beds and a full bed, built-in cabinets, and drawers. Shelves for books and knickknacks. Everything hand built with attention to detail. Only the finest for their guests.

The cabins had been built before plumbing, so there had been a shared outhouse, which was long since dilapidated. Now people would just go into the bathrooms on one side of the Lodge with full showers, toilets, and sinks. Each cabin had a small porch and windows on each side. Ledger pushed the windows open to air the cabin out and began ripping up rotten floorboards. He could hear Iris working in the cabin over from his. They weren't side-by-side but if he looked out the window, he could see hers through the woods.

His phone buzzed and he looked at it. Damn. His afternoon haul canceled on him. He seriously needed that money. He sat back on his heels and wiped the sweat off his face with a rag. Iris would pay him when the job was done but maybe she could front him until it was. They had almost no food in the house. He just didn't know how to ask her without sounding pathetic. He stood up and stretched his back, seeing her talking to a guest by the house. She was laughing, ignoring the man's arm intentionally brushing hers. She pointed down the path and toward the dock. Ledger could see the guests used the dock to sit out on, by the addition of a table and lounge chairs. He didn't know why, but it irritated him. He stepped out and waited for her to finish. She caught his eyes and smiled, taking her leave from the guest. The man watched her walk away and gave Ledger a snide smile. After all, he was just the help.

"Hey. Did you need me?" Iris asked as she walked up.

"Take a look and see if I got up the boards you wanted out."

She peered in and nodded. "Yeah, I trust you. Was that all you needed?"

Ledger felt his ears get hot, knowing it wasn't. He bobbed his head. "Yeah."

She frowned, resting her hand on his arm. "Ledger, you can talk to me. Was there something else?"

He stared at a knot in the wood on the wall, almost wishing he could just disappear into it. He cleared his throat. "I was just wondering if you'd be able to pay me some for the work I did today? My afternoon job got canceled. I was counting on that money."

Iris stared at him, then half laughed. "Of course. I was planning on it, anyway. I prefer to pay as we go, so I don't lose track. Sorry, I should've been clearer and not made you bring it up. That was stupid of me."

Ledger nodded, not meeting her eyes. "No worries. It's just that my mother's hours at the hotel got cut. It's kind of all on me now."

"I'm sorry. Yeah, I just had to cut my chef to one meal a day and I cover the others. It's tough when the season ends. Since your afternoon job got canceled, do you want to go with me to the beach after lunch? I need to get the guests set but after that, I'd love to walk down with you."

Ledger glanced at her and the earnestness in her face made him smile. "Sure thing. I think I have shorts in my truck I can change into."

"Yes! This will be fun. Hang out with someone my age for once!"

Ledger chuckled, he knew the feeling. He got back to work laying the new boards. Once he was done, he saw Iris had gone in to prep lunch for the guests. He moved over to the cabin she'd been working on and was impressed to see she'd pulled up all of the rotten boards. He laid the new boards and stepped out to drink water. Iris came out wearing a bathing suit and shorts carrying a picnic basket. Ledger tried not to stare. She waved at him.

"I packed us food and drinks. Get changed, so we can go down."

Ledger changed in the cabin, coming out in only shorts and a pair of sneakers. Iris stared at him and raised her eyebrows but said nothing. He felt exposed and wondered if he needed to put on a shirt. She led the way down the path, stopping to pick blueberries as she went. He watched her hair swing back and forth with her movement, resisting the urge to reach out and touch it. She turned her head to look at a bird flying by. Her nose was slightly upturned and her cheeks kissed by the sun. She seemed so pure and innocent, he felt a need to protect her, then laughed to himself. She was probably the strongest person he'd ever met. She glanced back at him and smiled, cocking her head slightly. He shrugged, then smiled back.

The path led to an old road that cut through the woods to the beach. It was picturesque and slightly eerie. As they got close to the beach, she quickly put her hand on his chest to stop him and pointed to the ground. It was covered in snails and perpetually wet.

"Their shells are super fragile. If you step on them, it will crush them. Their shells are like eggshells," she explained in a firm whisper as if not to disturb them. "We need to climb up on the bank and walk up there the rest of the way."

Ledger nodded and followed her, staring back at the snails. Why were they there on the road? Why were their shells so delicate? It seemed like an error of nature. A great cosmic mistake in design. He felt sorry for them but also slightly horrified at their plight.

A life of vulnerability.

CHAPTER SIX

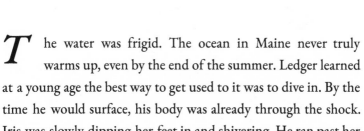

T he water was frigid. The ocean in Maine never truly warms up, even by the end of the summer. Ledger learned at a young age the best way to get used to it was to dive in. By the time he would surface, his body was already through the shock. Iris was slowly dipping her feet in and shivering. He ran past her and jumped into the ice-cold water, catching his breath in his chest. He pushed his face out of the water and shook his head, taking a deep breath. She was watching from the shore, wide-eyed and laughing.

"You just have to commit," he yelled back at her and dove under the water again. The water was dark and when he opened his eyes under, he couldn't see more than a few feet in front of him. He kicked back up and looked at her. She was now waist-deep and appearing miserable. "Just dive in!"

She watched him and took a deep breath. She closed her eyes and forced herself down under the surface. When she came up her mouth was in the shape of an *O* and her lips slightly blue.

Ledger laughed and encouraged her to move around to warm up. She started swimming and made her way out to him. As she got her blood flowing, a slight pink returned to her cheeks and she grinned.

"I grew up in the south. I am *not* used to this! It usually takes most of my time down here to get my body used to the water," she said through shallow breaths.

"You'll get used to it. We used to run and jump off docks straight into it. The first time under is shocking but you warm up quickly. The key is to keep moving and do it as fast as you can," Ledger explained.

They were both treading water and began swimming. The channel was much calmer than the ocean side. Iris dove under and came up about twenty feet from Ledger. He followed suit and they played a game of unintentional tag. She stopped and treaded water, looking at the houses on the other side.

"It's strange that the mainland is so close to over here, yet the ferry runs from the other side," she said, knitting her brows.

"The elite wanted it that way. This is all private land on both sides and they had no interest in having people shuttled in and out near their homes. Not so much on the mainland now, but this side of the island was traditionally the richest."

"Oh. So, like my family?"

"I guess. I mean, the Lodge catered to only the most hoity-toity guests, so maybe. It was like the country club of the island with its pool and tennis courts."

Iris turned and peered back at the Lodge, wrinkling her nose. "You know, my grandma told me they used to have some kind of meetings there."

"What kind of meetings?"

"I'm not for sure, but she said it was some dark arts type stuff. It's one of the reasons she didn't want anything to do with the place."

"Like Illuminati shit?" Ledger asked, snickering.

Iris chewed her lip, then nodded. "Something like that. Rich people would come out and dress up to do weird stuff. It's why she didn't come back once she had the choice. She didn't like how the place made her feel."

"So, your great-great-aunt? Was she into that kind of stuff?"

"I don't know. She never married and my grandma said she had a lot of lovers, men and women. But I don't know much else about her."

Ledger gazed at the Lodge and pictured ceremonies with rich people dressed up, performing different acts. It was too strange to imagine on their sleepy little island. He'd heard about those types of gatherings... just not on an island with less than three hundred permanent residents. His parents had never mentioned it. Then again, those things were typically kept highly secret, behind closed doors. He shuddered and watched Iris.

"And you wanted to come here and live alone. You're a strange one."

Iris laughed and started swimming back to shore. "Not the first time I've heard that about myself. Are you hungry? I packed us food."

Ledger bobbed his head and raised his brows. "I'll race you!"

"What are we, twelve?" Iris joked, then saw he wasn't kidding.

She swam after him as hard as she could, but he had the benefit of growing up on the ocean and his feet hit the shore before hers. She ran after him and made it to their spot seconds later. They grabbed towels and wrapped them around them, their teeth chattering. Iris twisted the water out of her hair, casting her pale eyes on Ledger. He wanted badly to grab her and kiss her but shook water droplets out of his hair as he plopped down on their blanket, instead. She watched him and smiled slightly as if she knew. She sat down next to him and opened the basket. She handed him food and they dug in.

"Twelve," Ledger said thoughtfully.

"What's that?"

"You asked if we were twelve. The age both of us were before our lives changed," he replied, meeting her eyes.

"Oh, yeah. I think I picked it randomly. Maybe not. Subconsciously. In all fairness, my father was abusive before then. Mostly at my mother. She always had bruises and I heard them yelling a lot."

"Why did she stay?"

"Who can answer that, right? I mean, she was the one who had the money. My grandma said that's why he pursued her. Because she came from money. After they had me, it got worse and she made sure she didn't have any more children. He yelled at me and was rough but never physically abusive. Until..." Her voice trailed off, her eyes flashing in fear.

Ledger reached out and took her hand. She let him but didn't look at him. "I'm sorry, I didn't mean for it to go there," he said quietly.

"No, it wasn't you. Honestly, I'm glad you let me talk about it. Anyone else would freak out and run. It is my reality, you know? I lived it, so whether or not it's brought up it's still in here." She tapped her head, then shrugged. "It's not like I can get away from it."

"If you need to talk about it, I'll listen. I know what it's like to not be able to say what happened to you. To feel misunderstood. I mean, it makes me angry, but I know you may need to get it out."

Iris turned her eyes on him and watched him, unblinking. "Thanks, Ledger. That means a lot. I don't ever intentionally go back there, but sometimes it just breaks through the surface."

Ledger thought about his own father and nodded. Sometimes it just surfaces. They ate in silence and made their way back to the Lodge. As they passed the snails, Ledger paused and crouched down, running his finger across one of the shells. He could feel how thin it was and it hurt his heart. He'd lived on the island all of his life and never known they were back there. He doubted the guests that stayed paid them any mind and probably walked across them, crushing their shells mindlessly. Again he wondered, why were they in this state? Were they lacking something they needed to strengthen their shells? Was it because they were here in the dark? But they could move, so why not go somewhere they would grow stronger? He was frustrated thinking about it.

"Sometimes I feel like them," Iris said, her voice low and soft. "Brittle and frail, stuck in one place. The wrong place."

Ledger nodded. He could relate. He could leave the island and have a life, however, he felt he *had* to stay. Like his father. His father could've packed them up and moved away but instead, he stayed until it took his life. Until *he* took his own life.

Ledger stood up and put his hand out to Iris, hoping she'd take it. She just might be the one person in the world who could understand him. She smiled, putting her hand in his and they walked back up to the Lodge. Ledger liked the weight of her hand in his and hoped he hadn't messed anything up. He felt like that a lot.

The guests for the Lodge were sitting on the screened-in porch. The man from before gave Ledger a haughty look even though he was sitting next to his wife. Apparently, the Lodge still attracted the same types. Those who thought they were better than the island people. Ledger eyed him and shrugged. The man turned away and said something in his wife's ear. She glanced over at Ledger, then snickered. God, he fucking hated them. Iris saw the exchange and squeezed Ledger's hand. She drew him around the side of the house and pressed herself close to him.

"Ignore them. Those people will always exist and only get true pleasure from making themselves feel better than other people. You are a genuine person, Ledger. That makes you miles above them." She reached up and brushed his hair out of his eyes, her own fastened on him.

Ledger felt the shame ease away and he nodded. He'd always be that kid who felt like he was being judged and ridiculed. Had his father not killed himself, he would've been different. Confident, popular, as he'd been before that horrible day. But that moment changed everything for him. He questioned everything about himself, even his existence. He always felt like he was one step behind the rest of the world, never able to catch up. He chewed his lip and shook his head, averting his eyes.

"My whole life here has been those people making me feel worthless."

"You aren't worthless. You know that. That man is just jealous. Jealous of your looks, your strength, your presence. Jealous of how I feel about you."

"I don't understand what you mean," Ledger replied, confused.

"Ledger, when you walk in a room, the whole air changes. You're one of those people. The ones the earth calls their own. I'm one of those people, as well. We belong less to the skin suits and more to the natural world around us. I'm glad we met."

Ledger laughed at the reference to skin suits and tipped his head. She was right, he'd always related more to the ocean and trees than other people. Except for his family. They were an island on an island. And now Iris. With her, he felt he could be himself, let his guard down. He met her eyes and smiled.

"Thanks. I'm glad we met, too."

"No problem. Now, are you going to kiss me or just stand there ignoring my advances," Iris asked, laughing but not joking.

Ledger leaned in and kissed her, the warmth of her mouth sending vibrations through him. She slid her hand around his waist and responded. His hand slid to the back of her neck and she stood on her tiptoes to get as close to him as she could. While over the years he'd hooked up with girls passing through, this was different. He wanted it to linger and wasn't hoping to just bed her. Not that he didn't want that, too, but at this moment all he wanted was to feel her lips on his and her hand pressing against his skin. He drew back and gazed at her.

Her eyes were half-closed and a smile played at the corner of her mouth. She met his eyes and slid her hand to his chest.

"You *are* coming to help tomorrow. We only have one cabin left, but I'm sure I can find other work to do," she teased, her eyes lighting up mischievously.

Ledger grinned, feeling his ears get warm, then bobbed his head. "You know it."

They pulled apart and let their fingers remain connected. One of the guests was calling her name and she rolled her eyes. She leaned up and kissed Ledger quickly on the lips, then let his hand go. He watched her disappear around the side of the Lodge and walked slowly to his truck. It all seemed so innocent, so easy. Like neither of them had been traumatized and left fighting for their place in the world. The scars they carried were invisible. On the drive home, he let his mind play their kiss over and over again. He was surprised when he drove up to the house to see the lights still on.

His mother was reading in the corner chair when he came in and met him with a smile. "There's my boy. How are you?"

"Good, Mom. Was working with Iris at the Lodge. Replacing rotten floorboards in the cabins out there, so she can rent them out."

"Oh? That's good. Is she a nice woman?"

"She is. Oh, also she paid me for today, so we can grab some groceries in the morning. I need to go back to finish the last cabin, but she thought she may have more work for me to do while she renovates the place. It will help since the hauls are dropping off. I do have a couple of tours at the end of the week though. Divers I think." He dug in his bag and handed her a wad of cash. "I have to go back in the morning, so can you go grocery shopping?"

"Of course. Wow, she paid you well. Sounds like she is good people."

Ledger blushed, cocking his head. "She is."

His mother raised her eyebrows and stared at him. "Oh? Your ears are a little pink there, Ledge. I'm guessing she is pretty to boot?"

Ledger laughed and looked away. "Mom."

"You can't hide things from me, you know that. Just be careful. People come and go from here. Don't invest your heart too much. Besides, that place, the Lodge? I've heard some dark things about it. Keep a keen eye out."

Ledger had, too, but didn't want to get into it. He shrugged and leaned down to kiss his mother on the cheek. "People around here, they like to talk. Take it with a grain of salt."

CHAPTER SEVEN

F all came in with bursts of color as the leaves changed and made the island transform into a postcard image. Iris marveled at the change since the south didn't get such a beautiful array. The leaves changed there, she explained, but nothing like the northeast; some years not much at all, depending on rainfall. She remembered years when the leaves pretty much turned brown, then fell off right after. Ledger took her to one of the smaller islands one afternoon and rowed in on a dinghy they'd towed with them. She stared up at the trees with her mouth wide open.

"It's like being part of a painting in a museum. Like we are the tiny, faceless people painted in the bottom corner of a massive painting of trees," she said, catching a leaf as it fell toward her.

"I can see that," Ledger agreed.

They dragged the boat ashore and hiked around the island, taking in the cool isolation. Iris was in jeans and an oversized beige sweater, her sneakers crunching on the fallen leaves. Ledger walked behind her, admiring how comfortable she was out there. She paused when she spied mushrooms growing and collected her favorite leaves. They'd spent almost no days apart since that day on the beach. He didn't want to admit it, but he thought he might just love her. She turned back to him and frowned.

"Who owns these islands?"

"Some are private, some are owned by Maine. The private ones typically have no trespassing signs," Ledger explained.

"Do people live on those?"

"Some. Others are just owned but empty. We used to boat out to them as teens just because we could. Throw big parties. To make a statement."

"Did you have a lot of friends?"

"Some. Honestly, after my father died a lot of kids treated me differently. I had a few close friends. The other ones who'd been through shit of some kind. I guess birds of a feather, you know?"

"I do. What about girlfriends?" Iris asked, winking.

"I mean, sometimes I went on dates but nothing serious. Girls liked me, but I think once they got to know me, and I was quiet and to myself, they moved on."

"Mmmm... they didn't care for the silent brooding type?"

"Less brooding and more leave me alone," Ledger replied, chuckling. He admitted he'd been in his own world and probably came across as self-involved back then. "I was probably a bit of an ass. What about you? Any special guys?"

Iris paused, then shook her head vehemently. "No. Men, even boys, scared me. I ended up homeschooled because it was too hard to be around people. Sometimes I'd lose my shit or space out and the kids teased me because of it. I was a total mess."

"Damn, that sucks. So, it was just you and your grandma?"

"It was until she passed away in the spring. I put her house there on the market and came here."

"Do I scare you? I'm a man... or maybe still a boy, to be honest," Ledger asked, making fun of himself.

Iris bit her lip. "No. You aren't like other men. You seem to come to things differently. More slow and thoughtful. You have this way about you."

From what it sounded like, Iris had never been in a relationship. Ever. Ledger frowned and thought about the repercussions of that. They'd kissed and held hands but he'd never pressed for more, even when she sent him signals. She was twenty-eight and had never been with a man. Well, a man had raped her when she was just a child. No wonder she hadn't been with anyone. This sent fear through Ledger. How would they ever get to that place after what she'd been through?

She reached back and took his hand. "Hey, a penny for your thoughts?"

"You don't want to know my thoughts. I was going down a dark path," Ledger replied honestly.

"Oh. You want to talk about it?"

He shook his head and sighed. "Not particularly. I was just thinking about what you went through, yet how you still find the world magical."

Iris watched him, then frowned. "I mean, not always. I have dark days, too. I just try not to dwell on it. I want to be happy, to find love. If I don't, then not only did he take my past, he'll have taken my future. I won't give him that power."

Ledger had no response and squeezed her hand as they walked along. They made it back to the beach and he got to work building a fire. She took out the food they packed and spread out a blanket by the fire he was building. Once it was raging, he sat with her and brushed the hair off her neck to kiss it. She leaned in, sighing softly. She sat back and met his eyes.

"Can I show you something?"

He cocked his head and blushed when she lifted her sweater up to show her abdomen. She ran her finger along a scar that went from the left rib cage up between her breast bone under her bra. "This is what he did to me. After he took away my trust and innocence, he wanted to remove the proof. I see it every day when I'm getting dressed. I can't get away from the reality of what I went through, but this is also a reminder I survived. That he didn't win."

Ledger nodded, not being able to take his eyes off of the scar. She had to have been sliced completely open. "What happened to him?"

Iris dropped her sweater and gave an eerie, dark look. "He was shanked in prison. He deserved it."

"He's dead?"

"Thankfully so. When my grandma told me, I was able to start sleeping again. He was gone. Straight to hell." Her voice was so hard and satisfied, Ledger almost didn't recognize her. She stared into the fire with her eyes glistening. "I hated him. I wanted him to suffer and die."

She had every right, yet it still threw Ledger off guard. She was always so calm and easy-going, this angry version of her was a side he'd never seen. This was the girl who'd had the strength to drag herself out of the woods. He reached out and rubbed her fingers.

"Hey, sorry. I didn't mean to bring it up."

"You didn't, I did. Remember?"

He watched her, she had. He still felt guilty about it, though. Her having to relive the memory of her father murdering her and her cousin. She turned to him and smiled gently.

"This is why I like you, Ledger. You feel things you don't have to. You care more than most. You're one of the sensitive ones, am I right?"

"I suppose." He didn't know. Life had made him different, he didn't know it made him more sensitive. He had no barometer for it. Iris slid closer and climbed on his lap facing him.

"You are." She kissed him deeply and he felt himself start to rise. He moved her away and shook his head, embarrassed. She looked thoroughly confused and reached out to touch his face.

"Hey, did I do something?"

"It's not that, Iris. It's just..." He glanced away and took a deep breath. "It was nothing you did. Just, um, my body responding to you."

She stared at him, then laughed. "Oh."

"Yeah. Oh."

"Maybe we should talk about things. I like you, Ledger, and would like to know you more," she replied, her voice firm.

"You do?"

"Of course I do. Just because I haven't been with anyone, doesn't mean I never want to. Are you afraid because of what happened to me?"

"Well, yeah," he replied, suddenly feeling stupid.

She slid her hand around his waist. "Me too."

He glanced at her and saw the fear in her eyes. He kissed her lightly, running his thumb across her cheek. "We don't have to."

"Eventually, we do. I want to."

"Maybe we can just, uh, you know, touch each other."

"Okay," Iris agreed. She slipped her sweater off and moved close to him. She ran her hands down his back. Ledger was too afraid to touch her and she lifted his hand to the scar. "Let's start here, point out the elephant in the room."

He traced the scar, frowning. It was raised and jagged. She pressed her hand on top of his and met his eyes. She unfastened her bra and took it off. Ledger stared at her breasts and felt like a schoolboy, unsure what to do next. She placed his hand over her warm breast and he felt the nipple get hard under his hand. He leaned in and kissed her, leaving his hand in place. They stripped down to their underwear and lay on the blanket. It was chilly and they pressed against one another for warmth. Iris let her hand drift down and feel his hardness, her eyes a mixture of curiosity and desire. She sat up and cupped him in her hands. He closed his eyes, trying not to go there, and felt her hands move gently across him. He felt himself coming to the edge and grabbed her hand.

"Wait."

She eyed him with her eyebrows raised. "Did I do something wrong?"

"No, you did something right. I'm about to uh... come."

"What do you mean?"

She couldn't be that sheltered. Even tv and books talked about it. He tried to think of how to explain to her what was going on with him. "You know... like I am about to release? Get off?"

She laughed, then nodded. "So, why did you stop me? Isn't that the point?"

"I don't know. It's just... I don't know what you're familiar with. On a guy's body."

"Let me find out," she said and put her hand back on him. Regardless if he tried to stop her, his body was committed. She moved her hands and he let go, moaning with his eyes closed.

Iris laid beside him with her hand on his stomach. Ledger put his hand over hers and smiled, opening one eye. "Was that weird?"

"Not really, kind of cool I have that power over you, to be honest," she said slyly.

He chuckled, rolling onto his side. He ran his fingers across her breasts, making her nipples erect. "Like this?"

Her eyes fluttered as she nodded. "Like that."

He leaned in and put his mouth on her breasts and she sighed heavily as her body both tensed and relaxed at the same time. She wound her fingers in his hair and closed her eyes. He let his tongue move around as she arched to meet him. He slid his hand down her belly and between her legs. All of a sudden, he felt her stiffen and push his hand away. He met her eyes and saw fear in them, then shame.

"Sorry," she blurted out and sat up quickly. She wrapped her arms around herself.

"Hey, nothing to be sorry for. We're both learning. What happened you didn't like?" Ledger whispered.

"It wasn't that I didn't like it. It's just. Ledger, I... he did that to me."

"Oh." Ledger felt stupid and dirty.

"I told him to stop and he didn't. I want you to but it just reminded me." Her words were fragmented and she'd turned bright red.

"It's okay. I won't do that again."

"No, I *want* you to do it again. I don't want the memory of *him* doing it to me. I just don't know how to move past it."

"What if you guided my hand, put it where you want it?" Ledger suggested.

Iris stared at him. She frowned as she considered it, then bit her lip. "Okay."

She laid down and Ledger rested next to her. She took his hand and placed it on her stomach. He gently stroked her with his fingers and she slid his hand a little further down. He made no moves that weren't led by her but kissed her as she guided his hand down between her legs. Her kisses became more fervent as his hand cupped her gently. He delicately moved his fingers over her and lightly explored her. She pressed his hand hard against her and lifted her hips to his hand. He made sure anything he did was soft and careful, finding himself getting hard just feeling the warmth of the folds of her skin.

She met his eyes. "Can we try? I want to. Just be gentle. Go slow."

Ledger rose and moved between her legs. He thought he was probably as scared as she was. He paused before entering her, looking to her for approval. She nodded and rested her hands against his buttocks. He entered her slowly and saw a flash of fear in her eyes.

He hated anything he was doing was causing her to be scared. "Hey, we can stop. It's just me and this is your call. I can wait for you, Iris. I love you."

Her breath was ragged but the fear faded from her face. She pressed her hand against his face. "No, I want you."

He allowed himself to go in, fully surrounded by her heat and she closed her eyes with the sensation. He moved as gently as he could but felt himself about to release and stopped for a moment.

She opened her eyes and smiled. "Keep going."

He slid gently in and out and groaned as he let go. She held him tightly inside of her and sighed. He'd been with a lot of women over the years but nothing had felt like this. The control, the desire. She ran her fingers across his lips.

"You told me you love me."

He pulled out and lay next to her. "I do."

"Not a heat of the moment thing?"

He frowned and propped himself on his elbow. "I don't think so. I thought about it when we were walking, too. Trust me, sex has never led to love for me."

"A lot of experience there?"

He felt his ears get hot. She was so blunt. "I mean, sort of. I won't lie to you. I definitely hooked up with a lot of summer girls and tourists. I'm not proud of it, but I was young."

"I'm not judging you. Just wondering. What about lately?"

Lately, he hadn't been with anyone. He was getting older and was more afraid of getting trapped in something he couldn't get out of. He laid back on the blanket and stared at the sky. "No one recently. The past couple of years I've been trying to figure out what the hell I'm doing."

Iris sat up and gazed at the fire. She slipped her sweater over her head. "I understand. I think I love you, too, Ledger."

"Think?"

"In all fairness, I was never shown what healthy love was. My father beat my mother. My grandma was alone for as long as I can remember. I don't buy into fantasies on tv. I know I like spending time with you and when something happens, you're the first person I want to tell. I knew I wanted you. To feel you inside of me. I know when you smile and the lines form around your mouth, I want to bury my face in your chest. I know I love putting my fingers in your salty, blond hair and when you turn those tea-colored eyes on me, my knees get weak. I know I could trust you with anything."

Ledger sat up next to her and smiled, touched by her words. "Wow."

"I know when you kiss me, there is no place in the world I'd rather be than with you," she said and squeezed his hand.

He wrapped his fingers around hers. No one had ever spoken to him like that. "I feel the same."

CHAPTER EIGHT

H e remembered the day like it was yesterday. He was fourteen and out in the yard, fixing the chain on his bike. His father hadn't been home when he was supposed to and his mother had called the island cop. There was only one. He could've had boat trouble, she said. The engine had been giving him trouble lately. Could they check nearby islands to see if he camped up there? He hadn't radioed, but that too was giving him trouble. There was just no money for repairs. They confirmed the boat wasn't in the marina and sent out patrols. It took a day before they found him, he'd drifted out into the ocean pretty far. The sheriff drove in and refused to make eye contact with Ledger. He knew something was up and followed the sheriff to the door, pausing by the bushes while he knocked. His mother answered and the sheriff told her something in hushed tones. She looked shocked and then set her face. She didn't bawl or fall apart. She nodded and met Ledger's eyes.

He knew then.

His dad wasn't coming home.

Ledger stared out at the ocean and shook the memory away. There was no point going over it again. It always ended the same. Snow had begun to fall and he needed to get back to the island. The pickup on the mainland was a double-door fridge and had been a beast to load. The owner was to meet him at the dock and help unload it. The hauls made decent money but he hated it. It was grunt work and not something he wanted to do the rest of his life. The work at the Lodge had been helpful but with winter coming on was becoming less and less. Even though Iris always found something.

He smiled and thought about her blue eyes. He and Iris had been inseparable and she'd pushed for him to start sleeping over, but he still felt uneasy inside the Lodge. Like they were being watched. He'd promised to have her meet his mother and Duffey and she wanted to cook for them. It was only dinner.

The place just gave him the creeps.

The owner wasn't there when he arrived and he called, cursing them as the snow came in heavier. They finally answered and said they'd send someone over. An hour later, someone finally arrived in a small pickup truck. Someone being a fifteen-year-old kid with spaghetti arms. Ledger swore he needed to stop doing the hauls and got the fridge out and onto the tiny pickup almost completely on his own. The kid waved and drove off, the fridge looking like it could flip the truck if he took a corner too hard. Ledger covered the boat with a tarp to keep the snow out and prayed his truck would have to problem starting. He shivered in the cab and turned the key. After a few unsuccessful turns, it started up, rumbling as it worked out the kinks, and he headed home.

Once he was in his warm bed, he checked his phone and saw he had a message from Iris. The last guest had left and she didn't have another one until the week before Christmas. Thanksgiving had passed, which meant she'd be alone for a few weeks. He shuddered at the thought and called her. She picked up immediately.

"Hey! I was hoping you'd call. You were out longer than I thought you'd be," she said.

"I was, too. People didn't show up until an hour after I docked. Was freezing my balls off out there."

"Well, bring them over and I can warm them up."

Ledger laughed, then sighed. "Would if I could but was having trouble with the truck. Need to see what's up in the morning with it."

"Mmmm that's too bad. I'm here naked and all alone."

"Don't tempt me, I'll end up broken down on the side of the road."

"Yeah, don't do that. Are you coming for dinner tomorrow with your family?"

"I am. Should be interesting," Ledger answered dryly.

"Why? Do you think they won't like me?"

"Hardly, my mother is thrilled to pieces I have a girlfriend. Duff will be their usually moody self, so don't take it personally."

"I won't," Iris replied. Ledger heard voices in the background and frowned.

"I thought you said the last guest checked out?" he asked.

"They did, this morning. Why?"

"Oh, I thought I heard someone talking on your end."

"Nope, just me."

Ledger felt uneasy and pressed. "You didn't hear anything?"

"Not on my end, maybe we are getting a crossed signal with another call. That used to happen when I was a kid."

He wanted to ask if it was before or after she'd been stabbed, but knew it wasn't appropriate. After all, he seemed to remember hearing people say that happened. Other calls bleeding through. He listened and only heard her breathing. He wished he could hold her but picturing her in the Lodge made his stomach flip.

"Do weird things ever happen there?" he asked, attempting to sound nonchalant and not freak her out.

"Weird how?"

"I don't know, like paranormal?"

"Not that I can think of. I mean, sometimes lights flicker and stuff, but I think it's just old wiring."

"Yeah, that happens here, too. Everything on the island is old," Ledger agreed.

"Oh, and sometimes I hear this horrible sound in the woods. Scares the shit out of me," Iris confessed.

"What kind of sound?"

"Like a woman screaming."

Ledger laughed. "Foxes. Red foxes sound like a woman screaming. I know that from growing up and camping around the island. It's pretty disconcerting."

"Ah, well that makes me feel better. I did see a fox with her babies one morning when I went walking. She hissed at me and I went the other direction."

"I can't wait to see you tomorrow, Iris."

"Me either. I missed you today. I don't think I have not seen you every day in months."

"Should we bring anything?"

"Not that I can think of."

"Okay, I'll see you then. I love you."

"I love you too, Ledger."

He hung up and turned over in bed. His mother would love Iris. Winters were hard on the island and getting them together may give them a better support system. Everything shut down or cut hours back, and by January the island hibernated until the end of March. He hated it every year. The short days, getting snowed in. One day, he was going to get on the boat and head down the coast to somewhere where everything wasn't so dependent on the weather. Maybe he could convince Iris to go with him. He breathed out heavily, it'd never happen. He'd always make an excuse to stay.

He'd die on this damn island.

The next morning, he checked out the truck and could see the alternator was going bad. He'd need to head to the mainland to replace it and didn't feel like taking the fishing boat. He headed down to the ferry on foot and got there as it was just about to pull away. He jumped over the side and sat by Leo, the ferry operator.

"Hey there, boy, haven't seen you on the ferry in eons. Everything alright with the boat?"

"Yeah, just saving the gas. This is a personal trip for me. Need to fix the truck," Ledger explained, tugging his jacket tightly around him.

"Good, good. How long are you going to be? I need to get home, so I may just wait for you."

"Running to the auto store and maybe grab a few odds and ends. An hour maybe? I need to get back for dinner at the Lodge."

"The Lodge? I don't know about that place. I've heard some things."

Leo was a good guy but a bit of a gossip. The whole island was a bit of a gossip. Ledger had not shared that Iris was his girlfriend and shrugged. "I know the owner."

"Oh, I heard it changed hands. Some pretty, young thing trying to run it. You know, back in the day a girl went missing there?"

Ledger felt the hair stand up on his arms and shook his head. "What do you mean?"

"They used to have these lavish parties up there. Rich folk. They'd bring in young women, girls really, sometimes to offer as a service."

"What kind of service?"

Leo eyed him and Ledger understood. Leo went on. "Anyway, after one of the parties, one of the young women wasn't accounted for. All the guests and the other women said they hadn't seen her. Just disappeared. They say she walks the woods screaming for help."

"Fuck, Leo, that's creepy as hell. It's just the damn foxes out there."

Leo chuckled and peered out across the water. He shook his head. "Maybe so."

They docked and Ledger bolted up into town. The story Leo told him made him jumpy, and he decided he most definitely would not share it with Iris. He grabbed an alternator, a bottle of wine, and a few items he couldn't get on the island, then headed back to the dock. The other passengers had left and a couple had boarded. Leo smiled at him.

"That was fast. You good to head back?"

"I am. You know I have dinner at the creepy Lodge," Ledger replied, grabbing a seat.

Leo laughed, nodding. "Better you than me, son. I wouldn't step foot in that place."

"Not helping, Leo."

Leo winked and eased away from the dock. Snow was falling again and Ledger had a feeling it was going to be a long heavy winter. A local was leaving the dock and offered Ledger a ride home. With the snow falling and his hands full, he gratefully accepted and they chatted about the weather on the way back. She dropped him at the top of the drive and he walked the rest of the way, enjoying the silent snowfall. The truck was in the garage and he spent the afternoon replacing the alternator. He was relieved when the truck roared to life. It was getting late; he still needed to shower and dress before heading to the Lodge.

After a shower and putting on a sweater and slacks, he checked himself in the mirror. He tried to smooth his hair back but it was just wavy enough to set itself free and curl around his face. At least he dressed nice.

He met his mother by the door with the bottle of wine and hollered for Duffey, who was listening to music in their old room. Duffey came out and glared at him.

"Chill your jets, I was finishing the song. Do I honestly need to go meet your girlfriend, anyway?"

"Please, Duff. It would mean a lot to me and to her."

Duff rolled their eyes and shrugged. "Fine. But there better be booze."

Ledger waved the bottle of wine and grinned. Duff came up alongside him and eyed him. "Just one bottle?"

"She'll have some, too. It'll be fun and I promise you'll be able to get a buzz, okay?"

"Good. So... are you pretty serious about this one?" Duff asked knowingly.

"I might be."

"Well, I've never seen you dress up for anyone. Not your usual t-shirt and shorts or jeans fare tonight. You almost look decent."

Ledger laughed. "You got me. Be nice, huh? Don't start any shit tonight."

"I'll try my best," Duff said in a way that sounded like they were lying.

"Duff!"

"Okay, if I can't say something nice, I won't say anything at all."

"Thanks."

The Lodge could've been a picture on a Christmas card with the snow falling around it if it didn't seem to hover menacingly over the landscape. Ledger knocked on the door and Iris swung it open, smiling from ear to ear. She was gorgeous in an off-the-shoulder cream and sage lace dress with her hair down. She waved them in and quickly shut the door to keep out the cold. A fire was burning in the large fireplace, giving the room a warm glow.

It also cast dark shadows on the ceilings, which appeared like a cross between people dancing and hands grabbing at things. Shuddering, Ledger averted his eyes and stared at Iris, instead.

"Welcome to the Lodge. It's nice to have you all out here. I've only been alone a day but already I'm hearing things, I think," Iris joked.

"Like what?" Ledger asked too seriously, Leo's story popping into his mind. Iris stared at him with a bemused look and laced her arm in his.

"Just the sounds a house makes when it's empty. Creaks and groans. I swore I heard a door slam earlier but I think it was just the wind. Anyway, I set dinner out on the closed-in porch. We can see the lights on the mainland from there. It's really lovely at night."

They made their way to the porch and somehow Duff already had the wine open and was pouring it. Ledger gave them a hard look and they grinned.

"Where are my manners, anyone else want a glass?" Duff asked serendipitously.

Ledger rolled his eyes. He motioned toward Duff. "Iris, this is my little ill-mannered sibling, Duffey."

"Nice to meet you, Duffey," Iris said with a twinkle in her eye.

"Likewise," Duffey replied and downed the glass of wine.

Ledger gave them a look and turned his attention to his mother. "My mother. Mom, this is Iris."

They shook hands and greeted each other politely. His mother gave him a quick look of approval, smiling. She was happy to see him with someone steady.

Iris pulled her chair out and chuckled. "Well, now that the first course of wine has been completed, shall we sit for solid food?"

Ledger busted out laughing and eyed Duffey, who was taken aback by the jab. Duffey grinned. "As long as you don't mind if I want seconds of the first course?"

Iris met Duffey's eyes and laughed. "By all means. Have at it."

Duffey looked at Ledger, shrugging with a half-smile. "I like this one."

"In all fairness, she's the only one I've dared let any of you meet," Ledger replied.

Iris took his hand under the table and rubbed his fingers. "In that case, I am honored."

CHAPTER NINE

D inner went off without a hitch and Ledger was relieved to
see his family immediately connected with Iris. The
conversation flowed and she was open about her life after she
moved in with her grandmother. His family was considerate
enough not to dig into why. She mentioned her parents were
dead and she was an only child but that was all. After dinner,
they sipped wine and stared out past the tall birch trees to the
channel below as the snow fell in delicate sheets around them.
For the first time, Ledger didn't feel uncomfortable in the Lodge
and thought maybe it'd all been in his head. The beauty of the
evening and maybe a little wine had made the Lodge seem almost
welcoming.

As evening fell, they moved in by the fire and Ledger
switched to coffee, knowing he had to drive his mother and Duff
home in the snow. Duff started playing the piano and Ledger
asked Iris if she wanted to dance. She grinned and took his hand
as they swayed to the music. Ledger eyed Duff.

"I always forget you can play."

"Forced lessons right, Mom?" Duffey joked.

"Kept you out of trouble. Well, sort of," their mother replied.

Ledger spun Iris and pulled her in close. She fit nicely with him. Duff finished the song and they drew apart, laughing. Iris went over and sat next to Duff and began playing a song. Duff's eyes lit up and they joined her in the song. Ledger took his mother's hand and led her to the floor. They started dancing to the upbeat song. As it finished, he hugged his mother tightly, kissing her cheek. He and Iris sat on the couch together and he slipped his arm over her shoulders as she leaned in against him. Part of him felt he could marry this girl and spend his life next to her. Another part of him felt he still didn't know all of her secrets.

The fire was warm and surrounded by his loved ones, Ledger wanted to hold onto the moment. Duff was buzzed and kicked their feet over the arm of the chair they were sitting in, leaning their head back to talk to Iris.

"Do you ever get freaked out here? Like being out here alone?"

"Not really. I think I'm always on guard anyway, so I jump at my own shadow as it is," Iris replied, then chuckled.

"I've heard stories about this place," Duff murmured, with an air of secrecy.

Ledger scowled at Duff and shook his head. Duff shrugged. "What? It's common knowledge. I mean, everyone knows rich people used to do shady shit up here. And that girl went missing."

"Where did you hear that?" Ledger asked, frustrated.

"Leo."

"Of course. That man can't stop running his mouth," Ledger said and squeezed Iris. "It's island tales. People here make up stories to pass the time. No truth to it."

"I like a good story. What gives?" Iris asked.

"Nothing really. They say young women were brought in to entertain some of the guests and one disappeared. The girls were young, too, mostly runaways. Easy to take advantage of." Duff waved their hand drunkenly in the air.

Iris shuddered and frowned. "Oh, that's sad. Poor girl. Do they say what they think happened to her?"

"Who's to say? I mean, who can say she ever was here or even existed? People get bored here and make a lot of shit up," Ledger replied, attempting to nip it in the bud before Iris got spooked.

"They say she walks the woods, screaming for help," Duffey added.

"Duff!" Ledger said sharply.

Duff side-eyed him. "Just saying."

"Well, don't. Iris is out here by herself."

"Sorry," Duff mumbled. "Maybe you should stay out here with her."

"Yeah, and who'll drive your drunk ass home, then?" Ledger retorted.

"Duff, Ledger, stop bickering," their mother said. "Sorry, Iris. These two are only happy when they're picking at each other."

"It's okay, kind of entertaining," Iris said and slid her hand on Ledger's thigh. "You all are always welcome to stay here."

"I appreciate the offer, but I can only sleep in my bed," Ledger's mother replied. It was true. Since his father had died, she could only sleep on his side of the bed.

"Besides, Duff may need to be close to the bathroom tonight, having drunk the lion's share of the wine tonight," Ledger added.

Duff bobbed their head and grinned. "That I did. You can thank me later."

Ledger eyed Iris, shaking his head. "I'd better get them home. Are you going to be alright tonight?"

"Of course. I know the stories and all the drama around this place. I take it with a grain of salt. I've been through worse."

Ledger pulled her close and kissed her temple. "I know you have. Still."

"Don't worry about me," Iris whispered, running her hand down Ledger's cheek. "Let me know when you are home safe."

Duff sat up and held their head. Ledger knew it was time to make an exit and get Duff into their own bed before the spewing or spins started. He jumped up and helped Duff up. His mother got on the other side and they guided Duff to the door. Iris followed them, pausing at the door. Ledger gave her a quick kiss and took his very drunk sibling to the truck, bracing them between himself and their mother on either side. Duff promptly passed out.

Once they got home, they practically carried Duff to bed and unceremoniously dropped them on the covers. Ledger grabbed a bucket and shoved it beside the bed, hoping Duff would discover it if needed. They left a lamp on and closed the door.

"Great first impression," Ledger muttered and ran his hand through his hair. Iris didn't seem to mind but he didn't plan on Duff getting plastered at dinner.

"Iris seems lovely. I feel like there are things you haven't told me?" his mother replied.

Ledger nodded. "Iris has been through a lot. Hell, honestly. But it's hers to share since it was pretty horrible. She is so strong and caring."

"You love her don't you?"

"I do."

"Like she may be the one?"

"I don't know, Mom. I don't know what that is, truth be told. I love her. I want to spend my days with her. But I feel like there is still a wall between us. Maybe what we both went through, but we're still figuring each other out. We're taking it slow."

"Just be careful. I can see your heart is on the line. Hers is, too. I can see how she looks at you. That girl loves you."

Ledger sighed. "I sure hope so. I worry about her, though."

"Then why do you leave her out there by herself? I can only assume you've already been intimate?" she asked pointedly.

"Mom!"

"It's not hard to see. You connect to each other's bodies as if you know them well. If you have, why not stay with her?"

He felt stupid for saying the place gave him the creeps. But maybe it was more than that. Maybe it was how he felt when he first heard about what had happened to her. Was he scared of her, too? No, she was Iris. His beautiful strong-willed girlfriend. His friend. But there was still part of her, he felt was hidden from view. Maybe to protect herself. He glanced at his mother, ashamed.

"Because I'm an asshole. I should go back."

"You should," she agreed.

He grabbed his keys and headed for the door. His mother was already heading to her room. He paused and looked back at her.

"Mom?"

"What, Ledge?"

"I'm sorry about Dad. I don't think I ever told you that."

"Me too, hon. But it wasn't on you to take care of me. We all lost him. We all miss him."

Ledger nodded and went out. He brushed the snow off the windshield which had fallen since he'd been inside and questioned if it was safe to make the drive back. He set his mind to it and got back in the truck. The Lodge was dark when he pulled in and he wondered if Iris had already gone to bed. He should've called first. As he walked to the door, a motion down at the dock caught his eyes and he peered down. Iris was on the dock, looking out over the channel. It appeared like she was in her nightgown and he wondered what the hell she was doing down there in the snow.

He ran down the trail and tripped right before he got to the dock, falling into the snow. He cursed and got up, brushing snow off his face and clothes. The dock was empty. He walked out and turned around, confused. She hadn't passed him on the trail. Had she skirted down to the beach and up the road, so they missed each other? He shook his head and glanced down the beach. It was empty. He turned and looked at the Lodge. A faint light was shining from one of the rooms and he headed back up the trail.

The door was locked when he got to the Lodge and he knocked. He sent her a quick message to let her know it was him, in case it freaked her out. A minute later, the door swung open and a very confused and sleepy Iris was standing there in pajamas. Pants and a shirt. Not the nightgown she'd been wearing on the dock. That had been long, with ruffles. Ledger frowned.

"I saw you on the dock and went down to meet you. When I got there, you'd already left. Did you go through the beach road?"

"What are you talking about? I didn't go to the dock," Iris replied, lost.

"I saw you down there, Iris. You were standing in your nightgown, looking over the water when I drove in," he said, pointing at the dock.

"Ledger, seriously? Even if I *had* gone to the dock, do you think I would've gone just in a nightgown? It's freezing out there. Come inside before you catch a cold."

Ledger stared at the dock and back at Iris. He *had* seen her. Her dark hair was loose on her back as she stared out over the water. It was her. "What are you playing at Iris?" he asked, irritated.

"What am *I* playing at? You are the one showing up at my door unannounced, accusing me of doing something I'd never do. I went to bed right after you left. I was reading and ready to doze off when you knocked. Look, Ledger." She was gesturing to the trail.

Ledger followed her hand and shook his head. "What?"

"Look at the trail. If I'd been down there and come back up right before you, wouldn't you see my footprints in the snow?"

Ledger peered at the ground and could see only his footprints being covered by the snow from when he went down and up. Maybe hers had already gotten covered by the snow? He rubbed his temples and groaned.

"What the fuck is going on? I swear I saw you down there. I'd bet my life on it."

"Well, please don't because I wasn't. Now, please come in out of the cold. Why are you here? Did you forget something?"

Ledger came in and Iris shut the door behind him. He took off his coat and stomped the snow off of his boots. "I was worried about you."

"Oh. Why?"

"I don't fucking know because apparently, I'm the one losing my mind here."

Iris laughed and wrapped her arms around him. "I'm fine, but I'm glad you came back. Do you want anything? Coffee?"

Ledger rested his head on the top of hers and held her tight against him. "No, I just want to be with you."

"Come on then. You can warm the other side of my bed."

They climbed up the stairs and went to her room. She had decorated it, creating a cozy, warm feel. Ledger slipped off his wet clothes and climbed into the bed in only his undershorts. Iris climbed in next to him and rested her head on his chest. She traced her fingers on his stomach and nuzzled his neck. He rubbed her back, wondering why he'd avoided this for so long. Being here with her.

In the middle of the night, he remembered why.

The sound of a woman screaming woke him out of a dead sleep and he sat straight up in bed. His heart was pounding out of his chest and he was drenched in sweat. He heard it again, feeling a cold chill creep down his spine. Iris stirred and sat up, staring at him blearily.

"What is it?"

"You didn't hear that?" he asked, his voice tight with fear and astonishment.

"What? The foxes? You told me about that, Ledger. I hear that all of the time."

"It sounds like that?"

"Like a woman screaming? Yeah." Iris laid back down and pulled him down next to her. "Go back to sleep."

Ledger lay in bed, staring at the ceiling. He'd told her about the red foxes and the sound they made. He grew up hearing them late at night. But those were no red foxes. That sounded exactly like a woman screaming in horror. Screaming for her life. He wrapped his arms around Iris as much for himself as for her, and wondered what he'd gotten himself into.

CHAPTER TEN

*H*e didn't sleep until dawn and even then jumped at every sound. He considered telling Iris the truth but realized it was better not to. She was blissfully unaware and needed to stay that way. By mid-morning, he got up and went downstairs. Iris was in the kitchen making food and smiled as he came in.

"Hey, sleepyhead, you're up! I was going to make breakfast but you slept so late it turned into brunch. Are you hungry?"

Ledger nodded and sat at the table. He peered around the kitchen and tried to imagine the Lodge in its heyday. The elite and all their creepy ceremonies. He shuddered and sipped the coffee Iris handed him. He knew he'd seen a woman on the dock, even if it hadn't been Iris. He knew he heard a woman screaming in the woods. It hadn't been foxes. He was beginning to believe the stories the locals told of the place and wanted no part of it.

"Iris, I can't stay here."

Iris turned, frowning at Ledger. "Oh. Is everything alright?"

He didn't want to scare her, so shrugged and glanced away. "I guess I just don't sleep well not in my own bed."

"Like your mother?"

"Yeah. You can always stay at our house, you know?" he offered.

"With your mother there? That seems kind of strange."

No stranger than ghost women and screaming, Ledger thought to himself. "My room is on the other side of the house. Duff is gone most days at school."

Iris handed him an omelet. "Maybe. I need to be here to keep an eye on things most times, though. Pipes freezing, that sort of thing."

"What about Bertie? You still use him?"

"Sometimes. He's getting old and not getting around as well. I suppose I can talk to him and see if he can check on the place now and then. I'd still need to be here some nights, though. Keep a presence about the place."

Ledger nodded. After the holidays, she wouldn't likely have any bookings between January and March. Maybe he could talk to his mother and see if Iris could stay with them during that time and have Bertie keep an eye on the place. They could come during the day to the Lodge but stay the nights at his house. He suggested that as an option but Iris didn't seem so convinced. She eyed him as she sat down.

"Ledger, is there something you aren't telling me?"

"Not other than what I have. I just don't want you alone out here but I can't sleep here. Iris, have you ever felt anything strange here? At all?"

Iris thought about it, then shook her head. "No."

Ledger stared at her and tried to read if she was hiding anything but her large, blue eyes were open and honest. How could that be? How could he be on the edge and seeing things and she was perfectly fine by herself here? He finished the omelet and stood up.

"I have a haul today. I'll be hitting the mainland, do you need anything?"

"If you can get me some broccoli that would be great. The store here has been out for weeks. Honestly, any vegetables. I need to learn to can or at least freeze things during the summer. I'm craving fruit and veggies."

"Will do. I can see if Mom has any canned vegetables, too. She usually tries to store about half of what she gets from gardens. I'll be back around four. Do you want to get together for dinner?"

"Yeah, I have a frozen lasagna I can throw in. Maybe grab some garlic bread?"

Ledger leaned down and kissed her, running his hand down her back. "It's a date."

The haul was a large wood stove and he was surprised to see Bertie waiting with it on the mainland dock.

"Bertie! Hey, this for you or an installation?"

Bertie stood up and stretched his back, making it pop. "Installation. The Darnell's one finally bit the dust. Glad you could come help bring it over. My back is killing me."

"Come on old man, let's get it on board," Ledger joked. He was glad to have a chance to bend Bertie's ear. Once the stove was loaded, they hunkered under the standing shelter of the boat and headed back.

"Someone meeting you on the other side?" Ledger inquired.

"Their son. At least he'd better. I'm not loading this in my little truck," Bertie said matter-of-factly.

"Hey, can I ask you something?"

"Shoot."

"You were the caretaker for the Crowley Lodge all these years?" Ledger watched Bertie's face to see if he could detect anything.

"The Crowley place? I was. Still help now and then."

"Were you when it was active?"

"When the rich snobs stayed there? Near the end, yes. I didn't like to go there, though. They spoke to me like I was mentally retarded and made fun of me. Those people detested the locals, saw them as dirty and stupid. They liked to pick on me."

"About what?" Ledger asked, confused.

"How I spoke, how I dressed. They were a right mean bunch. I helped Miss Crowley with some tasks around the place. When she died, her niece asked if I'd keep it up. It was easier then because it was just me out there."

"You had a key?"

"Ayup, I did. I'd go out about once a week and check on things. If I saw repairs that needed to be done, she'd wire me money in addition to my monthly check."

Ledger tried to think about how to word the next question. He played it over in his head, measuring the words. He didn't want Bertie thinking he was off his rocker. "Bertie, at any point when you went out there, did you feel or see anything strange? Out of the ordinary?"

Bertie eyed him and grunted. "Everything about that place is out of the ordinary and strange. What do you mean exactly?"

"Did you ever see anyone, or anything, that shouldn't be there? Hear anything?"

Bertie laughed, but without humor. He met Ledger's eyes. "Like ghosts?"

Ledger felt his face get hot. He felt stupid but there was no going back. "More or less."

"Son, you may be going down a tangled road here. That place... it was used for dark matters. Them people probably opened it up to things neither you nor I want to know about. I kept my head down and did what I was told."

"You didn't answer the question, Bertie. I wouldn't ask but I'm worried about Iris."

Bertie shifted uncomfortably and glared at Ledger. "This had better not come back on me. I don't want no part of it. You hear?"

"Okay?"

"After she died, Ms. Crowley, I went to close the place up for the winter. It was a clear day and real pretty. I went around and boarded up the cabins and once those were done, I went inside. I covered all of the furniture and left the water dripping. I went upstairs to check all the rooms and make sure the windows were sealed. I kept having this feeling I was being watched, you know? Like someone, or something, was following me around. I chalked it up to being alone in a big, spooky place. But when I got to the last room and opened the door, I about had a heart attack."

"What do you mean?"

"I swung the door open and there was this girl with a noose around her neck. She was hanging from the ceiling, that iron light fixture. I screamed and slammed the door shut. Then I called the sheriff. He came out and I told him what I'd seen. He went upstairs with his gun drawn and swung the door open."

"What did he do with her body? Who was she?" Ledger choked out.

"That was the thing. There was nobody. No girl. He told me I must've seen the curtains fluttering and thought it was a body. There was no sign of anything. Just an empty room. And the windows were closed, so the curtains weren't fluttering. But I know what I saw. I can see it until this day. It haunts me."

"Why did you keep going out? Weren't you afraid to be out there?"

"I was. But my pride told me I was being ridiculous and the money was good. She paid three times what anyone else paid. Times were tough."

Ledger focused on the shoreline of the island and pondered what Bertie said. Bertie was one of those old Maine fellows. No drama, say it like it was. He believed he saw what he saw. Ledger was inclined to believe him after last night. They fell silent and Ledger dreaded the question niggling at his brain. He knew he needed to ask and bit his lip hard.

"Bertie, what room was it?"

"Oh, yeah. It was the last one on the end with the windows on either side."

Iris's room. Ledger fought back tears. How could he protect her if he didn't know what he was fighting against? A missing girl, ceremonies that sounded like black magic, a woman screaming. A woman who looked like Iris on the dock. The

100

shadow he saw behind her that first night in the window. What the hell was actually going on? Even the guests who'd stayed recently seemed meaner, as if something was controlling their thoughts. The Lodge seemed to attract a certain kind of folk.

"Bertie, do you know anything else about the place?" Ledger asked, not really wanting to know.

Bertie sighed. "I guess it's time to get it all out there, huh? I know they brought young girls out there sometimes. As young as thirteen or fourteen. They seemed to be on their own, maybe girls who didn't have someone looking out for them. Runaways, orphans, I suppose. They never left the Lodge while they were there. They were heavily supervised and when they left they seemed different."

"Different how?"

"Like not there as much, as if part of them had been taken away."

Ledger shuddered and felt sick. "How were they being brought on and off the island with no one knowing or making an issue of it? It seems like the locals would've made a fuss about it."

"These people, the ones with money. They'd offer a good sum to the fishermen to transport them from the mainland directly to the dock."

"The fishermen? Didn't they know what they were doing?" Ledger practically yelled.

Bertie put his hand on Ledger's shoulder. "It's a small town. Bad things happen elsewhere. They didn't know what was going on up there, did they? How could they have? It was two separate worlds. Maybe they were told it was the girls of the families. Or girls coming for fun by choice. Who's to say? I don't think they had a clue. If they did, the money probably spoke louder."

"But when the girls left?"

"Ledger, I don't know. I think people like to believe those types of things can't happen in their town. Call it denial, call it stupidity, call it trust... but I believe they just saw it as some extra money to help their families."

Ledger nodded. He knew what Bertie was saying but no one had a clue? Girls were being shuttled on and off the island and not one person questioned it? A sudden thought hit his stomach like lead and he caught his breath. "Fishermen? Like who?"

Bertie met his eyes and tipped his head slightly. "Ledger, don't go down a road you can't come back up. Maybe it's best to let it go."

"Bertie, was my father one of the fishermen?"

Bertie set his mouth and stared out over the water. He remained silent and Ledger cut the engine. "Tell me. Did my father shuttle girls on and off the island on this boat? Was he part of this fucking darkness?"

Bertie glared at him and huffed. "Damnit, Ledger. I don't want to get into this."

"I won't start the engine until you tell me." Ledger gritted his teeth.

"Fine. He was. There were a tough couple of years with disease and shortages. This was right around when you were born and everyone was struggling. They likely just thought they were bringing people to the Lodge for a stay. No one knew what was going on up there. The girls were silent. It wasn't like they knew and did it anyway. It stopped when that girl went missing."

So, a girl did go missing. It wasn't an urban legend. Girls were brought in to do who knows what and one never left. Ledger felt flashes behind his eyes and leaned over the rail to vomit. His father may have brought that girl to her end. On this boat. The one he treasured and felt connected to; a part of his father. The one his father blew his brains out on, maybe because he knew he'd a hand in what happened. Maybe he wasn't so unaware, as Bertie was saying.

"Ledger, it stopped after that. They closed it all down. The Lodge wasn't used again and those people left."

"Until now," Ledger said miserably.

What had Iris unintentionally reopened? Panic filled him and he knew he needed to let her know. To get her out of there. He fired up the engine and got back to the island as quickly as he could. There was someone more sinister at play in the Lodge, he knew it in his gut.

They unloaded the stove and got it onto the Darnell boy's truck. Bertie followed him out to install the stove and Ledger headed home. He needed to regroup. To come to grips with his father's involvement and the disturbing past of the Lodge. The stories he'd heard weren't just island talk or gossip. They were real and his father had been part of it.

Did his mother know?

A loud buzzing started in his head and he barely made it home before it turned into a full-fledged vomiting migraine. He stumbled up the path, his head feeling like it would crack open. No one was home and he just made it through the door before collapsing on the floor.

The last thing Ledger could remember was seeing a demonic face hovering over him as pain shot through his skull down into his body. He couldn't move, paralyzed in fear. The face came closer, its gaping mouth almost touching his face. Ledger felt like he was dying as it dripped words like acid into his brain.

"She killed him and is coming for you."

CHAPTER ELEVEN

*T*he doctors said it was meningitis. Ledger knew better. He was hospitalized for over two weeks and when he was allowed to come home, he was so weak he could hardly stand. Brain inflammation. The holidays were a blur and his short-term memory was shot. Duff came home over the holidays and helped their mother take care of Ledger. The person who did everything around the house and supported the family was practically an invalid. Iris had a full house the week before and after Christmas, so Ledger didn't see her. He wasn't sure he wanted to. Whatever was going on at the Lodge wanted him out of the way.

Him and Bertie.

Bertie's body was found in his truck the day after Ledger was hospitalized. Heart attack, they said. Pushing himself too hard. While that much was true, Ledger had a suspicion the thing that visited him that night had probably overcome Bertie as well. They'd talked about secrets long since buried that day, and Ledger feared it marked them in some way. Bertie hadn't wanted to open up about it, yet Ledger had pressed and now wished he didn't know what Bertie had told him. Bertie had said he wanted no part of it. Now, he was dead. Some things just were meant to stay buried.

The thing said she was coming to kill him.

She. Iris? The missing girl? Something more sinister? He was terrified, either way. As much as he didn't want to confront Iris, he knew there were secrets she was carrying he needed to uncover to stop this. To protect his family. He heard his mother come in and got himself out of bed to talk to her. He'd dropped weight and his legs could barely hold him up. It took him three tries to stand from the edge of the bed; even then his legs felt like they may give out. He used the hallway wall to brace himself and crept along, each step zapping him of energy. His mother was setting groceries on the table when he made it through the door. She saw him and gasped, running to help him.

"Ledge! What are you doing up?" she admonished, bracing him with her arms.

"I need to talk to you."

"It can't wait? The doctors said you need to rest."

"It can't wait," he sputtered.

She watched him, then nodded. "Come sit down. Let me make you some tea."

"Mom. No. Please just listen."

She sighed and guided him to the couch. "Okay. What's going on?"

Ledger leaned back against the cushions, feeling like he'd just run a marathon. He looked at his mother, his eyes large with worry. She needed to know the truth. As much as he feared opening up the conversation might put them in danger, or hurt her, he also knew they might be the only ones to stop whatever had started at the Lodge.

"I talked to Bertie the day before he died, or maybe he died the same day. I don't know. He was my haul that day, a wood stove."

"He always did too much, Ledger. He was getting old and shouldn't have been out hauling a wood stove."

"Maybe. But he told me some things. Some serious horrible shit. About the Lodge."

"Oh? I mean, rumors have always gone around about that place. People like a little drama."

Ledger coughed and shifted on the couch to try and sit up. His back twitched with the exertion and he gave up. "I know. These aren't rumors, Mom. People did weird things there. Bad things. Ceremonies in black magic. They brought girls there and did things to them."

"What kind of things?"

Ledger shrugged, not wanting to open that box. "You can only imagine. The thing is, those girls were brought on and off the island directly through the Lodge dock."

She frowned and leaned forward, her brain starting to piece things together. "By who?"

"Paid for by the rich people at the Lodge. Transported by fishermen."

They both sat in silence and dread crossed her face as it sunk in. "No."

"Mom, Bertie told me Dad was one of the fishermen. He said they probably had no idea why the girls were being taken to and from there, however, anyone with half a brain would have some sense it wasn't good."

Her face was pale and her hands started to shake. "Ledger, your father was a good man. He cared about people. He never would've done anything to hurt anyone. Not intentionally. You need to believe that."

Ledger sighed and shook his head. "Maybe the fishermen had some sort of spell cast on them, maybe they were just trying to take care of their families. I don't know, Mom. But I do know Dad did it. It's how he got through those years. Maybe it haunted him. Maybe it's why he took his life. He brought those girls on the boat until the one went missing and they shut it all down."

"That story is true?"

"Apparently."

She put her head in her hands and began to weep. Hearing the man she loved, and had children with, may have been part of something that harmed young girls, and eventually took his life, was too much. Ledger waited and allowed her to absorb what he'd told her so far. She took a tissue and wiped her eyes, shuddering. She lifted her eyes to Ledger. He reached out and took her hand.

"Mom, there's more."

"Ledger, I can't. This is too much to process."

"I need to tell you. Something happened to Iris that same year, the year Dad died. Two months after Dad took his life, Iris's father raped her. She was just thirteen. When she told her mother, they ran but he chased them down and murdered her family. He thought she died too but she didn't. Or she did and came back from the dead. Her father was sent to prison where he was killed. After she was released from the hospital, she was sent to live with her grandmother, the niece of the woman who ran the Lodge."

"Do you think the two are somehow connected? Your Dad and Iris?"

Ledger laughed bitterly. "If only it was that simple. I think everything is connected. I think Iris's great-great-aunt brought a dark cloud on that family which attracted other bad people, like her father. I think Iris did die and come back, but maybe not alone. Maybe something latched onto her and the Lodge knows it. I've seen things around her."

"Do you know how crazy this sounds?"

"I do and would doubt myself if something hadn't happened to me, as well. Something wants me out of the way."

"The Lodge?" she asked, furrowing her brow.

"I mean, maybe. Or whatever they opened there in those ceremonies. Maybe opened a door to another realm. I think Iris is the key to reopening the lock. Every time I'm there, I feel or see something, an overwhelming presence. That night after I talked to Bertie, on the drive home my head started hurting. Buzzing and flashing."

"The meningitis?"

"Mom, I wasn't sick. I helped Bertie unload the wood stove and felt fine. No fever or anything like that. On the ride home, I decided I was going to tell you and then go to the Lodge and insist Iris come home with me. To leave and stay here, for her own safety. I never made it there. I collapsed by the time I got here."

"But why do you think it was something trying to stop you?" she asked fearful and confused.

"Because I saw it. Right before I blacked out, this thing hovered over me, got in my face, and told me she was going to kill me. That she killed him and was coming after me." Ledger shuddered with the memory and felt a wave of nausea pass through him.

"She? Iris?"

"I don't know. I don't think so. Iris says she doesn't feel anything at the Lodge. She's never harmed anyone as far as I know. Nothing strange has happened to her and she hasn't seen anything. She thinks it's all in my head. Ha, maybe now it is. I could feel that thing going into my brain that night."

"Ledger, that scares me. I can't have anything happen to you."

"Mom, I think the only way to get this to stop is to confront it. It's not going to just go away on its own."

"But what is it?"

"I have no fucking clue," Ledger replied, exhausted. "As I said, I think Iris is the key. It needs her and maybe if I can get her away from there, I can stop it."

A voice laughed caustically from behind him, making them both jump. Duff came into the room. "What the actual fuck? Are you serious? If any of this is true, you need to stay the hell away from her. She's poison."

"Duff-" Ledger started.

"No. Fuck that, Ledger. You almost died. Mom was crying and freaking out. You aren't going back there. Fuck Iris and her bullshit," Duff spat.

"Duffey, watch your mouth," their mother said.

"Mom! That's what you are worried about? Ledger almost fucking died. Now he wants to be some kind of fucking hero and go back? Our family has been through enough and if Dad was involved, fuck him then, too."

"Duffey!" Ledger yelled and tried to get up. His knees buckled and he fell back.

"Ledge, look at you. You can hardly stand up. Mom, maybe it's time to say goodbye to this fucking island and move in with me. I hate it here. The small-minded, gossipy locals and the weird shit that has gone on here for years. I say let it goddamn burn."

Duffey stormed out of the room and slammed the door. Ledger looked at his mother who was openly crying now. He felt bad for bringing this all on her but knew there was no other way. He may have brought attention to his family, however, they were marked anyhow. His father had done that, whether he'd known or not. His mother got up and left the room and Ledger laid down on the couch, no longer able to keep himself upright.

Duffey was right on that front. He couldn't save anyone if he couldn't even stand up. He didn't know when he dozed off or how long he'd been asleep, but when he woke up he was covered by a blanket and it was dark. He went to get up and when he put his feet down he felt something soft and warm.

"Ow, bigfoot," he heard from the floor below. He peered down and saw Duff lying on the floor right next to the couch.

"What are you doing down there?" he asked, moving his feet.

Duff sat up and brushed their hair out of their face. "I didn't want you getting any hero ideas. I figured I could take you in the state you're in."

Ledger laughed and cocked his head. "Fair enough. I think a toddler could take me at this point. Come sit with me."

Duff climbed on the couch and sat next to Ledger, who slipped his arm around them. "You know, I was six when you were born. I was not thrilled with having a little sister and you pestered me endlessly."

"Well, at least I took care of the sister part for you," Duff teased.

"That you did. But you know, sometimes you'd climb on the couch with me to watch tv and snuggle up next to me. It made me feel big and powerful. I started liking you then. You mean the world to me, Duff. You and Mom. I'm not trying to do anything to hurt our family. I need you to know that. I'm trying to save us."

"You wouldn't have to if Iris hadn't come into your life."

"Look, Duffey, it's easy to blame her but she is a victim in this. If anything, Dad put us in this, to begin with. She is like us; wrong place, wrong time."

"Ledge, could this all be in your head? Maybe you were sick and didn't know what was happening. Maybe the bacteria was causing delusions in your head for a while? Have you considered that?"

"I have. And it's a possibility, but I don't think so. I'd honestly prefer that scenario. But I do know what Bertie told me and he's dead. Died at the same time I ended up in the hospital with brain inflammation. Would be a hell of a coincidence, no?"

Duffey hugged him tightly, then sighed. "It is strange, I'll give you that. It's this fucking island. It's always been off. When I go to school, I feel like this is someplace I made up in my head."

Ledger chuckled and kissed Duff's forehead. "I can see it. This shit is out of a creepy book."

"Except it's not. It's our home and our family. Have you ever thought about leaving?"

"Just about every damn day. Then part of me feels this unexplainable loyalty to being here. The generational commitment to continuing our family saga on the land."

"That's some Dad bullshit, right there." Duff snorted, sitting up. "I guess I didn't know him as well since I was only eight when he died. He did a serious number on your head."

Ledger thought back to the times his father took him out to check the traps and do hauls. How his father talked about how their family was one of the first on the island. How they made the island what it was. It'd instilled pride in Ledger. Now it instilled something different. A heavy horror in his gut. His father had fed them off the suffering of those girls. He may not have known it, but it still happened. Those girls still suffered. The island wasn't this quaint village of neighbors. It had secrets and many of the residents were part of what happened.

It was up to him to undo it all.

CHAPTER TWELVE

I t took weeks until Ledger was able to physically be up and moving around without needing to stop and rest every few minutes. The labs came back negative for meningitis which was no surprise to Ledger, however, this deepened his family's belief in what he was telling them. Once the last guests left the Lodge, Iris came by to check on him and stayed each time for a few hours to help get him better. He avoided any conversations about what he knew, not wanting to exacerbate the situation until he was strong enough to fight. He loved her and knew he couldn't walk away from her but eventually, the truth had to come out. Duff went back to school and avoided being home when Iris was there, knowing being silent wasn't in their wheelhouse. Their mother acted the same to Iris when she was around. No matter how long Iris stayed during the day, she always went back to the Lodge at night.

After she left one evening, Ledger's mother came into his room and handed him a small pile of pictures. He raised his brows, then frowned. They were of him and Iris dancing the night they all had dinner at the Lodge.

"Thanks? I didn't know you took these."

"You seemed so happy that night, I snapped a few. I had them on my phone. But that's not why I'm giving them to you. Look closer. Something is off about them."

Ledger turned his bedside lamp on and moved the pictures under the light. At first glance, they were romantic and made him smile, however, something about them made him feel strange. It was almost like they were slightly out of focus, but that wasn't it. He peered in closer. In each photo, it was like there was a slight double exposure on Iris. Like she was there twice but just faintly.

"Could it be double exposure?" he asked.

"I don't think so, because the rest of the photo is clear and crisp. Plus look at the last photo," his mother said, her voice quivering.

Ledger pulled the last photo out and stared at it. It was him and Iris as he swung her around. She was looking at him and laughing. He didn't see anything out of the ordinary. He glanced at his mother and raised his hand in question. She pointed at the picture, to a mirror in the background. He peered closer. It was Iris's reflection. Or was it? He took out a magnifying glass from his bedside table and hovered it over the image. It looked like Iris but somehow different. It was a girl with long, dark hair, but the reflection didn't match Iris. The girl wasn't laughing and her head was cocked differently than Iris's. She had her hand outstretched like Iris did, however, it didn't connect to Ledger's hand. Her eyes were fastened on his but there was no joy in them. They were hollow and pleading. The image of the demon from the night he collapsed flashed in his mind and he shoved the picture away, feeling like he was going to vomit.

It was the girl from the dock.

His mother sat down next to him and put her hand on his back. "I think you're in danger."

"Well, I could've told you that. I think we all are. But something wants me gone, so it can get to Iris. To control her."

"Ledger, maybe you should leave the island. Just walk away from all of this."

"Like Dad? Mom, I don't think there is an out on this. I love Iris and would never forgive myself if I let this thing take her. I also think it's using her to open a door of some kind. If I walk away, it's going to destroy a lot of lives. On the island, who knows where else? And it will come after me. I can feel it in my bones. The only way out of this is to fight it."

"This isn't a movie, Ledger! If it took your father, it will take you, too. Iris made her choice to come here. She doesn't have the right to bring this on you. That family has a lot of dark secrets you don't need to try and fix!"

"Like our family?"

Her face fell and she bit back tears. "That's not fair. It's different. Your father was just trying to make sure his family was okay."

"Well, are we?"

He knew his questions were harsh but his mother had to face they were not innocent in all of this. Not that it mattered anyway. Innocent or not, now they were knee-deep in it. She shook her head and wiped her cheeks.

"No. I guess we haven't been. You know your dad tried to send us away. Told me to go back to my family in Vermont. I thought he was being ridiculous and told him I wouldn't go. He told me he was afraid things would get worse. I thought he meant just fishing. He became so distant near the end. Stayed out on the boat longer. Begged me to take you kids to Vermont. I was being stoic. Standing by my man. When he didn't come home that night, part of me knew. I refused to believe it. We were always so madly in love. Right up until the end. It's why I wouldn't go. I believed love could conquer all. It can't, Ledger. Some things are bigger than us. Sometimes you can only save yourself."

"Sometimes you can't even do that. One way or the other, Mom, this is going down. I can either try to stand and fight or lose the battle on the run. Dad should've stood and fought. At least then if he died, he would've done something to undo the wrongs."

"You don't know that he didn't try to make things right," she pointed out.

"I don't know that he did, either. Regardless, I'm going to do my best to end this once and for all. Whatever this is, it's coming after people I love and it's time to fight back. You should go and stay with Duffey, but it may come after you. Now that it knows you know, you're at risk."

"Ledger, you're my baby boy. The best gift ever. I won't leave you. If I lost you, it would be the end for me," his mother said, her voice resigned to the reality of what was going on. She met his eyes, her own fixed and determined. "So, now what do we do?"

Ledger laughed softly, swinging his head back and forth. "I'm not sure, to be honest. I think I need to talk to Iris. Make her tell me everything about her life. About what happened to her and after. There is something in that which is a catalyst for this."

"Do you think she'll tell you?"

"She thinks these are all stories. I need to approach it from a different angle. What I need to remember is that anything that transpires between us is not just between us. We're being watched or listened to. I can't put her in danger but I need to dig out the truth. In a way, I'm doing it out of love. Putting us in danger to find a way to make us safe."

"Well, you do love her, so follow your heart. But watch your back. Make sure your head leads your heart and not the other way around. What do you need from me?"

"Mom, I need you to believe in me. No matter what happens or what I tell you. Knowing you and Duff are there for me despite everything, is giving me the strength to face this. You're all I have. If I call on you, please come. But if I do call on you, I'll tell you what you used to say to me when I was little and was scared, okay? If I don't say it, don't trust it's me. I won't say it now, because something is listening."

She gripped his hand tightly, then nodded. "I remember."

Ledger knew he needed a set plan to talk to Iris, so he took a walk around the property to test his strength and think. He needed her to trust him because he didn't think he could save her if she didn't. Whatever lured her to the Lodge was playing it safe, not involving her. This made it harder for him to convince her it was real. The game was played in secret, in mirrors and minds. He closed his eyes and leaned against a tree. It was him against it. Iris was just a pawn, a tool to get what it wanted. He needed to figure out how to get the upper hand. What was it?

He heard a faint sound coming from up in the tree and wondered what kind of bird was making it in the middle of winter. He peered up but didn't see anything. He heard it again. He stepped back away from the tree and stared up to where he thought it was coming from. It was silent. Convinced he was hearing things, he heard it one more time and shook the tree frustrated. Snow fell and the sound got louder. He glared to the top of the tree and spotted it. A tiny, orange, fluff of a kitten, its fur iced with snow. It was almost to the top of the tree and he doubted it knew how to get back down. He shook the tree again and the kitten held on for dear life.

"Goddamnit," he muttered and considered just leaving it up there, but knew his heart wouldn't let him. He started a weak and slow climb up, pausing every few branches to catch his breath. The branches began to thin and get weaker. There was no way it would hold his weight. He eyed the kitten who eyed him back.

"Come on, little dude, meet me halfway."

The kitten didn't budge. It meowed at him pitifully and he glanced around to figure out what to do. There was only one option and it was a crapshoot. He grabbed the tree above him and shook as hard as he could. The kitten attempted to hold on but lost its grip and began to fall. As it fell past Ledger, he stuck his hand out and snagged it before it whipped past him to the ground. He barely caught it and pulled it quickly to his chest as he gripped onto the tree with his other hand.

"Gotcha!"

The kitten dug its claws into his arm and cried out. Ledger shoved it in his jacket and began the descent down. It was all fur and claws inside his coat and he could feel it digging in as he moved. He jumped down the last few branches and his legs buckled as he hit the ground. He peered in at the kitten, who stared back terrified.

"You're safe now. You didn't make it easy on me, now did you?"

It blinked back at him and relaxed its grip on his skin. He headed back to the house and went to his room. They'd had a dog that was old and passed away when he was about ten, but never a cat. He knew there was a reason but couldn't remember exactly why. The kitten made itself comfortable on his bed and he went to find his mother. She was in the kitchen and almost immediately started sniffling when he came near. Then he remembered. She sneezed and peered around.

"Were you touching a cat?" she asked, doubting the question.

"Uh, yeah about that. I rescued one from a tree when I was out there."

Her eyes grew big and she shook her head. "Just don't bring it in the house. I'm severely allergic."

Ledger made a quick exit and grabbed the now sleeping kitten off his bed. He ducked out of the house and went to his truck. He couldn't stick it back outside in the weather and couldn't leave it in the house. It left only one option. He dialed the phone and held his breath when she answered. He eyed the small creature.

"Hey, Ledger. How are you?" Iris asked cheerfully.

"Iris, you aren't allergic to cats, are you?"

"Nooo. Why?"

The kitten started to cry out in the background. Ledger laughed and sighed, rubbing its head. "That's why. I found a kitten in a tree and my mother is allergic. Any chance I can bring it there?"

The line was silent and Ledger looked to make sure the call hadn't dropped. Finally, she answered. "I guess so. I've never had any animals, so I'm not sure what to do with it. How to take care of it."

"Me either. We can figure it out. I'm on my way."

"Okay, see you in a few minutes."

The kitten crawled up to his shoulder and sat there as he drove, meowing incessantly in his ear. It was probably hungry but he'd no way to get it food. The store was closed until morning. Maybe Iris had something to tide it over. By the time he got to the Lodge, it was curled in his hair and he needed to detangle it to get it out. Iris met him at the door and stared at the pitiful creature. Her face broke out in a smile and she rubbed its head.

"Oh, it's so tiny. How did it end up in a tree?"

"Most likely chased there by a fox or something. It can only be about two months old." Ledger didn't know cats but it seemed really young.

Iris scooped it up and held it close to her face. "Boy or girl? Name?"

"Don't know and haven't named it."

"It looks like a little lion. Maybe we could call it Roar?"

"Fine by me but it makes more of a cry than a roar," Ledger said, laughing.

"Come in, I have the fire going. Let's put Roar by the fire."

Ledger didn't relish going in but agreed and followed her. She put a blanket by the fire and placed Roar on it. The kitten yawned and laid down after batting at one of the strings for a moment. Somehow Roar being there made the Lodge seem more friendly. Ledger knew better than to let his guard down, however. Iris turned her eyes on him.

"So, this is what it takes to get you out here. A wayward kitten?"

Ledger watched her and his heart filled with love. He smiled at her, then nodded. "It definitely forced the issue. Iris, something happened since I was last here. Some things have come to light and we need to talk. Roar just brought me out a little sooner, but I've been needing to speak to you."

Her face looked worried and she bit her lip. "Is everything alright?"

Ledger grasped her hand in his, meeting her eyes. "I love you. I'd do anything for you. But I need something from you. I need you to tell me everything about that day. The day you died and what happened after."

CHAPTER THIRTEEN

I ris seemed unsure she wanted to go down that path and it took some convincing on Ledger's part. He explained he was simply trying to piece something together and didn't mention the picture or demonic face he saw. He asked her to trust him. Iris met his eyes and knitted her brows, her face growing dark with the memory.

"I'm not sure what you want to know?"

"I suppose first tell me about your family. Your great-great-aunt owned this place, right? Or, I guess it was in the family? So, was your family from here?"

Iris thought back and shook her head. "I don't think so. I mean, I think some were from Maine but not the island."

"Hmmm, so how did she end up here?"

"Well, it was her and my great-grandfather in that generation. She never married or anything. They had money, that side of the family. She had this place built, so I guess being a spinster, she took that money and bought this land. I don't think we had any other connection to it before that. Maybe they came out on a vacation and she decided to buy land. I honestly don't know, Ledger, and I'm not sure why it matters?"

"I don't know if it does. Just making a trail, so I understand how you ended up here. Okay, so her sibling was your great-grandfather and he had nothing to do with the place?"

"Nope, he and Iris were siblings and he joined the army and got married. He and his wife had my grandmother."

"Wait, so her name was Iris, also? Your great-great-aunt?" Ledger asked, chilled by the thought.

"Yeah, I was named after her. My grandmother used to come here sometimes as a child to visit but her children never did, so my mother named me a family name to make that connection, I guess."

"Do you know why they never came?"

"No. It was never brought up. My grandmother moved south with her husband and their two little girls, so maybe it was just too far," Iris suggested.

"Alright, so by the time your mother was an adult and had you, it was no longer being used for guests. Were you ever told why they stopped?"

"Just that she got too old. My grandma was pretty tight-lipped about it."

"And it was left to you when she died. Do you know why she left it to you?" Ledger asked, trying to put the pieces together.

"She left everything to me. I'm the only survivor in my family. It was more because I was the only family to give it to. End of the line." Iris shrugged.

Ledger nodded. Everyone else had been slaughtered by her father. He cleared his throat. "Do you mind talking about what happened the day your father... um, this is hard to ask. I'm sorry. The day your father came after you. I mean, I know the basics, but after you came to in the woods. What do you remember?"

"You know the part of him coming after us and what he did. After that, I remember being in the woods and I felt like my body was made of shredded fabric. Like it wasn't held together anymore. Everything in me was on fire. I was choking on my blood and had this mixture of searing pain and numbness. I focused on my nails digging in the cool dirt and moving each inch forward. I thought about the worms in the dirt and hoped they weren't getting into my body. It was like it wasn't my body anymore. Like my mind was in charge and it was something I had to transport."

"Did you feel like you were alone, or like someone was with you?"

"Someone like how? Remember I was the only survivor?"

"Like watching over you, or pushing you along?" Ledger asked, careful to not suggest anything.

Iris shook her head. "No, I felt completely alone. In the whole world."

"You told me the sheriff came and you were taken to the hospital. You had surgery to repair your liver, kidney, and lung, right?"

"Surgeries. The first one just kept me alive. I had a couple more over the next few months."

"What for?"

"To be honest, not a hundred percent, but I know I lost part of my liver, one of my kidneys, and part of my lung. Oh, and I can't have children."

"What? Why?" Ledger stared at her, attempting to figure that out from what she'd told him.

"Doctor said too much scar tissue."

"Were you stabbed there, too?"

"Just the one stab and he pulled the knife down."

"How far down?"

Iris cocked her head. "I guess far enough."

It didn't add up. The scar ended where her liver and kidneys were but didn't go past. Ledger rubbed his head, then sighed. "Can I see the scar?"

Iris laughed and shook her head. "Ledger, you have seen me naked a few times."

"Still, I just want to understand."

She lifted her shirt and leaned back on the couch. He traced the scar. Kidney to the breastbone. Nothing near her ovaries. A light glint of white skin caught his eye near her belly button and he peered closer. Right under the navel was a straight white scar about an inch long. A clean incision.

"What is that from?"

Iris glanced down and frowned. "I'm not sure. Maybe part of all that."

Ledger knew better. The scar from being stabbed was jagged and darker from being stitched together as the wound had been. This was an intentional surgery scar. He grabbed his phone and typed in *scar below navel* which brought up pages on hysterectomies and tubal ligation. He ruled out a hysterectomy because she wasn't taking any kind of hormone replacements.

Tubal ligation said there would be another small scar on the abdomen. He scanned her stomach and saw a slightly raised bump of scar tissue no bigger than a pencil eraser. Dread filled him when he realized what the doctor had done. They'd forced sterilized Iris. But why would someone do that? On a child, no less?

She was watching him with a confused look on her face. "Ledger what is it? Is everything alright? You look like you saw a ghost."

"Do you have your medical records?"

Iris laughed and sat up, pulling her shirt down. "Of course not. Not something I carry around with me. Do you have yours?"

Ledger stared hard at her and realized she'd no clue about any of this. "No, I guess not. Do you think you could get them?"

"I have no idea. Why?"

"Just wondering," Ledger replied, coming to grips with it probably being pointless. If they did it, they weren't going to put it on paper. "The doctor. It was the same one every time who did your surgeries?"

"Yeah, I think so. He was like a middle-aged, balding guy with glasses and a mole on his nose. Why?"

"Do you remember his name?"

"No, just that he had a mole and glasses because it reminded me of that game *Guess Who?.*"

Ledger remembered the game, each player had a set of faces and the other had to narrow it down through features until they had the same person on each side. Middle-aged, balding male, glasses, mole. He made a mental note.

"Georgia, right? Do you know what town or hospital?"

Iris shrugged, thinking back. "Not really. My aunt lived in the country. I guess it would be the closest town to that. Why are you asking all of this? Is something going on I need to know about?"

Ledger considered how much he should tell her. How much he *could* tell her. He felt safe in asking questions but after what happened last time he found out things about the Lodge, he didn't think he should talk about anything specific about what happened there. He didn't know exactly what the line not to cross was, but he'd talked to Iris before about her past and nothing happened. He talked to Bertie about the Lodge and almost died. Again, he felt Iris wasn't the issue, she was the key to something. Something that wanted to keep her in the dark.

"No, I'm just trying to understand everything. What about before? Was life pretty normal?" he replied.

"Normal? No. My father was a raging asshole and took it out on my mother. She tried to reason with him but he was flying off the handle at the littlest things. Every day was walking on eggshells, trying to not set him off."

"Was she afraid to leave?"

"I suppose. I think she thought she'd bear the brunt of it, but when he came after me, she knew she needed to run. To keep me safe."

"God, I'm so sorry Iris. That you went through all of this," Ledge said miserably. Until he was fourteen, his life had been great. Loving parents, stable home. Or at least through his eyes.

Iris nodded and chewed her lip. "It was horrible but after... after he attacked us and it was just me, my grandma took very good care of me. I was in the hospital for a couple of months and when I was released, she took me to her home. She was so loving and supportive. She was my best friend."

"I'm glad you had her."

"Me too."

"Since then has anything weird happened to you?" Ledger asked.

"Weird how?"

"Like seeing anything, strange dreams, anything unexplainable?"

"I had nightmares for years, obviously. Kids were terrible to me. But other than that, no. Never saw a ghost if that's what you're asking. Sometimes I'd beg my mother to come to me but she never did. Not even in dreams. Maybe she was trapped."

Ledger could relate. He'd sometimes talk to his father, to ask him for guidance but was greeted with radio silence. No words from the great beyond. Once his father was gone, he was just gone. He rubbed his eyes and yawned. Roar came over and meowed at him.

"Hey, do you have anything we can give this guy to eat? He's pretty hungry, I think."

"Maybe. Let me go look in the fridge. Do you think it's a boy?"

"As much as I think it's a girl. I have no idea how to tell the gender of a cat."

Iris laughed and got up. She scooped Roar up and carried it to the kitchen. "Okay, either way, come on. Let's get you something, little lion."

They looked in the fridge and gave Roar some cheese and bread, which the kitten happily gobbled up. Iris set a bowl of water down and looked around. "I'd better find something for it to poop in before I find little presents everywhere." She went to the mudroom off the back and came out with a shallow plastic bin and a dead plant. "Ha! Good thing I don't have a green thumb for inside plants. I can put this dirt in the bin and *viola,* a makeshift litter box!"

Once the box was ready, they put Roar in it who stared at them and jumped out. Ledger chuckled, stroking the kitten's fuzzy head. "He'll get it."

Iris picked up the kitten and turned it around, lifting its tail. "She. She'll get it."

"How can you tell?"

"Lina showed me on kittens they had. See? It has an upside-down exclamation point as genitals. That makes it a girl. If it looked like a colon it would be a boy."

"If you say so," Ledger replied, not seeing much difference.

"I do," Iris assured and put Roar back in the litter box. This time the kitten sniffed around and used it. Iris grinned and slipped her arms around Ledger, resting her head against his chest. "I'm glad you came over. I've been missing you."

He sighed and rested his head against hers. "Me too. Just a lot going on."

"Are you feeling better?"

"Pretty much. Still not as strong as I was, but every day I'm getting closer."

"You want to stay the night? It's after midnight."

A knot formed in Ledger's stomach. Being there awake was one thing. Sleeping was another. "I can't, but we can stay up and talk longer if you want."

"I want you."

Ledger chuckled and rubbed her back. He felt the same, but there was no way he was going up to her room. She drew back and kissed him deeply, getting a rise out of him. He knew he couldn't resist her and slid his hands across the skin of her back. She pulled him out of the kitchen and toward the stairs when he stopped her. She frowned and he motioned to the couch. She dropped one eyebrow and smiled. They made it to the couch as they took off their clothes and explored each other's bodies. Iris pushed him back on the couch and straddled him. He was more than ready and moaned as she guided him inside her depths. The heat coming off her made his head dizzy and he buried his face between her breasts as she ground her hips against him, raising and lowering slowly. The sensation was mind-blowing and he came hard and fast as she tipped her head back and cried out. He wrapped his arms tight around her waist and held her there. She bent forward, kissing his neck.

"Sorry," he murmured. "You drive me crazy. I didn't think I'd get there so quickly."

"It's fine, I got there, too. Just being around you keeps me about halfway there anyway," Iris teased, running her fingers across his lips.

"Really?"

"Really. I'm always a little breathless around you, Ledger."

He had to admit, hearing that felt pretty good. He'd been with other women, but none came remotely close to what he felt for Iris. With her, he was fully engaged. He craved her when they were apart, mentally and physically. When they were together, he felt fully connected to himself. To both of them.

He met her eyes and smiled. She tipped her head and let a grin play at the corners of her mouth. As he slid his hands down her spine, he swore he would do anything to keep her with him. To protect and love her.

Even if it meant fighting the devil.

CHAPTER FOURTEEN

*L*edger woke up on the couch with Roar on his chest. They'd stayed up and talked until dawn when Iris insisted she could no longer keep her eyes open. Roar had already taken her place on Ledger's lap and he used the kitten as an excuse to stay on the couch when Iris went up. Iris paused at her room door and blew him a kiss, then a small one for Roar. Ledger didn't remember falling asleep but when he awoke, the sun was high in the sky. Iris came in from outside and stomped the snow off her boots. She was carrying wood and he jumped up to help, upsetting the kitten who yawned and glared at them. They built up the fire and Ledger messaged his mother, so she wouldn't worry. She'd messaged him multiple times and he felt bad for not having responded sooner.

He wondered if he could convince Iris to come home with him. Probably not, especially since she now had Roar to look after. He didn't want to fight about it and stayed until lunchtime, helping her around the Lodge.

"Hey, I need to head home. I'm picking up some groceries for my mother. Do you need anything?"

Iris thought and nodded. "I guess I need cat food and cat litter for Roar. I didn't think through the whole bike thing for the winter months. Would you mind swinging some by?"

"Sure. I'll go to the store first and swing back by before heading home."

"Are you sure? I don't mean to have you run around."

"And miss a chance to see you again?" Ledger winked at her, rubbing Roar under the chin. He wasn't lying, either. He meant it. He'd never want to be away from Iris if it wasn't for the Lodge.

Iris watched him with a half-smile. "You truly are the sweetest guy. I'm surprised you weren't already married with kids by the time I met you."

"Mmmm, don't be so convinced about that. About my temperament, not the married thing. Never married and no kids I know about," Ledger joked. "I think I've been an asshole in the past. Probably put my needs above other people's."

"I find that hard to believe," Iris replied.

"That, my Iris, is because you bring out the best in me. I want to always have you look at me like I'm worthy of your love."

Iris came over and ran her fingers into his hair, smiling up at him. "You are. You're part of me."

Ledger felt a tingling sensation in his cheeks and grinned. "Stop, you're making me bashful."

Iris stood on her tiptoes and kissed him. "Maybe that's why I was called here. To meet you."

"Iris-" he began and his words cut off. He wanted to say he wanted to marry her, to run away with her. That she'd opened a part of him he thought didn't exist. But first, he needed to figure out how to get her away from the Lodge. To set her free.

She cocked her head and chuckled. "Ledger, I know. I'll see you in a bit?"

He nodded, drawing her close. He liked how her body curved into his. "You will."

He headed out and climbed into his truck, then sighed. How did he find the woman he loved and she was not truly his? Yet. He started the truck and drove out as a red fox darted in front of him. He tapped the brakes and watched it scamper into the woods. In moments like this, he could convince himself he was making this all up. But then his mind flashed to the picture his mother had shown him of the girl in the mirror and reminded him that was tangible. There was no denying what could be physically seen.

The grocery store was the only supply store on the island and was no bigger than a convenience store. Luckily, they had cat litter and food and he stocked up on any items either Iris or his mother's house needed. Being the only store, they made sure they had all the essentials, plus some. Once he checked out, Ledger sorted the bags outside and stuck a little collar for Roar in Iris's bag.

Iris was outside shoveling the walkway when he pulled up. She stopped and leaned against the shovel to catch her breath. Her cheeks were flushed and her eyes stood out against her ruddy cheeks and the snowy landscape. She pushed her hair back and smiled. Ledger admired her for a moment before getting out of the truck. He wished he didn't have to leave again. He grabbed the bags and carried them in, with Iris following behind him.

"I grabbed some extras for you. Noticed your cabinets were getting low and we're due for a pretty heavy storm tonight," he explained, unloading the bags. He began filling the cabinets and turned to face her. "I don't suppose you want to stay at my house to be safe? I'm sure my mother would be delighted."

Iris shook her head. "I wish, but since your mom is allergic to cats and I can't leave Roar alone, I think I'd better stay here. You want to stay for dinner?"

"I can't. I need to get wood and food to my house. Duff is coming in on the ferry this afternoon and I need to pick them up. I can come by in the morning... if I can get out."

"Okay, breakfast it is. Do you think we'll lose power?" Iris asked, her face lined with concern.

"Maybe. My logic is if you prepare you won't, and if you don't you will."

Iris laughed at this. "Good advice. I guess I'd better check everything then. This is my first real storm. I just got used to all of the snow, so this will be an adventure. Roar will be great company, either way."

Ledger finished unloading and helped her stack wood by the fireplace. He went around and checked her storm windows to make sure they were secure. He saw the time and he had just enough time to get to the ferry.

"Hey, I have to go pick up Duff. Message me tonight and let me know how you're doing or if you lose power. I looked at your generator. It has gas and fires right up if you need it. It's supposed to come in hard and heavy after eight. Let me know if you need anything."

"I will. Give your mother and Duff my love."

Ledger watched her as she sorted the wood stack and admired how her hair twisted in waves from the snow melting. He wanted to grab her and demand she go with him, but she was strong-willed and would resist. Instead, he walked over and wrapped his arms around her, burying his face in her damp hair. She turned around and rested her head against his chest. He thought about the future.

"Do you think there will ever be a time you won't want to live at the Lodge? Like, hand it off to staff or someone?" Ledger asked, hoping she saw a future outside of running the Lodge.

She knitted her brow and shrugged. "I don't have much else. I mean, my grandma's house in the south, but it's small and I don't love it there. I have it up for sale. Why?"

Ledger knew he'd show his hand if he said anything else and shook his head. "I don't know if I want to be here the rest of my life. On the island. I wonder what's out there, away from the island. Thinking out loud, I suppose."

Iris watched him knowingly. "We can cross that bridge when we get to it, Ledger."

He kissed her forehead and let go. "Alright, Duff will have my hide if they have to wait in the snow for too long. I love you."

"I love you, too."

He ran to the truck, knowing he was cutting it close. He made it to the dock just as the ferry was pulling off and Duff was standing there with their bag and a scowl. They climbed into the truck and made a noise of disgust. Ledger laughed and tousled their hair.

"Hey, I'm here, so don't give me shit."

Duff stared out the window and shrugged. "Sibling rights to give you shit."

"I can drop you off here if you want and you can walk," Ledger offered.

Duff eyed him, their green eyes twinkling. "You wouldn't."

"You know I would."

Duff laughed nervously and nodded. "Fine, thanks for coming to get me."

"Now, was that so hard?"

"A little."

The weather forecast was right and the snow started coming down in thick sheets after eight at night. Ledger made sure they were stocked on wood and was glad he'd bought extra food at the store. It was heavy enough, he doubted he'd be able to get out the next morning. He messaged Iris to let her know and she sent back a sad face. She let him know the power was still holding and Roar was oblivious by the fire, which made him laugh. The power went out around midnight. Iris sent a picture of her starting the generator. She could hold her own.

What Ledger didn't count on was that it ended up being the worst storm the island had seen in a decade, and they weren't able to get out for a couple of weeks. Iris assured him she had plenty of food and company with Roar. His mother's house was set with canned goods and the root cellar with canned fruit and vegetables. People on the island knew to stock up when they could because the winter months were feast or famine. The power was out for four days and everyone cheered when it came back. Most people had backup generators but used them sparingly because of limited gas.

Two weeks later when he was able to dig the truck out, they were down to mostly canned vegetables and frozen fish. He never cared for fish in the first place and now he dreamed of a place where maybe fish wasn't the main item on the menu. The store had been picked pretty clean, but he was able to scrounge up ingredients to make biscuits and gravy. It would be a refreshing change. He swung by the road to the Lodge but it was still buried and could only be cleared with a plow. He could snowshoe in but didn't have them on him. A quick message to Iris and she assured him she was okay. He let her know he was leaving cat food, litter, and a bag of groceries at the end of the drive. She thanked him and said she'd ski out later to get them.

He headed home and their conversation about the doctor crossed his mind. Once he got home, he began researching the attack to see if he could narrow down who the doctor was. He couldn't find much other than a blip about the crime and that one survivor was taken to Bryman Memorial Hospital in Bryman, Georgia. He found it odd it hadn't made bigger news, but then again domestic violence was still treated as something the victim brought on themselves. He clicked on the hospital page and searched for any doctors who fit the description Iris had given him, but none did. It'd been fifteen years, so he may have retired or even died. Ledger hoped he hadn't died.

He called the hospital and tried to get information but the very bored girl who answered wasn't much help. He asked how to obtain medical records and she read off a monotone script of the process. Iris would have to fax them a copy of her identification and twenty-five dollars to request them. Ledger didn't want to involve her at this point and doubted the records would be very helpful. He racked his brain and came up with an idea. He typed in the year in the town's paper and the word doctor. It was a long shot but if it was anything like their area, doctors found ways to make the news.

Nothing came up for that year so he went to the following year. A few search results came up. "*Doctor Speaks at Local Elementary School*", "*Dinner Held by Hospital Board Honor's to This Year's Top Doctors*", and "*Free Vaccination Clinic Held by Area Doctors*". The first showed a dewy-faced young female doctor surrounded by children. The second showed a row of old white fuddy-duddy men otherwise known as the hospital board and the last showed probably the area's only long-haired doctor. He was getting nowhere. He erased doctor and changed the search to surgeon. One article came up, "*Local Surgeon and Church Leader travels to Haiti.*"

He clicked on the fuzzy photo and stared at it. The description fit and the article went on to talk about how this fine man of God was sacrificing his precious time to go help the impoverished country through surgery and mission work. He was a balding, middle-aged man... with a mole on his nose. He didn't look like a happy person and maybe a little pious. The article said he was Dr. Arbuckle. Dr. Eugene Arbuckle.

Ledger typed that in the search bar and pulled up the white pages. There was a Eugene Arbuckle in Tennessee. Sixty-nine years old. The age seemed about right. He couldn't find much else with the name and jotted the number down. No other sites had a Eugene Arbuckle except old links to his connection to the Bryman hospital. No modern pages or social media sites. He prayed this was the right one and closed the search. He wasn't ready to call yet. He wanted to make a list of questions and figure a way to get the doctor to talk to him if it was in fact him. He couldn't approach it as her boyfriend or anything like that. He'd have to pretend to be some type of professional.

He pondered it over dinner. He scribbled down everything he knew about her and her family. What did she say her grandmother's name was? Or did she? The great-great-aunt was Iris but that didn't help. He wondered how he could gather info on her grandmother without letting her know. The grandmother had left the Lodge to Iris, so the island town hall should have a record of her. He felt sneaky and ashamed for going behind Iris's back, but he knew if he brought this to her she'd close off, or worse. Something might happen to either of them. He couldn't risk it.

He messaged her before bed and she said she'd skied out for the cat food and litter. She thanked him for the extra treats he'd put in the bag. He'd scored chocolate, crackers, and cheese for her. She sent a picture of Roar who was very much at home in front of the fire, a small round bread loaf with pointy ears. Then Iris sent a rather explicit picture of herself to which he blushed and slammed his phone closed since Duff was sitting just feet away. He'd save that for later when he was alone. He opened the phone once Duff got up to go to the kitchen and texted Iris back.

"Dinner at your place tomorrow?"

"I'd love that. Did you get my picture?"

"Uh, yeah. Duff almost saw more of you than they would've known what to do with. Hopefully, they didn't see me turning red."

"Oh! I guess I should send a warning message first. Did you like it?"

"Why do you think I asked about dinner?" Ledger replied. He could still feel the heat in his face.

"Ah. Am I dessert?"

"God, I hope so."

CHAPTER FIFTEEN

*T*he next morning, Ledger went to the island city hall and spoke to Brenda. He didn't even lie or try to cover up what he was doing. After all, most of it was public record and he'd known Brenda his whole life. She'd been in high school when he was little, the island babysitter. The island city hall was literally a room at the back of the library, which was no bigger than a large living room. Which was technically a living room, dining room combo, since the whole shebang was in an old house converted into the library and city hall. He waited at the chipped laminate counter while Brenda pulled up the records on the Lodge. She peered closely at the screen, then wrote down some notes.

"Okay, originally was in the name of Iris Crowley who passed it on at her death to Darcy Cantrall. It recently changed hands again to an Iris Brubaker."

"Thanks, Brenda! That helps a lot. How's your father doing?" Ledger inquired.

"Oh you know, mean and befuddled. How about your mom?"

"Good. Winter is hard when she is out of work, but she's keeping busy at the house."

"Tell her I said hello."

"I will. I'd say tell your dad the same but his only recollection of me is screaming at me to get my bike off his lawn," Ledger joked.

Brenda laughed lightly. "That sounds about right. His lawn was his pride and joy. Now that he's in the retirement village, he doesn't know what to do with himself. So, he yells at the television."

Ledger chuckled and said his goodbyes as he headed out the door. He let his mind drift back to a simpler time on the island. The Fourth of July parade where all the kids would decorate their bikes and ride in the parade at the beginning, so they could stop to watch the rest of the parade after. In the last few years, very few kids participated and the last year was just one of the summer children. The kids now were more indoors, in front of screens. Those that were left. When he was a kid, they were always out exploring and getting into trouble. In the winter months, they broke into the summer people's homes to see what treasures they could score. He liked the idea of raising kids on the island but it wouldn't be the same. Then again, if he married Iris, they may not have any children. He stared at the name of the doctor and took a deep breath. He needed to be convincing.

The phone rang multiple times before an answering machine picked up and he let out the breath he'd been holding in. Should he bother leaving a message? It might become evidence if he did, but if he didn't, he wasn't sure he'd ever get through to the doctor. He was probably a screener. Ledger thought about what he'd say.

It beeped and he made a quick decision.

"Hello, I'm trying to reach Dr. Arbuckle. Dr. Eugene Arbuckle, who was a surgeon at Bryman Memorial Hospital in Bryman, Georgia. If this is Dr. Arbuckle, can you please call me back at your earliest convenience? It's in regard to a patient you treated about ten years ago. I need some information to help in their current care. Thank you!"

He fudged the timeline and didn't mention Iris, knowing for sure he wouldn't get a call back if he did. He made it sound like he was in the medical field, hoping this would urge the doctor to call him. He saved Arbuckle's number in his phone, as he was a screener, too, and couldn't miss the call when, or if, it came through. Brubaker. He wasn't sure he'd even known Iris's last name. Maybe from the original pick-up, but he hadn't stored it in his memory. Obviously, her father's name since her grandmother's name was Cantrall. Ledger wondered why she kept it after what her father did. Then he wondered if Iris even knew his own last name.

Later that evening, he drove out to the Lodge for dinner and was glad to see someone had come and cleared her road with a plow. Island people were like that. If it didn't require investment or emotion, they'd be there for you in a heartbeat. Not to mention, everyone that met her seemed to take a shine to Iris. She had that way about her. The Lodge was glowing and smoke was coming out of the chimney. Despite her history and being a petite woman, Iris could more than take care of herself.

She greeted him at the door with a kiss and a beer. "I've missed you!"

He wrapped his arms around her and grinned. "Same. The good thing is we're getting to the tail end of winter, so at least we shouldn't have too many more major storms. It still snows on and off through March and into April, but we get some warmer days in there as well. Warmer being above freezing."

"Good to know. My grandma's house is in Tennessee, just over the Georgia border, and we saw snow maybe once or twice a year. I was not ready for this."

"Still, you've adapted well," Ledger responded with admiration.

"It's one of my superpowers. Somewhere I have a cape with an A on it."

"For Adapting?"

"Yup," Iris replied, grinning with her eyes sparkling. "What's your superpower?"

"I don't have one," Ledger said, wrinkling his nose.

"Sure you do. Let's see. How about Persistence?" she offered.

Ledger laughed and took a sip of his beer as they moved toward the kitchen. "If you mean persistence as in stubbornness, I think my mother would be inclined to agree. She used to say I'd cut off my own arm just to prove my point. She's probably right."

Roar came bolting out from behind the piano, jumped on Ledger's feet with her claws out, then ran off. Iris shook her head and sighed.

"She does that all night long. I can hear her tear-assing from one end of the Lodge to the other. Then she sleeps all day. Little shit."

An orange flash sped past them and into the curtains. Roar had clearly made herself at home and somehow her presence seemed to take some of the Lodge's power away. Ledger waited until he saw she was going to zip by again and snagged her as she did. She blinked at him with big, golden eyes and batted his nose. He laughed, holding her up. She was purity in its simplest form. Not able to be tainted or convinced otherwise. She began to purr and he put her against his neck to feel the vibration.

"I wish I'd had a cat growing up," he thought out loud. "We only ever had a dog and he was more my dad's companion on the boat until he died. The dog, I mean. It died when I was ten or so. We never had anything after that."

"Yeah, animals have a way of keeping things grounded. Can't take myself too seriously with this little spitfire running around," Iris agreed and rubbed Roar's head. "People say they can see spirits."

Ledger frowned. "You think so?"

Iris shrugged. "I don't know. I haven't seen any proof of it, but she freaks herself out with her own reflection if that counts."

"Does she sleep with you?"

"No, she's up most nights acting like a maniac. She actually won't even go upstairs. Not sure if it is the stairs or not. She just won't."

Ledger could relate. He doubted it was the stairs because he'd seen the kitten scale the curtains to the top. He went to the stairs and set the kitten on them. She immediately stopped purring and bolted off them. Electricity came off of her as she brushed his hand.

She knew.

Iris watched her run off and laughed. "See?"

Roar jumped on top of the piano bench and started grooming herself. She looked miffed. Ledger thought back to Bertie's story about seeing the hung girl and shuddered. He stared at Roar, who stared back like she could read his mind. They both knew the truth about the Lodge. He shook it off and took a deep breath in.

"Smells great! What are you making?'

"Ah, a very southern meal. Baked macaroni and cheese, green beans, whiskey baked beans, and cornbread."

"Damn, that sounds good. Were you able to get groceries?"

"Yeah, I ordered some from the mainland and my neighbor Edgar brought them by from the ferry."

Edgar Simpson. He was a nice guy and lonely since his wife passed. Ledger had gone to school with his youngest, Marie. All his kids moved away after graduation. Edgar chose to stay and was all alone. It was the same story over and over. The island needed something to invigorate it before it dried up. Iris pulled the macaroni and cheese out of the oven and Ledger's stomach growled. She heard it and laughed.

"Good. I was afraid I made too much."

"Uh, never. I don't have an off switch."

They took the food to the enclosed porch and left the door propped to let heat move out to it. The sun had warmed it during the day, but with it going down it was rapidly cooling. The sun was setting, casting an orange glow across the channel. With no leaves on the trees, Ledger could see the houses on the other side well. Barely more than a stone's throw away, but a completely different reality. Everything there was accessible. It was like they lived in a different century.

He ate way too much and still wanted more. He groaned and stood up, trying to make room in his abdomen. He rubbed his stomach and stared down at Iris. "If you keep cooking like that, I'm going to get fat."

"Well, I hope you saved room for dessert?"

He hadn't seen any dessert and peered at her with question. She raised her eyebrows, biting her lower lip. Oh, yeah. *She* was dessert. He chuckled and shook his head.

"Give me a bit to digest this food and you're on."

She play pouted, then stood up. "Well, then let's clear the table and I can put some coffee on. Don't want you falling asleep on me between now and then."

"*That* you don't have to worry about, Iris."

"Alright, Mr. Elliot, let's have some coffee and play Scrabble until you are ready to rumble."

"Mr. Elliot is my father."

"Well, then, Ledger, you ready to get beaten?"

He laughed and picked up dishes to take to the kitchen. So, she did know his last name. Probably a good thing since they were sleeping together. No. More than that. He was going to spend his life with her. There was no doubt in his mind about that. Iris Elliot. That'd be if she wanted his last name. Times had changed and women taking a man's name was somewhat outdated. Maybe she didn't. He thought she might not want her father's either, though.

"My parents joked they gave me and Duff last names as first names since we had a first name as a last name. That way we wouldn't have two first names," Ledger said half to himself, remembering his father and mother telling them that when they were little. He hadn't gotten the joke then. But he liked seeing how his parents kidded with each other.

"That's funny. Your parents sound like they were close," Iris murmured, her thoughts seeming to go back to her own parents' relationship.

"They were. Or at least I thought so. They were always teasing each other and you know, connecting. They'd stare at each other across the dinner table and it was like they were sending secret messages. We were a super close family and they treated each other with such love."

"Aw. That's really sweet. I want a love like that."

"Me too. I want to be old with someone and still be cracking up."

Their eyes met and they both saw the potential there. The only thing in their way was the Lodge. Ledger knew Iris couldn't see it and he couldn't move forward as things stood. He needed to find a way out of the maze for both of them and not lose Iris in the process. He leaned in and kissed her softly, brushing her cheek with his thumb.

It was about strategy. Even though they were both affected by the outcome, he was the only one fighting for their survival. Iris didn't know what lay underneath. He needed to lead the way out of the woods without her knowing they weren't just going for a stroll.

They put everything away and sat with coffee to play Scrabble. Iris was smart and knew how to manipulate the board to her will. Ledger quickly saw she was going to easily beat him at the game. She swiftly won and wasn't polite about it. She jumped up and slammed her hands down on the table.

"In your face!"

Ledger busted out laughing, shaking his head. "I'd hate to see you when you lose."

"That's the thing," she retorted. "I don't lose."

Whatever it was, seeing her like this turned him on and he stood up, grabbing her hand. He dragged her toward him and kissed her firmly on the mouth. She responded, letting her hand drift under his shirt. Blood rushed between his legs, making him so hard, his pants felt constrictive. He led her to the living room, reading the heat on her face. He laid a blanket out in front of the fire and pulled her down on it, pressing her to him. He couldn't wait any longer.

"You may have won, but I got the prize."

CHAPTER SIXTEEN

*T*he next couple of months went on like totally normal life. It was as if whatever had existed before moved on. Spring was coming and with it, the relief from snow and restriction. Ledger tried to set himself free from the worry and fear about Iris's past and the Lodge, but when he was alone in bed at night, it crawled in and buried in his chest. The weight reminding him nothing had changed.

He figured he'd hit a dead-end with the Eugene Arbuckle he'd called, either because it wasn't the right doctor, or it was and the doctor was on to Ledger's true purpose. He considered just letting it go, though deep down he knew that wasn't the correct answer. Either way, he shoved it to the back of his mind and found new hope in the delicate buds he saw on the trees.

Nothing weird had happened since the night Bertie died and Ledger had been visited by the terrifying vision. He still refused to sleep in Iris's room but she'd quit asking. They found ways to be together without it causing an issue and neither wanted to give up their time together.

It was a warm spring evening when Ledger headed to the Lodge for dinner. It'd become so common, they were beginning to feel like they were married. They made dinner, she beat him at Scrabble. Sometimes they made love, others they just relaxed until he got ready to leave. The Lodge bookings were filling up for the next month and soon he wouldn't be able to hang out there. He didn't like the guests and Iris would be too busy to relax.

Ledger was just about to head out for the night when his phone went off. He'd saved the number, so when he saw Eugene Arbuckle on the screen, he knew he needed to take it. Iris had gone to the kitchen to put dishes away as he stepped onto the porch to answer the call.

"Hello?"

"Hello, this is Dr. Arbuckle. I received a message from this number. I apologize for the long delay, I vacation out of the country for the winter months."

"Yes, thank you so much for calling me back." Ledger put his hand over the mouthpiece as Iris came back in. "Can you hold just a moment? Or can I call you right back? I'm just finishing up something."

"That would be fine. I will be up for the next hour or so. After that, it will need to wait until tomorrow," the doctor explained.

"Thank you, I'll call you in a few minutes."

Ledger hung up the phone and smiled at Iris. "Hey, I'd better go. Thank you for dinner. My mother wants you to come out for dinner this week."

"Great, I'll be there! Just let me know what night. I think Roar can handle being alone now," Iris replied and leaned up to kiss him. "Important call?"

"Not sure. It's one I've been waiting for. Probably nothing, truthfully." Ledger knew she could read him and it was best to stick to the truth with omissions.

"Not another girl is it?" Iris asked, eyeing him playfully.

Ledger grabbed her, pulling her tight. "Never. You are my one and only."

She grinned and pushed him away. "I'd better be."

As he was about to head out the door, Roar jumped up from where she'd been sleeping and hissed, her back arching. Ledger and Iris stared at her, then to where she was looking but there was nothing there. Iris laughed and shook her head. Roar's gaze was fixated toward the piano, growling low. The hair on Ledger's arm raised as he watched the cat.

It wasn't nothing.

It was just something they couldn't see. He could feel it, though. They weren't alone. Roar could sense it, and now he could as well. He wavered, wondering if he should stay, but Iris practically pushed him out the door.

"She just had a bad dream is all. She isn't right. She does stuff like that all of the time."

Ledger paused at the door and for a second Roar turned her head to him, then back to the spot. She was letting him know something was there. Iris scooped her up, distracting the cat, then waved him off. He wanted to talk to the doctor and knew he was running out of time. He left reluctantly and went to his truck. He dialed the number as he drove, relieved when the doctor picked up.

"Dr. Arbuckle? Hi, it's Ledger. We spoke a second ago."

"Sure, sure. You said in your message you were calling about a mutual patient?"

"Sort of. Sorry if I gave the impression I was a doctor. I'm not. However, I'm calling about one of your past patients."

"This is highly unusual and possibly unethical. What patient?" Arbuckle asked, his voice irritated with the dishonesty.

"Before I tell you, I need you to know this may be a matter of life and death. I wouldn't reach out otherwise. This patient is someone very dear to me and I fear they are in danger," Ledger explained.

"Alright then, go on."

"About fifteen years ago, you performed surgery on a girl who was attacked by her father. Iris Brubaker. I need to find out why she was unknowingly sterilized. Given a tubal ligation as a child?"

The line was silent but Ledger could hear the doctor breathing. Short, nervous breaths. Arbuckle cleared his throat and whispered in a low southern drawl, "I had a feeling this would come back to haunt me."

"What do you mean? Why did you give her a tubal ligation at thirteen years old and then lie about it? She has no idea that it happened to her. I figured it out."

"Look, son. I do not know how you know this girl but if I were you, I would run as far away from her as I could. *Your* life could be in danger. There are other things at play, and she is the doorway."

"What do you mean doorway? Can you just tell me what happened?" Ledger gripped the steering wheel with his free hand.

"That girl, she was barely alive when they brought her in. Cut wide open. I was a surgeon but not that kind. I did mostly routine things, minor. They did not think she would survive being transported, so I did what I could. She died on the table. I should have let her stay that way. However, she was just a child and I felt for any family she had left. We revived her and she died again. We revived her again but this time the surgery room filled up with the most sulfuric smell I had ever experienced. Like we were being gassed. No one could breathe and our eyes were watering, swelling shut. I quickly closed her up and decided if she survived, it would be on her own."

"So, she pulled through obviously. What was the smell from?"

"Honestly? I think we opened the gates of hell. I did not make her live. I put her together the best I could, but something else pulled her through." Arbuckle made no apologies with his explanation.

Ledger swallowed hard, remembering the first image he had of her coming out of the woods. A creature crawling its way out of the depths. Not Iris, but also *not* not Iris. "I don't understand how she was sterilized, though. She said had a couple of surgeries?"

"She did. After she survived, I saw her sweet face and I felt differently. So innocent, so unaware, I knew we needed to help her. I do not think she is evil, mind you. I think, well... I do not know what I think."

"Why did you sterilize her then?"

"It's not so simple. After that first surgery, I kept having these visions. This demon would come to me when I was sleeping. It seemed to enjoy its existence and would taunt me

The Book

That Told On Me

True Justice

THIS DIARY BELONGS TO:

This diary belongs to every woman who fought to get out of bed this morning because pain always has a tendency of making sleep impossible. This diary belongs to every woman who has smiled every day while crying in bathroom stalls on breaks and on drives from work. This diary belongs to every woman who has been wounded by family, friends, lovers and even our own selves. This diary belongs to all mothers and mothers of no children. But most of all, this diary belongs to every woman who has decided that her purpose is greater than her pain and that her mistakes have only paved the way for her to look inward and reclaim the power that was placed there from the beginning. This diary belongs to you.

Contents

Promise you won't tell ......

Monsters..6

Silent soldiers.....................................9

When it hurts 11

Autumn...13

His voice 14

Right turn 16

Wants 18

War on us 20

Her 24

Rumors 25

My world 27

Paper 28

Thought to call 30

True story...32

The bed you made 34

The truth 36

Bumping heads...........................37

When he never said 38

Midnight thoughts 41

Simply stupid 43

Reflections 46

Alone 47

Today 48

Life 49

Hannah 50

Super hero 53

Dear Diary,
I just wanted to forget about the …

<u>Monsters</u>

Mommy always told me monsters were not real
But I swear
I hear them creep into my bed at night
So I lay ever so still and try not to make a sound
Because I know if I get up and run
This monster will just take me down and turn me
around and that will be the end of me
And I'll scream
Scream like I always do
"Mommy, Mommy!"
But it's as if she can't hear me and she's only in
the next room
That's okay because I know that soon
Prince charming will burst in my room
Just to save me
He will pick me up and say
"I'm so sorry for all the bad things you had to go
through lately "
And he'll take me far far away from here
A place where monsters cannot go
Or maybe!
Even Dumbo will swing by my window
Just to pick me up
And I know!
I'll say Rumpelstillsin three times just to give me
luck

Rumpelstillsin, Rumpelstillsin,, Rumpelstillsin
But now he is here again
And I feel his hand on my skin
Mommy always told me that Monsters are just not
real
But I see the strange look on her face when she
washes the "kool-aid"
Stains from my sheets away
But it's real crazy because I never had Kool-Aid
in the first place
And if I did
Why would it fall only from between my legs so
far away from my face?
See Mommy,
Monsters are real
Real enough to see and they love to rub and touch
little girls like me
And I know you see him because you treat him so
nice
And I know you heard me cry for you at least
twice the other night
But you never said a word
Not even to make the monster stop
Do you remember what you told me Mommy?
"Listen here little girl, you don't pay enough bills
in this house to keep your door locked"
So mommy do you see how you made it easy for
this monster to get in and on me
So see mommy monsters are real
Real enough to see and they love to rub and touch
little girls like me
And I know you see him and everything that he

7

does
But this is what happens when moms fall in
monster love
Because you never made him stop
Mommy always told me monsters are just not real
But I don't believe her.

Secret: Monsters are real and they don't live under our beds they sneak in them.

Dear Diary,
What we learned never to talk about.
<u>*Silent Solders*</u>

The first words I wrote in my first poem was
"I feel like dying, 'I was ten then
Sweaty hands clenched to my gel pen
But I never felt more free
I never wanted to utter words that would make
Anyone mad at me
So, I wrote to cope
It was the telescope to my soul
And it hurt a lot less than words spoke
But sometimes silence becomes too loud
And in an instant flashback, I could recall the
sound
of hands slapping faces
Torn clothes, and tears of me and siblings leaving
Traces of things we would never talk about when
we were grown
Because what happens at home stays at home
I learned to escape the way that my brother did
As he used the beat from this beating
to help him create a new song
That would drown out my step mothers cries
I could never forget as he wrote a love song
Tears welled in his eyes
Because there was nothing loving about this
But we knew that by morning
Scratched faces, busted lips, and moved furniture
Would all be dismissed
And sealed with a kiss as my father left for work

Leaving us as silent solders to imaginary wars
And the thought that we are just kids
Who understood that bruises heal
And cuts don't bleed that long
But this is where they were wrong
Because we were left open and wounded
each part of us becoming infected
Replaying our own childhood in our relationships
as if we never left it
and now, "why are you so violent," becomes
parents questions
but we respond with no words
but thoughts of "why you didn't expect it"
yet, we dare not speak on the things that you
wanted us to forget
But you shared in your rage
how about sharing that switch?
that can make everything okay by the morning
Because now we give kisses and close doors
To children who are left as silent soldiers to
Imaginary wars.

Secret: What happens at home...stays with you..

Dear Diary,
Something hurts …

When it hurts

When it hurts to write
When my pen can't extend pass this eight by ten
And write all the wrongs in my life
It's at that moment I wish I could sing
Release all this pain over my steady heartbeat
Compose a lullaby to soothe my pain to sleep
Or maybe a gospel would do
A song to the heavens just to remind God all the
Things that I've been through
Then maybe just maybe then
He would send something
that I can clap my hands
And stomp my feet to
And dance this pain away
Never learned how to sing on key anyway
And the only note that I know is the one I wrote
And the only instrument I can play
Is this voice that I own
And my message may go undelivered
Because of my tone
But this is the sound of pain being strung to long
A song of pain in the form of a poem
So tell me, God is you listening?
Cuz I would love if you could tune in
And if you forgot why I hurt
I can replay it again
If that helps you better
And I've never felt more alone

So, I sing my song acapella
God just let me know when you hear it.
I just want you to turn this off in my spirit
Because I never liked this song anyway

Secret: God never seemed so far.

Dear Diary,

I've got used to having no one but sometimes hurting alone hurts too much.

Autumn

I had fallen into autumn.
My body floated down below the trees
I reached out to those who loved me,
But they all just turned to leaves.
Had they forgotten our summer days?
And how we once shared the tress
It was autumn that changed me,
Made me, fall to my knees.
Brown and orange bruises
Some say how beautiful I bleed …
I was dying in autumn just trying to make it to Spring.

Secret: People tell me how beautiful I am and I think to myself... it must be hard to tell when beautiful things are dying

Dear Diary,
I hear love cures all wounds .... I think I need
It ....

<u>*His voice*</u>

Today, I thought I heard love
It was beautiful,
  Yet gritty like the sound of a Negro
Spiritual on Sunday
Filled with feelings,
  the sound stopped me in my tracts
It gripped my heart and it tore into my unbelief
The sound was so loud
I couldn't even hear my thoughts
Only my heart beating to its rhythm
This sound
Moved mountains that blocked sunsets
And uncovered oceans where lovers spend their
Nights and kiss slow
It rang in my soul
So deep, that it spoke not only to who I was
But also, to the people I had been
We all heard it
It was a sound that we knew but never heard
So together we prayed for arms like a bird
Just to catch what we heard
or at least find where it lands
So maybe then I could touch it with my hands
Because I never knew what love felt like anyway
I moved closer, but the closer I came
It faded away

Leaving me open and listening
To nothing because nothing could compare to this
sound
It left me
Lost but found
Because at least now I knew I could hear it.

Secret: Love was my answer...

Dear Diary,
I think I made a Right turn.
<u>*Right Turn*</u>

Aw damn. I'm sorry so late, I'm a mess
I'm still trying to figure out this love GPS
Sorry it's new
But I kind of got lost coming from my last
Relationship because I left then made a U
Only to turn around
 and comeback and arrive at the same truth
I should have left, right like the GPS told me to
Because you can't expect your love to take a
Different direction if you don't even move
But I knew
That he couldn't be my final destination
But I drove myself crazy
 Trying to love him through
Dead end streets and recalculations
Wrong ways. And his way highways
And I can't even expressways
 Of the many tolls I've
Paid ...
Just to go nowhere and I swear
All I ever wanted was to make it to loves home ...
But trying to reach him drove me wrong
My love GPS ringing like a cell phone ,
"Wrong, wrong, wrong way"
But I would ignore it, shut down and deactivate
And that's how I got lost

But I never meant to make you wait
And I know my accuracy must recalibrate
But I apologize for taking so long
But this time I followed all the sighs
I almost got lost at the roundabout street "of just
Looking for a good time"
But this time my landmarks
Are no longer broken hearts
I'm speeding to you, no breaks
No detours
Getting out of my own lane just to merge to yours
Ready or not ...
Just tell me, I haven't fallen into your blind spot

Secret: He made me so happy that I forgot about the monsters and I was no longer a soldier of pain. Who needs pain when you found someone who can make it go away? Right?

Dear Diary,
  So, I ignored who I was just so I could be who he
  wanted...

Wants

Simply tell me who you want me to be
I can be your sexy school teacher,
Who never gives you a "B"
Because, she
Just wants to "F" you
Or I can be your Chinese masseuses
 Sent all the way
From china
Just to please you
"Cu me love you long time"
So tell me who you want me to be?
I can be your hood bitch from the streets,
The shy girl who never speaks,
Your loyal wife who goes to church every
Sunday
Or your mistress who's a freak
Your French maid who only gets paid by your
 Oh la we-we
See baby you can have all three in me,
Have you losing your mind by all the people
Who live in me
I aint lyin
Make-believe starts to seem real, real with me
Just enter my world one time
So just tell me who you want me to be

Cuz aint no need for you to be in them streets
Because I got your love
And if you start to get bored
Forget it;
 I'll turn this whole damn living room
Into a strip club
So baby take a seat..
And rest assured these ones you throw
Will be spent on the food we eat
So throw generously
I want steak tonight
But seriously, I need to be
Just what you want
So say it

Secret: It was better to pretend. I didn't know who I was anyway..

Dear Diary,
He was supposed to heal what hurts but then why am
I still bleeding.... We were dying before we met and
together we murdered each other.

War on us

Would you at least look at me?
Please understand that our relationship has
Reached an all-time high state of emergency.
And something in me tells me
  this won't end good.
So would,
You please put your weapon down,
  and stop pacing
  I need you to understand that this is my last
Attempt at any negotiation.
Because (warning, warning)
I'm really starting to lose my patience
I see you ready for war, cocked and loaded
But you know my words can be radiation
So, what you want to do???
Ohhhhhh, fuck me huh?
  Well,
Since we are on this topic hell
I'm tired of fucking you
It's not like we're making love,
  it's not passionate,
  we just sexing
And then you always give me
  that same lame excuse

That you never knew love growing up,
so you don't know how to show affection.
Well, question?
Is that what you tell these hoes via text message?
But you know what? You don't know love
I remember you told me
you cried everyday growing up
Praying to God for your mama to give crack up
But look at you selling the same drugs
Let me back up
Hell, that's enough to make me crack up
Oh so you big mad or naw?
What you going to do now huh?
Barricade me with your silence
Hell, that's better than 2 weeks ago when you put
Your hands on me
And I told you I would never tolerate domestic
Violence
See I aint like my mama
cuz see I FIGHT BACK!
And please understand
you can't sneak attack me.
I see the artillery that you gave to your family,
Telling them I'm messed up because my daddy
Touched me
Nice try, but baby I'm bullet proof vested ...
Cuz the truth is between me and you
I aint the only one that been molested.
You just let it hold you captive,
allowed it to feistier
So tell me how does that make you any better..

When it's something we both went through..
Yea I knew that's the real reason why you beat up
that gay dude
Cuz yall made eye contact
and you felt like he knew.
So to hell with you!
And let me say this before I go
Consider this a terrorist attack on your ego
Fuck this and this relationship,
Cuz my love for you has grown absent like your
daddy
So yea, yea call me crazy
But you threw in the hand grenades
When you said if I was a real woman,
I would have had your baby

And this is just how we blew up .....

We never grew out of the pain of our childhood we
just grew up
Trying to love each other through shit that we
couldn't even get through
We learned to soothe our wounds with "I LOVE
YOU'S "
But both of us defeated,
See he just needed the love of a mother
And a father to show him direction and patience
But every day he was forced to stare down the
barrel of my expectations.
And if he didn't love me the way that I wanted my
Parents to do
I would shoot

Open wounds never healed
See we mastered the art of blowing each other up,
Never trying to build
Bleeding all over each other
 and hurting each otherstill
"Love me until I don't feel empty",
 Just became the deal
That we couldn't possibly ever fulfill
So our love was a causality of hurt
You can't stop the bleeding of someone else's heart
Until you stop your first.
Enough was enough
This war was on us.

Secret: I hated him for not being able to fix everything inside me that broke ...and he hated me for the same reason ....

Dear Diary,
  We couldn't fix each other so he found her ....
HER

So can you get out tonight?
Say you're chilling with your boys, or start a fight
Bump it, tell her you're just going down the street
but then bust a right
Towards me
And come love on me
not for long
Turn your phone off to turn me on
Until there is no time left
Drive home with the scent of me on your breath
A guilty man under an innocent protest
But you can't avoid this flesh on flesh
Cuz we get so close it's like incest
So lets
Just do what we shouldn't
Let me take you were your wife couldn't
Reach
The deepest part of your soul
Where the pastor couldn't preach
Hard enough to make you stay away from me
But I warned you before trying this ecstasy
So now I'm a habit and you're an addict on "E"
You can feel wrong but that's all right with me
See you tonight ....

Secret: I want to kill him..

Dear Diary,
I can feel her on him even right now as he lies next to
me...something in me knows..

Rumors

FYI, just to clarify
The Rumors well
They started with the pillow
He told me He just wanted to give me the heads up
He told me he heard your thoughts of infidelity at
night
And he told those thoughts to shut up but,
They wouldn't listen
Oh and by the way he didn't fail to mention
That he told you that if you chose to bring another
woman into our bed
That he would get ahead and tell on you
Look at you straight in the eyes and ask "what the
Fuck are you going to do?"
Yea, we got one bad ass pillow, that nigga
comfortable too
And our sheets
Man they expose you like open lids on toilet sheets
And exposed all the shit you did
Like it or not
They were even nice enough to show me all the wet
spots
From you and her
They even showed me a slight rip
Where they tried to pull away from her grip
As they rolled down as of not to touch her
And the comforter told me that you were

comfortable enough
To tell her
You loved her as you fucked her
And the mirror cried when she showed me that
Night's reflection
And the AC cut off cuz she knew your actions
Weren't cool
And left yall sweating while sexing and turn the
Heater on
And the CD player made sure that she skipped on
Every song
Just to make sure your love making was off beat
And the floor cried with the sheets as she squeaked
as to tell on you
Oh and by the way
The throw rug told me to tell you
That she is through with your dirty ass too
The phone let me hear her moans when I thought
I got a call for you
But instead of voices I heard bodies
In motion like Pilates
The bed squeaked from impaction
You loving that ass and
I hold the phone to my ear
And I'm like damn justice
I thought love was everlasting
But I guess it's not true
But a special
Shout out
To the rumor
Of the room
That told on you.

Secret: Give a man the moon and he'll wish for the stars.. Somehow I was never enough...

Dear Diary,
I just want to escape....

My World

Sometimes, I wish that I lived in between the sheets
Of my poetry book
Because there,
Words comfort me like hugs.
God, never seem so close
Love comes easy
And only tears of joy fall from my eyes
Blurring any disappointments, I've ever had.

Secret: I was lost ....

Dear Diary,
The very thing that I thought would heal me has
ripped me and tore into my soul like ....

<u>Paper</u>

See he told me that our marriage was simply just
Paper
And maybe that's why I cry on empty sheets
And maybe that's why I couldn't read between the
Lines when you were trying fuck over me
And I allowed you to poke these three holes in me
Like,
I – love- you
Because if it were true,
I'm sure I'd be much more then paper to you
But I've been penned and marked and erased so
much
I can't even use context clues
To realize whose name was on this paper
in the first fucking place
And I've given you,
all of me for the last four years
And all you can do is throw paper in my face
Because I've been crying for weeks
And I want to rip you like you've ripped me
So be on the lookout for this loose leaf
Because I am more than fucking paper
I was your lover, your wife
Your personal freak at night
Your lawyer, your doctor
Your supporter in your darkest hour

Yet four years later
You refer to me as fucking paper
Torn by you bit by bit
But I refuse to be your toilet paper
and take this shit
Just remember this
our children's name would have been printed on
birth paper
I only pushed you to get a better job to get a little
more paper
So one day our love can be in the paper
As the love that made it
But now it become folded and faded
And you've thrown it like some type of
Paper boy
But I refuse to allow anymore construction to this
paper
So baby, do me this favor and sign these divorce
papers
Don't worry it's just papers

Secret: I hated being alone ...

Dear Diary,
I held the phone to my ear, but my hands refused to
dial. It hurts to call maybe silence is better. This is
just how we disconnected …

Thought to call

I thought to call, but somehow my words slipped
Through the cracks of the phone and fell
Somewhere in between the dial tone and operator
"If you would like to make a call"
I would
But I need help
Then the voice on the other end said,
"Then redial your operator"
But what if I can't operate
Because it's been too long this time
So, I thought to call you unknown
I am now, so I press *69
But as a coward,
I hang up before connection.
Then instantly I start text messaging
But I can't send any more apologies because my
Memory is low.
I can't erase the memories of you
Never did let go
So….
Can I reach out and touch you like AT&T?
And can you sprint my way?
Can you be my metro off the clock, so we can talk
all day?
Can I say hello, so you can hear me better?

Like T-Mobile I'm saying, can we stick together?
If I call will you answer, by luck?
Or should I just hang the thought of you and I
Up...
Because I never liked feeling this disconnected
Anyway
But I thought to call...

**Secret: I always had a tendency to clinging to
people who hurt me the most...**

Dear Diary,
Maybe I'm just hard to love either way I'm getting
real tired of this shit ...

True story

I dedicate this entry to the men in my life who
Simply couldn't love me
Shout out to the dude
Who said he had no kids
Only to find out he had three
One time, for the men who use their birthdays as
their cell phone IDs
The real MVPS
Now, I really appreciate you.
Three times, to the dude who dressed up every day
Like he was going to work
But was only employed in his mind.
Now triple time to the dudes who said they were
single
But they girlfriend's sending "I love you's "all on
they timeline
You must have forgotten we were friends huh?
Now that's funny
Shout out to the dudes that got mad
When they found out my vagina
wasn't attached to money
And a big up to all the phone calls
I got from girlfriends
Hey, we had something in common or whatever
And this goes out to the dude who wants to talk

But keeps his phone on silent
So, I guess nobody calls you,
Really like, ever?
And kudos to the men who only wanted to give
Me the world after I already let go.
Yall know you on the block list, right?
Call, I won't know
And one shutout to the dude who lies so much
Hell, I don't even know his real name.
Let alone where he stay
And finally, I have to acknowledge the pretty boy
Who only liked me because he thought I could
Make him straight
DAMMN ....

Secret: I became angry ...

Dear Diary,
Now why would this nigga call me now? As much
I love him. I still won't answer....

The bed you made

Sometimes I wonder
Do you think of me in between sentences spoken?
For her?
Do you really love where you are?
Or would you prefer where you were?
All those times we never left our beds
Mangled in our minds our legs intertwined
Who needs food, our bodies were fed
Never board in our heads
But our headboard stayed
Banging
Leaving only the neighbors to decipher what they
Were saying
Because all we heard was love
And we never cared how loud that was
So, I wonder
Do you fuck, or do you make love?
In the synonymous way that we use to
So, tell me when your bodies touch
Does it resemble our union?
Do you make love to her in remembrance of me?
Like Holy Communion
Do your bodies share in confessions?
Is God, called in your sessions?
Giving reverence to every position
Fulfilling our mission

Both visionary
Cuz you know that our love making extended
Missionary
So tell me, has your love for her also become
Religious
Have you given her all our offerings?
That was made for our business
And when she asks you, "whose is this"
Do you remember that you gave it to me first?
Does the thought of losing her hurt?
Or is the pain of what we had worse?
And I wonder
Still smelling like her
What makes you dial my number?
I'm simply the miss that you didn't take
An ex with no cape or superpowers to make you
Forget
So we can avoid all the pleasantries of
"I miss you and shit"
Because I was left, and I guess you chose right
So I won't pick up this call
Just to let you wonder what life would have been
Like.

Secret: A part of me feels like he chose right
because.... Hannah

Dear Diary,
I aint playing with these niggas.

The Truth

He told me a story of hero's and dragons
I told him a story about virgins and queens

WE BOTH LYING...

Secret: when you can't beat them join them..

Dear Diary,
I was doing better. I could finally feel my heart
again. I smiled more and felt myself blossoming into
the universe until I bumped into him …

<u>Bumping Heads</u>

I guess I was tripping when I fell for you
Cuz you went under and I was over you
I pushed but you pulled too
So, we are both responsible for this collision.
Bumping into you was never my intention
You went right
I was right
We made the same decision
And now we've bumped heads
And I hate it when mistakes hurt.
Do I stand up brush this off and part ways?
Or do I stay and play in this dirt we've made
But I hate getting dirty, don't you?
But hell, I tried to signal you
Do I apologize or am I owed to?
Did we move to fast or
did I slowly crash into you?
Or maybe I wasn't paying attention to
Your signs
Like I tend to
Either way, I never liked falling for you.

**Secret: love don't love nobody so I tried to
fight it.**

Dear Diary,
I never wanted to love him. I just wanted to laugh,
dance in his living room and never get hurt....

What he never said

I never heard what he said until he touched me.
His lips pressed against my skin
His fingers wandered to where I've been
And his standing ovation told me that he loved me
So, see words weren't necessary.
Although he heard me
Crashing against his being
Searching through the green of his eyes to
Understands what he means
Meanwhile,
I expressed how much I loved him
Through the love making
That matched the Rhythm
To his heart
And I could have sworn
His heart talked back to me.
Told me, I could never beat this feeling from the
Start
My skin dripped to his lips
And they told me I tasted
Different then all the other women
The pulsate of him
told me that if we didn't calm down

Our time would be ending.
But his slow strokes of my hair told me
 we were just beginning.
Oh, how much I missed him
And the words he never said....
But his hands said
"l love you", as they dominated mine
Placing my hands around my head
And my body spoke of submission
Perfectly position for this needed incision of what
He failed to mention.
Words weren't necessary,
When it came to this feeling.
So, "I love you," simply became the fill in to what
he didn't say
And I was filled to the brim with him
And maybe he confused my tears with all the other
Wetness that surrounded him
Enjoying yet ignoring
Every moan that called out to him
I just wanted him to love me as deep
As he knew I was...
What could this be if it wasn't love?
And hadn't he heard too.
Or had it been that "I love you" can easily be
Misheard with "I just love fucking you".
Cuz maybe,
That's what he said from the beginning...
But I only paid attention to the tips of his lips.
Abandoning all sentences of
"I don't want relationships".
That he did mention.

Thinking that somehow the Rhythm of my sea
Might sway his decision.
But then again,
I was just a friend with a feeling...
With hard situations
And blank spaces between us.
I just wanted to fill em
With words that exceeded body manipulation
I just wanted him to catch these feelings like my
Tears that caught his pillow
Due to my naked expectations
Of words he never said...
So, I never said a word.
Put on my clothes and vowed never to see him
Again.

Secret: I wanted to be numb...

Dear Diary,
  The afterthought always hurt worst.

Midnight Thoughts
 Damn, I wanted him to ask me to stay
But naw, I can't seem pressed,
I'll just grab my bag and my keys
And slowly walk away
Give him a kiss on the cheek
Maybe?
Or would he look at my crazy
Naw, crazy would be if he knew
How in my mind
I've seen our wedding and our baby
Naw I'm just playing
She was cute though
Carmel complexion,
 big brown eyes and a curly fro
Man, I'm tripping
Keys in my hands
His hands on my waist
Damn now we're kissing
Caressing my face, and he is telling me to stay
Fuck!
Is this really what I want to do
Pull away
I do
But now he is whispering in my ear
You know I'm really into you
Naw I didn't know
But I know what you trying to get into
But that's not where my heart is

Although these days they both are split
As he glides his hands up my dress my thoughts
Scream
"Girl, remember niggas aint..."
Shit, why does this feel so good?
I forgot what it felt like to be held this tight
Maybe he could feel the real me
If we lay naked and just cuddle all night
I always wanted someone to love me naked
Please love is far from his mind
Aw here we go ,
What you said?
Lay on your bed
I mean I am kinda tired
I guess that seems fair
Ten minutes later
You biting my neck and pulling on my hair
How did we get here?
And you coming where?
Did I call for you?
Did he just tell me to stop running?
Well I was trying to
Out run these thoughts
That got me in this bed
But now you're sleeping
And I'm left with these thoughts in my head
And the least you could do is turn over

Secret: I gotta do better ...

Dear Diary ,
One day it just clicked . I've spent my whole life
just trying to be loved. I wanted my parents to love
me so I was good. I wanted a man to love me so I
was even better. I had been held captive by this prison
that I created. I was a fool ....

Simply stupid

Simply stupid I got a jones for you
Simply stupid one day we will be through
Simply stupid
Love
Simply stupid
Me
But now we hugging and touching
We aint loving but lusting
So tell me
Has anybody seen me?
Cuz I was last seen
Holding dreams
And insecurities
Stitched in the side of my jeans
With a white tee that
Screens
"Do me wrong cuz this is what love means"
And see its okay if you screen my phone calls
Cuz latter on tonight
you'll have me riding up the walls
And then I'll know that you love me
And when you're at home
Laughing at how dumb I am

At least you're thinking of me
Cuz we've got that, not quite commitment
Don't really mean shit
But you care about me though
And I know I'm special
Because you kiss my lips
And you even go low
So I understand that
You're just afraid of relationships
And that's why we are on this friend with benefits
Tip ,
But we gonna be together right?
Simply stupid I got a jones for you
Simply stupid one day we will be through
Simply stupid
Love
Simply stupid
Me
But now we hugging and touching
We aint loving but lusting
So tell me
Has anybody seen me?
Cuz I was last seen
Holding dreams
And insecurities
Stitched in the side of my jeans
With a white tee that
Screens
"Do me wrong cuz this is what love means"
And I understand
that you have to glide through my thighs
To realize how good I am on the inside

In that case I want you to go so deep
And touch me heart and tell me what it looks like
Cuz I just gotta be everything that you like
Cuz I just gotta be your type and
I'll be your receiver and your tight in
Ill be your mighty tight in
But now its 4 am and Carolyn is calling again
Sending you text messages
"come over boo where you been?"
So I guess we are both your friend and I can't do
this again
So tell me
Has anybody seen me ?
Cuz I was last seen
Holding dreams
And insecurities
Stitched in the side of my jeans
With a white tee that
Screens
"Do me wrong cuz this is what love means"
But now we not hugging and touching
We aint rubbing and lusting
Cuz simply stupid
Im leaving you
Simply stupid this time it's true
Simply stupid
 love
Simply stupid
Me
Simply stupid
Love yourself

Dear Diary,
I've been looking for pieces of myself in other people
but I'm starting to understand they have been within
me this whole time.

<u>Reflections</u>

I fell in love with a man who couldn't speak
I got tired of the silence
So, I left him
For a man who could talk to me all day
But had no feet
But I wanted to dance
So, I couldn't resist the romance of the man who
Could move his feet
But at the end of the night,
I could not feel his touch
because he had no hands.
I wanted to be felt.
Got upset with the cards I had been dealt.
So, I found a man who could touch me
but nothing else
I just wanted all their pieces that they lacked
So, I grabbed my heart from all of them
and stuffed it in my backpack and
Cursed them for not being whole
But I only left before they could notice my missing
Pieces truth be told

Secret: I was missing me the whole time ....

Dear Diary,
I just needed sometime alone..

Alone

She has morphed
she went from ugly to beautiful
Sad to happy
Learned to accept things that she cannot change...
And sometimes in the mist of the storm...
She found peace.
Right in the middle.
With no one beside her
Alone

Secret: what we run from will chase us. I had to find
me.

Dear Diary,
The truth is life had been pushing me this whole
time. Pushing me to a place of solitude,
comfort and peace that did not require the presence of
anyone or anything . It was here I found GOD and
LOVE .

<u>Today</u>

I woke up this morning and didn't paint my face
Just to admire how beautiful I was without it
I didn't weigh in
to hate myself for the things I ate
Today I could do without it
I sat at my alter, meditated,
And forgave everyone you would think I shouldn't
I laughed
I cried.
I danced by myself while I listened to music
Closed my eyes passionately
Liked the way you would
the moment before a kiss.
And I wrote, "life isn't always bad"
Just to remember this

Secret: Therapy helped but when I came to
understand who I was and what I was....I finally
felt free ....

Dear Diary,
My life is nothing I thought it would be. But I'm okay with that.

Life

My expectations have been interrupted
by things I never expected.
I've traveled roads of routes I've never looked for
I've morphed from ugly to beautiful
Just to find out how synonymous the two can be.
I've cried Rivers of tears
And use the same tears
to dance in on days I wished for rain
But oh, not once have I given up
All is well with my soul

Secret: when you war with life it will war back with you .when you accept the present moment there is peace ...

Dear Diary,
Sometimes there is no peace without war. This killed
me but sometimes you have to die to really live...I am
a mother of no one but I give life to many..

Hannah

See this poem is not intended for the easily
Offended
But rather pure motivation for those that suffer
from involuntary menstruation of pain
For those of you that this doesn't apply to
I understand that you won't conceive this same...
All I ask is for your undivided attention
 as at every gender reveal
And baby shower we give you the same
We play your games, eat cake, and Offer names.
Became god and step parents in exchange for our
pain.
And after we cried for hours
We collect the tears from men, who leave us,
Doctors who claim to have powers
 and on negative days
Well
These tears form baby less showers
I'm sorry but we normally don't invite anybody to
Those
Ignore pregnant bellies in grocery stores
Quickly turning from any isle that has baby
clothes...
Meanwhile smiling at your kid's parties
As your complaining about how much work you

had to do
We just praying for one of those
Just trying to compose ourselves
So, no one knows.
Makes you want to hug your kids a little tighter
Tonight, right?
But I digress
back to what this poem is intended to do
See girl this poem is for you
And every hardship that you've had to go through
I know what it feels like
dying just trying to put life into you
The insecurities that bear in your womb
The worry not only that he may cheat,
But he may find a woman
To give him something you were intended to
Knowing that your "I love you's" are purely
conditional to what your body can do
He can't even see how your value extends your
womb
But hell, he's been socialized too.
He sought you but now he only succumbs to what
Your body can do
I'm here to remind you,
Baby, there ain't no body better then you
It's just that when god has compacted you with
some much greatness
It's kinda hard to break that it two
I know it hard but hold on to your light
Understand that the man that the universe has for
you will love you more than life
Because that's what you deserve.

You are a woman of value
Forget what you heard.
Let this penetrate, conceive these words
And may they keep you pregnant all the time
See you are not on any doctor's biological time
line
YOU are not flawed
Yet perfectly built in design.
Always remember a mother is not a state of being
but a state of mind
So, give birth to whatever you got
And remember to love yourself despite anything
else, never stop
Even when times get tough
Never give up
Hannah, you are enough.

Secret: I had to die to give life

Super Hero's

Extra, Extra read all about it
Somebody stole the "S" off superman's chest
Did you hear about it?
Yes, I did I confess
I'm the one who ripped the "S"
Off superman's chest and I brought it here today
now I see the strange look on your faces
First let me explain
See I had a vison,
Is that a bird? is that a plane?
No, it's my grandmother
Flying by with the speed of light
Just trying to make it to the bus stop
Four children following behind her all carrying a
Pal of meat and rice
That was scrapped from the bottom of the pot
But each having more than enough to leave her
hungry
Yet satisfied
that her children had something to eat
And it's amazing
How her stomach laughed at hunger
Her body defeated sleep
And she succeeded the two jobs that antagonized
her feet
See, she was super
I mean like supernatural

Even when she was attacked by single parenthood
Domestic violence
Thrown her down to the gravel
But with a prayer cloth and a bible
She won every battle
She fought many that were not even her own
And see my grandmother never needed a telephone
booth to change
Because she knew that change started at home
That's why she had
an x ray vison for family division
And out of text intellect
To help you make any needed decision
See she could transform on any given day
And I don't know about yall
But I aint never seen superman act this way
Now or then
My grandma's only disguise
Was that she was a woman
In a world that said men are heroes
And women just need to be saved
Well I'm here to let you know today that
It didn't matter how much kryptonite
Got thrown my grandmothers way
She would defeat it and beat it
And then turn around and teach her enemies how
to pray
See, she was super, I mean supernatural
So yes, I did it I confess
I'm the one who ripped the "s" off superman's
chest
Because I wanted to give it to someone who was

more deserving
Because I never got a chance to see her name in
lights
And I never got a chance to see her name in the
newspaper
Until the day that she died
And still then
They never acknowledged the fact that she was a
superhero
Capable of everything that superman did
So I wanted to take this "s" and place it between
The date she died and the date she lived
But since I can't
I decided that I'll simply
Give this "s" to every woman
who will never receive
Credit for being a hero
In a world that's indebted to the male race
They say men run this world
But come on ladies; tell me how men got here in
The first place
So women wear your "S" and wear it held high
And if someone has the nerve to question your
Confidence
Stare them straight in the eye
And let them know that you deserve this "s"
Just like my grandmother did
So take it with you
Everywhere that you go
And every time your super powers start to show
In everything that you do
Because I'm here to scream it at the top of my

lungs
WOMEN ARE SUPER HEROS TOO!

Secret: Your Pain has Purpose and Power ..USE IT !

This Dairy is not just about me but every woman who has experienced these feelings or experiences. I am you. This Diary is not intended to relive those hurtful experiences but intended to show you just how strong you really are and how much love you deserve from

you. This diary is not meant to magnify your pain but exalt your purpose. YOU are still here, stronger, wiser and more powerful then you have ever been.

This is the last page of this diary but not the end of your story. No matter what, hold on to your light, hold on to love and the relentless spirit that is guiding you, every step of the way. You deserve a happiness that is not attached to anything or anyone but you and the GOD that lives in you so I urge you to own it now. It belongs to you

Special acknowledgement: GOD (my source, thank you for this spirit). My parents (Tony Kennedy and Deborah Guillory) for being my portal to this life.

All my siblings because I am only an extension of who you are. Nidia Bates(Tu-tut)because you first loved me. Sonya Clarke for being the first person to see light in me. Shatoyia Falls for igniting the fire in me. Special thanks to Aileen Byron for always reminding me of my power just when I thought I lost it. Portia Knight for treating me like your own. Joyce Peterson for just being who you are. Knowledge (twin flame lol) for allowing me to laugh through the pain. And special Thanks to all my friends and loved ones who spoke life to all dead situations in my life.

> **For booking contact:**
  Ebonykennedy47@yahoo.com
  True-Justice Poetry on FACEBOOK

Made in the USA
Columbia, SC
21 March 2023

about her. I cannot really put it into words. It just kept showing me that she had brought it to life. Brought it here. Finally, I spoke to her grandmother about the girl. She was healing and doing fine despite having seen her family murdered. I told the grandmother about the visions and dreams, but rather than laughing in my face, she grew quiet and asked for specific details. On the next surgery, I performed the tubal ligation on the girl. It was against my beliefs, but it had to be done."

"Did her grandmother know you'd done that to her?" Ledger asked, horrified.

"Son, I think you misunderstood what happened. Her grandmother was the one who signed off on it. She *asked* me to do the surgery. I had her consent as the girl's guardian," Arbuckle replied.

"But why? Why would she ask you to do something so horrible?"

"She said the family was cursed. That someone in her family, an older relative, had welcomed them in. She was terrified for the child, she was afraid any children she might have would be possessed. By the ones the grandmother's relative had welcomed into their lives."

"Welcomed who?"

"The demons."

Ledger wiped his brow and slowed the truck to a stop at an intersection. His heart was racing and fear had overcome him. The demons? What the actual fuck was going on? He glanced up and stared at the stop sign. Some kids had added graffiti to it which wasn't unusual but the words were. The sign now read *STOP now or dead-end.* The road did cross to a dead-end but the timing was eerily accurate. He took a deep breath.

"She said demons?"

Arbuckle cleared his throat before he answered. "She said the family had a place, and her relative in question held ceremonies there with the intent to commune with hell. Some sort of black magic that would give those involved power. I would have thought she was off her rocker except I had seen the visions. She was afraid for the girl. Afraid if she gave birth it would be to a demon of sorts. She thought the attempted murder on her life and her dying then coming back had reopened the door. I did not like doing it, but I did not doubt for a second she was probably right. I think she was truly trying to save the child."

"Save her? Jesus," Ledger whispered with disbelief.

"Yes, Jesus. I don't know if you are a religious man, but if you are not, I would become one as quickly as possible. If they know you know, they will find you. My visions stopped after the surgery and becoming a devout baptist, but every now and then, I feel like I am being watched, being followed. Like it is not over yet. Talking to you will probably be my death sentence... and yours."

Ledger thought of Bertie and knew this was likely true. Whatever was at the Lodge, whatever had a hold on Iris, was not going to let him intervene. "I'm sorry Dr. Arbuckle for dragging you back into this. I love Iris and can't let her get taken by this. I appreciate the information and hope you will be alright."

"God help us both," Arbuckle replied and the line went dead.

Ledger stayed on the side of the road, trying to figure out what to do. A car pulled up behind him, its headlights shining in his rearview mirror. He waved them around and as the car passed, a man inside stared at him knowingly, his face set in a serious scowl. Ledger didn't recognize the man and knew he wouldn't. The shift between planes of existence was beginning to happen. Iris may have been the key to the door, but Ledger was pushing it wide open. He was the target now. The only way to survive was to take the key out of the lock. Iris needed to be removed from the Lodge and she needed to come to grips with how she was being used. He had to find a way to make her understand.

He turned the truck around to head back to the Lodge and the engine stalled. He got it going and made it a short distance before it stalled again. He'd replaced the battery and alternator, so knew it wasn't those. He climbed out and popped the hood. Everything seemed in order. He checked cables and fluid. Everything was how it should be. He climbed back in and turned the ignition. It sounded like it was going to start and died. He was being fucked with. Panic rose in him and he decided maybe he should walk home. Fear kept him in place, however, and he tried to get his mind off everything. He thought about calling Iris but didn't want to scare her. She couldn't help, anyway. He texted his mother that he was having car trouble. She asked where he was and said she was on her way.

He saw headlights coming toward him and told her to wait and he'd see if he could flag someone down for a jump. He got out and waved his hand at the oncoming car. It slowed and the driver rolled his window down. It was the man from before.

"Hey there, son. I saw you earlier and thought you might be having trouble. Do you need a jump?"

Ledger gulped past the tightness in his throat and nodded. Tourists were starting to come onto the island and maybe this was one of them. His gut told him differently. This man was here for a reason. The man got out and searched his trunk for jumper cables.

"Looks like I don't have any cables. Do you?" he asked, more than friendly.

Ledger went to the back of the truck and dug around. He thought his mother had them but there they were. He carried them back and held them toward the man awkwardly. The man took one end and watched Ledger with a sense of humor.

"Have you never jumped a car before, son? You look like you don't know what to do with these."

"Uh, I have. Sorry, let me pop my hood again." Ledger had jumped his mother's car a hundred times and knew how to do it with his eyes closed. The man hooked the ends up to his as Ledger made sure his were secured. The man got into his car, turning it on and Ledger climbed in to start his, praying for it to turn over. It started right up. He climbed out and quietly thanked the man.

"Ayup, glad I could help," the old man answered, his eyes fixed on Ledger.

"Can I give you anything for your help?"

"Nope, we have to watch out for each other, you know?"

Ledger nodded and headed back to his truck. The man called out.

"Hey there, son. You forgetting something?" The man's voice chided.

Ledger turned back and realized he'd left the jumper cables. The man watched him hard and handed his ends to Ledger. Ledger grabbed them, lifting his hand in a small wave. "Thanks again."

"Sure thing. I knew your father. Good man. Always there to help. Glad I could get you back on the way home." The man said home like it was an order.

Ledger watched him get in his vehicle and drive off with a wave of his hand. Knew his father? Ledger was sure he didn't recognize the man. He wasn't a local or a summer person. Tourists came and went, but his father didn't know them more than in passing. He considered going home but he felt like he needed to get to Iris, so he headed for the Lodge.

The thing was, he never got there.

CHAPTER SEVENTEEN

*L*edger came to in a pool of his own blood. His head felt like it'd been cracked open and his vision was blurry. The one thing he did know, was he was on his boat. The familiarity of growing up, touching every inch of the boat made it easy to recognize. At some point, he must have vomited as it was dried to his hands and shirt. He pressed himself up and groaned as lightning shot through his head. He rolled over and leaned his back against the bench seat in an attempt to get his bearings. He was on his father's boat, far out on the ocean from what he could tell. Nothing else seemed familiar.

Ledger forced himself up to look over the sides and was immediately confused by what he saw. Or didn't see. Land was nowhere in sight. How did he get there? The last thing he recalled was driving back to the Lodge. Or toward, he never made it. He vaguely remembered something dark, like the shadow of a very large bird, passing in front of the truck. That was it. It'd been night, so he wasn't sure if his headlights had cast light on the trees, somehow tricking his eyes. Now, he was here. But where was here?

He managed to get himself upright and checked the ignition for keys. There were none. He felt in his pocket but he had nothing on him. No keys, no wallet, no phone. The boat radio responded with heavy silence when he attempted to call out. Not even static. Ledger had no clue how long he'd been on the boat or where it'd drifted to. All he knew, was that he couldn't see land, couldn't radio, and had no recollection of what'd transpired. He touched the gash on his forehead and winced. Or where that came from.

He dropped the anchor and made his way into the boat's storage area, finding a jug of water and compressed meals he kept on board for emergencies. There was a flare gun, but was he too far out for anyone to see it if he shot it off? He decided to hold off until he could assess where he might be. He pulled out a compass and map to see if he could lock down some coordinates. Nightfall would help by seeing the stars and where they were. He jotted down a general idea of where he might be and shook his head. This far out would mean he'd been on the boat for at least a couple of days. If he was even close on his assessment.

By nightfall, the stars' alignment confirmed his fears. He'd been drifting and unconscious for days. He was close to a hundred miles out to sea. He'd called his mother when the truck wouldn't start. She'd been expecting him home. By now, she would've alerted the authorities. He pulled out a blanket and wrapped himself in it, feeling shivers coming on. The night would be cold and he was already weak. He needed to conserve food and water because it could be days before anyone found him. *If* anyone found him.

Three days later, he knew he was fucked. Without keys, he couldn't start the boat. He ran out of food by the fifth day and didn't see a sign of anything. No ships passed, even the birds were out of sight. It was like the world had disappeared, or been covered up in water. It was just him and the vast open ocean.

He started hallucinating after a week. His water had run out and he'd given up any hope of being rescued. He opened the engine and tried to figure out a way to start it, but his brain couldn't make heads or tails of what he was looking at. It just sat, gaping back at him. He shot the flare gun off in the hopes someone would see it, knowing they wouldn't. Whatever wanted to get him out of the way succeeded. Ledger was fucked.

The first time he saw his father, he was sure he wasn't seeing him. His father was at the front of the boat, peering out and turned back to wave at him. Then he was gone. The next time was in the middle of the night and he awoke to his father sitting, watching him. Ledger jerked and blinked his eyes. His dad smiled sadly and nodded.

"Dad?" Ledger croaked between his dried and split lips.

His father nodded and pointed to the engine. Ledger shook his head.

"No keys."

His father disappeared into the night like he hadn't been there. Ledger started to cry then. He truly was alone in the world.

When he opened his eyes later, his father was there again. Or maybe he was dreaming because the sky seemed off. Devoid of stars. His father reached out and touched his shoulder. Ledger felt it, the weight of his hand. Had he died and was with his father now? His father spoke.

"I was always so proud of you. You never got caught up in bullshit, Ledge. Good head on your shoulders. Until now. There are some things you can't beat."

Ledger frowned. "I don't understand."

"You should've left that girl alone. They need her, they don't need you."

Ledger felt anger rise in him. "Who the fuck is *they*? I will protect Iris. Well, maybe not now. Who are you to lecture me anyway? You took girls into hell."

"I didn't know, Ledge. I didn't know why they were going," his father replied, his eyes carrying the weight of reality.

"Bullshit, Dad! You may not have known exactly, but you knew something wasn't right. You just didn't care."

"I had a family to take care of."

"That's your excuse?" Ledge asked, his words hot and bitter. "Blame us because you chose to do something horrible?"

His father sighed, then looked away. "I suppose you're right. I made excuses then. I wasn't part of what they did, just so you know. Had even one of the girls told me, I would've rescued them. Did I get a bad feeling about it? Sure. Did I know? Of course not. How could I have? They always had adults with them. It was easy to reason it was their parents or guardians. Never once did any of them say or do anything which led me to believe they were in danger."

"Yet, you still had a feeling." Ledger's words cut through the dark.

"Yes, I can't deny that, but feelings are often our minds making up stories. Ledger, I loved my family and was trying to give you a good life. A chance. The money was good and until that girl went missing, there was no concrete evidence anything bad was happening."

"Was she on your boat?"

"Who's to say? Before long, they all ran together. The girls. Did I take a group out around that time? Probably. But I don't know who she was. I didn't know any of them. They were just girls being shuttled back and forth."

"I fucking hate you," Ledger spat, feeling the fear and suffering of the girls.

His father nodded. "That's fair. I hated myself for it. That's why I did this."

In an instant, his face transformed into how it was after he shot himself. The back and top of his head were blown off, his jaw hanging loosely. Ledger glanced away and wished it would all just end. That his father would go away and leave him to whatever came next.

"I don't care," Ledger muttered. "Just fucking leave me alone."

When he looked up, his father was gone. He closed his eyes and wished for death. He lay on the floor of the boat and sobbed. Maybe he should've left Iris alone. Maybe it took him being with her for all of this to happen. He pictured her face laughing and his heart shattered into pieces. He would miss her. If the sun rose and fell, he didn't know it. He just lay on the boat, waiting for the end. Nothing mattered anymore. He was delusional to think he could save anyone. He couldn't even save himself.

The next time he saw his father, it wasn't of this world. Ledger was walking along the beach, collecting sea glass from the edge of the water. He was maybe eight or nine years old. His father was ahead of him and turned, smiling. "Did I ever tell you what to do if you lose your keys and you are out to sea?"

Ledger shook his head and stared up at his father. "No?"

"Well then, come on." His father laughed, his face young and happy.

All of a sudden, they were on the boat and his father was pointing at the engine. He rubbed his hands together, forming a small ball of light. "Energy is everywhere. You just have to harness it."

Ledger wrinkled his nose and shook his head. "You need a key."

"Do you, though? Maybe you need to see things differently."

He placed his hands on the engine and it lit up, a glow spreading from one end to the other. Ledger watched in amazement as the engine sputtered and came to life. His father nodded and grinned.

"See? I knew you could do it."

Ledger stared at him, shaking his head. "I didn't do anything. You did."

"Are you sure about that?"

Ledger looked down and his hands were on the engine, glowing. He yanked them away and shoved them in his pockets, scared of what was happening. His father tipped his head back and laughed.

"Why are you afraid of your own power, Ledge?" he asked.

"I'm not, I just... I didn't do that."

"Oh, but you did. The key may start the boat, but you opened the engine."

Ledger had no clue what he was talking about and rubbed his small nose. "You opened the engine. I saw you do it. You put your hands there."

His father's face shifted and turned hard. As if he wasn't quite himself anymore. "That may be true, but it wouldn't have started back up without you. Key or not. Take responsibility, son."

Ledger felt scared and wanted to be away from his father. This version of his father. He didn't understand what he was saying and wanted to go back to collecting sea glass on the beach. He closed his eyes and imagined himself there, the waves lapping at his bare feet. When he opened his eyes his father was driving the boat and turned to wave at him, fading in and out. Ledger stared at his hands and he was no longer little. His father set the boat to its course and moved over to Ledger.

"You're in trouble. You need to leave that girl alone. You two together are opening the floodgates and it will consume you all."

"I can't, Dad. I love her and she needs me."

"Does she, though? Love is a trick. I need to go. I can't help you if you won't listen." His father walked to the edge of the boat and drew a gun out. He smiled and put it in his mouth.

Ledger ran toward him as he pulled the trigger and pieces of his skull exploded behind him. His body fell overboard just as Ledger tried to reach him.

"No!" Ledger screamed and peered over. The water was still except for a reflection. A scared little boy, peering back at him. There was no sign of his father.

The boat was cruising along the water and Ledger went to the helm. When he put his hands on the wheel, the boat lifted out of the waves and took flight. He was looking down onto the world and saw the island as a blip in the expanse of sea. He could hear people laughing and crying. His mother crying. He tried to guide the boat back down to the island but it rose further and further into the sky. He was leaving them all behind. The wind cut through his hair and he experienced a lightness he'd never known. A soul without a body. He laughed and embraced the feeling. Nothing mattered anymore.

In a flash, the boat lost altitude and Ledger found himself rocketing toward the earth, toward the sea. He cried out and grabbed onto the rails, knowing it wouldn't help. Even though it was water, the boat would hit it like concrete and he would disintegrate into a million pieces. As the water drew closer, a large hole opened and the boat fell through the surface. The ocean closed over the top, enveloping the boat.

Ledger was drowning.

Water filled his lungs and the salt burned his insides. He clawed his way to the surface, feeling the darkness take him just as his fingers broke through. He became weightless and floated, his body moved only by the water. His eyes were wide open, staring emptily.

It was over.

The boat was discovered just offshore. They'd called off the search and assumed it was lost at sea. Then it was just there within sight. Ledger's body was recovered and he was pronounced dead. As they moved him to the rescue boat, the paramedic gazed at him and felt sorry such a young guy lost his life like this. She placed her hand on his cheek and sighed. It never got easier. Something told her to try CPR again, even though they'd tried for twenty minutes to no avail. Her partner looked at her like she was crazy when she leaned in and began the count. After five minutes, she knew it was just that thing in them of feeling like God. Thinking they had more power than they did. She sat back and resigned herself to her humanness.

As she reached across to pull the bag closed, she saw it. A tremor. Like the air off a butterfly's wings. His eyelashes moved. It could've been the wind. She waited and leaned in close. That's when she heard it. A gurgle from his throat.

"He's alive!"

"Pam, you know it's just a death gurgle."

"No, it was a word or words. I heard it."

"Yeah? So, what was the word?"

"I think he said "I wish" or "Irish"." She started CPR again. "Get the paddles."

The other paramedic eyed her, sighing. "Fine, but I think this is all in your head."

Pam leaned in close but felt no breath. "Give me those."

They put the paddles on his chest and fired them up. Ledger's body jumped with the electricity but went back to its current state. They tried again and Pam felt his wrist artery. A grin broke out on her face.

"We have a pulse!"

CHAPTER EIGHTEEN

*W*hen his eyes finally opened, he saw his mother reading beside him. His mind immediately went back to the boat and he gasped. His mother jumped up and stared at him, her face contorted in shock.

"Ledger!"

"Mom?"

A grin broke out on her face and she kissed him on the cheek. "I knew you could do it."

"Do what?" he whispered, his voice unfamiliar and broken.

"Make it back."

Make it back. He remembered. He was on the boat in the middle of the ocean. His father was there. The boat flew and crashed. As he replayed the memories, he realized it couldn't have happened. Boats don't fly and his father was dead. He must've been hallucinating.

"What happened?"

"No one knows for sure, but you called me and said your truck wouldn't start. You said someone was driving by and you'd flag them down. After that, who knows? You showed up on the boat over a week later on death's door. They'd been out looking for you all that time and then you just showed up offshore."

"So, I *was* on the boat?"

His mother knitted her brows, seeming confused. "Well, yeah. I don't understand why did you take the boat out that night?"

"I didn't. I was driving my truck and then..." There was no *and then*. It's all he could remember.

"Ledge, how did you end up on the boat?"

"Mom, I have no clue. I woke up in the middle of the ocean with a gash on my head and no recollection. No keys, phone, or anything."

She sat back down and stared at him. "Do you think there was foul play? Should we call the police?"

"And tell them what? That I woke up in the boat a hundred miles from shore and didn't know what happened?"

"I mean, maybe?"

"It gets weirder. I saw Dad. He talked to me. He used some kind of magic or energy to get the boat started and then it flew. I don't think the cops would think I did more than drop acid and took my boat out."

His mother laughed unintentionally at this and squeezed his hand. "They said you hotwired the engine. You don't remember doing that?"

"I didn't do that. Dad put his hands on the engine and it started glowing. I would've died out there without him. I'd no fucking clue what to do."

"Technically you did die out there, Ledger. When they found you, you weren't breathing. They pronounced you dead but kept trying. They used the paddles on you and somehow got your heart to start. Thank God."

Ledger listened but wasn't sure how to respond. He'd died? He sort of remembered that. Now, he and Iris had something else in common. He could see the fear in the memory in his mother's eyes and smiled at her.

"Well, I'm here now. I don't understand any of it but I'm here."

"Do you think the man who stopped to help you had anything to do with it?"

The man's strange smile flashed in Ledger's mind and he sighed. On some level, yes, but he wasn't going to tell his mother that. "Nah. He jumped the truck and left. I got back in the truck and started driving."

"Home?"

"No, to the Lodge."

Her face dropped. "What have you gotten yourself into, Ledger? You were heading home. What changed?" she asked, her brow furrowed with concern.

"I can't get into it, but I got some information that night. I don't want to tell you and drag you into this or put you in danger."

"For fuck's sake, Ledger, leave it alone! This is twice now you have dug in about the place or Iris and almost died. Whatever is happening there, it's not going to let you close or stop it. You're not as strong as it is and it *will* kill you." Her eyes were pleading with him and he nodded, knowing he wouldn't let it go.

He was aware of something she didn't know, however, it sounded too crazy even considering what'd happened already. He needed to let his mind process and accept it to fully understand. Something that happened out there. Something that happened when he died.

Duff appeared at the door and cleared their throat. "Hey."

"Hey."

Duff came and stood by the bed. "You decided to fucking join us?"

Ledger laughed. "What, was I late for the party?"

"You are the party. An event all to yourself."

"Sorry. I didn't mean to worry anyone."

"Well, you did. Ass." Duff stared at their shoes, then eyed him warily.

"Nice welcome, Duff."

"You are lucky that's all I did. I should shake the shit out of you," Duff replied, their eyes glittering.

"I deserve it." Ledger knew it was true. He'd put them through an all too familiar hell. Like after his father died. He was ashamed.

"You do."

"Okay, you two. Knock it off," their mother chided. "You know you love each other."

Duff wrinkled their nose. "That's debatable."

Ledger grabbed their hand and squeezed it. "You love me."

"Fine, I love you but it doesn't make you any less of a turd for worrying Mom like that."

"It doesn't. Just Mom?"

Duff squinted at him, then sighed. "Yeah, don't push it. I have a limit of sappy stuff. What the fuck is wrong with you?"

Ledger chuckled and shook his head. "Even I can't answer that. Knight in shining armor complex?"

This made Duff crack a smile and they bobbed their head. "That's an understatement. Knock it off, will you?"

Ledger nodded again, knowing he wouldn't. If anything, he was going in full force. What was affecting the Lodge and Iris was bigger than all of them. He wasn't trying to save just Iris anymore, he was trying to save everyone. What he'd come to see was that the Lodge was an entity.

Its own life force.

Almost like a mother hen with a brood of chicks under her. Iris was feeding them. The people who'd stayed there before had ignited the fire which kept them warm. Even the island was part of it, each person connected, helping them to grow. He used to think the Lodge was just a portal, but he realized it was more than that. It was alive. It was watching and protecting whatever it intended to put out into the world.

Ledger couldn't tell his family any of this. Ignorance was their only protection. He'd no doubt had his father not come for him, he'd be dead. His father had known on some level in life and now wherever he was. He could see Ledger was fighting a beast bigger than all of them. He put Ledger there. Ledger didn't know if he'd ever see his father again, but he knew it wasn't just hallucinations from dehydration and exposure. His father had been there. He was attempting to make things right. To undo the wrongs.

"Hey, I'm pretty tired. I need to rest," he whispered.

"Okay, well, the doctor is on his way to check you over. They were just waiting on you to wake up to see where you were at," his mother replied.

Ledger frowned. He was home, which seemed odd, to begin with. "From the mainland?"

"No, there is this guy who lives here on the island now. I didn't recognize him but he showed up at the hospital to offer his services. He said he is semi-retired but knew I wanted to get you back home, and he said he could sign off to come to check on you here."

Something about the whole thing didn't sit right and when the doctor showed up Ledger knew why.

"Why hello, son. We just keep crossing paths don't we?" the doctor said and smiled.

Ledger felt ice run through his veins and his mother stared from the doctor to Ledger. "You know each other?"

"Mom, this is the man who stopped to jump the truck," Ledger said casually, so as not to show his hand.

"Oh! That was very nice of you. I don't suppose you know what happened to my son that night?" his mother asked, her eyes darting between them.

"No, sorry, I don't, ma'am. I guess I should've stayed around. I got him going and headed out. He said he was heading home."

No Ledger hadn't. The man had said home to him. An awkward silence filled the room. Ledger met his mother's eyes and she understood.

Let it drop.

"Well, anyway, thank you for getting his truck going," she responded, smiling without emotion.

"That's what neighbors do, am I right?" the doctor said genially.

She nodded and Ledger waved her away. "It's good Mom, you can go if you need to do something. He can check me over, then I'm going to rest."

"Are you sure? I was going to get dinner on."

"Dinner sounds great."

She left the room, pausing at the door with a frown. She was trying to figure out what was going on between her son and the doctor. Ledger ignored her and turned his attention to the doctor.

"So, my mom said you showed up at the hospital? Did you know I was there?"

"No, no. Like I told your mother I am semi-retired, so I drop in now and then and heard a local boy was there. Was just trying to help a neighbor out."

"That was very thoughtful of you. I know she was happy to bring me home. Not sure how she did it." Ledger had a feeling she didn't do it alone.

"I signed off on it. Small hospital, I think they were happy to have the bed back. Leo was kind enough to make a special round trip to get you transported home. I came along to help." And there it was.

"For sure, much appreciated."

The conversation felt scripted and contrived but Ledger wanted to make sure he came across as nothing but grateful and friendly. Now, more than ever, he needed to play things close to the vest. He didn't know who this man was or why he suddenly showed up in their lives.

"I'm sorry, I didn't catch your name?" Ledger asked.

"Oh sorry, how rude of me," the doctor replied and stuck out his hand. "Dr. Gotzon. Mike Gotzon."

Ledger took his hand and shook it. The doctor met his eyes and energy passed between them. A force, drawing him in. Ledger wanted to yank his hand away but knew that would show weakness and resisted the urge.

"I'd say nice to meet you but since we've already met, I'll ask how you knew my father? That night, you said my father was a good man?"

The doctor flinched and dropped Ledger's hand. "Oh, sure. Back in the day, we crossed paths a few times. Small island, as it may be."

"Are you from around here?" Ledger asked pointedly.

"Can't say that I am. However, I've been around the island for years. In and out. I love it here."

"Oh, because I didn't recognize you?"

"I don't imagine you would. I don't think you and an old fella like me run in the same circles."

"No, you're right there. So, my dad-"

The doctor cut him off, looking at his watch. "We'd better go ahead and get you checked out. I've got to get on my way."

Ledger let him look him over and noticed how the doctor's hands never rested on him for too long. He watched the doctor from the corner of his eyes. He was an older man with white hair and ice-blue eyes. His face seemed friendly enough, but something was under the surface. The doctor caught him looking and stared back.

They both knew this was part of the dance. Forward, back, side-step.

"Healing nicely. You almost didn't make it. Well, I guess you didn't but thanks to modern medicine, right? Maybe now, you'll stay home and keep yourself out of trouble, son?"

Ledger nodded and looked away. He saw something in the doctor's eyes, making him feel exposed. The doctor knew something only Ledger had known to this moment. A secret he intended to keep. A truth that gave him the courage to keep fighting.

Ledger did not come back from the dead alone.

CHAPTER NINETEEN

*T*he moment breath started back in Ledger's body, even though his eyes didn't open, his mind did. He was taken on a journey in which he saw his life and the lives around him as a passenger. Kind of like riding through the dark tunnels of an amusement park ride. In the snap second between never coming back and being shocked back into reality, everything that ever did happen, or would happen, flashed through him. Even though in a human sense these would be years of information, he saw and understood it at that moment. Who he was, what he was supposed to do. He was never meant to be a fisherman or exist solely on the island. Iris was no more the reason everything was coming to the surface than he was. It was predestined and as much as she was being used by certain forces, so was he.

There'd be no choice, no options to select. He had a path and he'd be on it whether or not he wanted to be. In the moments between his soul being in and out of his body, he was shown to understand he was there to fight. However, one wanted to determine it. Good versus evil. Survive or succumb. It just was. The thing which shook him the most when he came to and remembered was how it all had been determined. Iris had died and something came back with her. Something dark, evil, and focused. It was a random parasite that hooked its teeth into her because of her journey. It'd been waiting, planning, messaging. She needed to die and come back. It was the only way it could get to him.

See, Ledger was the actual mark. From birth, and maybe even before, he'd been called to set things right. To undo the wrongs. He didn't know it, of course, and until his father died, had no sense of himself as more than a child, safe under his father's shadow. When that shadow lifted, he was left exposed and needed to find a place for himself and his family. To fulfill his destiny. Once he felt the full sun on his face, the purpose laid out for him began to come together.

Thus Iris had to die. It wasn't hard to arrange. Her family had already made the connection with that side. Her father was an angry man and easy to manipulate. He'd already danced in the dark corners of his mind, allowing those forces in. He liked the feeling. The vile, impure thoughts that fueled his obsession with power. The feeling of being God. So, when he welcomed in the thoughts of his own volition, it was easy to push the boundaries and get him to embrace the rancid, putrid thoughts, which drove him to violate and kill his only child.

Iris died but was forced back as a vessel to tear a hole in the planes of existence to allow the monster through. It needed to get stronger and the Lodge was the motherland. The key was to lie dormant until the grandmother died. Then Iris would be on her own. Why her grandmother left the Lodge to Iris was a mystery, knowing the history. Maybe she thought Iris would just sell it off and use the money to have a life. Or maybe she thought Iris could somehow bring a change to the place. Surely, she didn't know the evil which existed, lying in wait.

Ledger's first breath into the world was a joy to his parents and set a course meant to end the storm brewing under the surface once and for all. Iris was born a year later simply to be a way to get to him. His father's death had not been part of the plan and made Ledger a stronger adversary than could've been expected. Still, not knowing his calling or his strength, he was almost defeated. So, on his second first breath into the world, he brought backups. There was no way to put it into terms, except he was no longer alone. Almost like angels on his shoulder but more as if they lived within him. And not angels but vapors of light. He couldn't wrap his brain around it, but when he felt them join him, it made total sense.

The doctor had sensed something. Ledger knew to act like his old self and shrug it off. After all, how could he even explain what he knew?

Hey doc, these little, like wisps of light invaded my body and made me stronger. No, not stronger, like more clear. Maybe not more clear. Like, more me. No that's not it, either. Anyway, it's pretty cool. Don't you think, doc? Little bits of me that aren't me, but are.

Not to mention, he didn't trust the doctor and felt like he was there to keep tabs on Ledger. Or stop him. For all he knew, the doctor could've been the reason Ledger ended up on the boat. He'd been the last one to see Ledger before his disappearance.

Or was he?

Ledger remembered the marina installed cameras a couple of years before when it was becoming clear local kids were using the boats for make-out spots. Hell, even Ledger had done that, and not just as a kid. Leo managed the marina in addition to running the ferry. Ledger would reach out to him and see if he could recover the tapes from that night. Why hadn't the police looked at them?

The next day Ledger called the marina office, hoping to catch Leo before his first run on the ferry. He got the answering machine and left a brief and non-descript message. "Hey-o, Leo. It's Ledger. Was wondering if you got that part in yet? Anyhow, give me a holler when you get this."

There was no part and Leo would know that immediately. It would pique his interest and make him more likely to call back. Ledger had almost died, well did, but felt like his body was healing at record speed. He was up, moving around when the phone rang and he saw it was Leo. He shut his door and locked it. He picked up the phone.

"Hey, Leo."

"Ledger! Good to hear from you. Didn't think you'd pull through."

"Thanks for the vote of confidence, Leo."

Leo chuckled. "You know me, call it as I see it."

"Hey, I was wondering. Do you by chance have the footage from the night I disappeared?"

"Yeah, I do. Just got it back from the police a few days ago."

Ledger was surprised. "Oh? They never came and talked to me or anything."

"That so? Well, maybe because of the tape."

"What do you mean?"

Leo paused. "Ledger, were you drinking that night?"

"I mean, I had a beer with Iris but nothing to write home about," Ledger replied, his brain trying to think back. "Yeah, no. I knew I needed to drive, so I had just the one. Why?"

"I need to show you the tape then. Are you going to be home tonight? My last run is at six."

"Leo, where am I going?" Ledger teased. "I'm sure I'll be back from my triathlon by then."

"Smartass kid. Alright, I'll come by then. "

"Thanks, Leo."

He let his mom know Leo would be by later and she smiled. "I like that Leo. Always with a smile and a joke."

Ledger noticed she seemed a little flushed and grinned. "Mom, you have a thing for Leo?"

"Stop it, Ledger! He's just a nice man."

"Gross."

His mother set her mouth and raised her eyebrows, trying not to laugh. She acted like it was nothing, but Ledger noticed she'd changed into a different blouse and freshened up before Leo arrived. Not to mention, Leo had clearly stopped home before coming over and was showered and clean-shaven. She welcomed him in and they made small talk until Ledger took control of the conversation before it degraded into a couple of high schoolers at their first dance.

"So, Leo. You brought the footage?"

He looked over from staring at Ledger's mother and nodded. "I did. But let me warn you, it doesn't shed a good light on you. The police wrote this off as you being drunk and taking your boat out for a midnight spin."

Ledger frowned. That didn't make sense. He took the recording and put it on the television. It was dark and grainy and at first, all they could see was the boats swaying slightly, tied off to the docks. The sway increased and a figure appeared in the right corner. It was Ledger but something wasn't right. He was moving in a jerking manner, almost like he was drunk but more like he was a marionette being controlled by invisible strings. It appeared he was alone but it seemed all off. Nothing about his movements seemed like his own, drunk or not. Almost Frankenstein-like. All of a sudden, the Ledger on the screen stumbled and fell, smacking his head on a metal dock cleat, splitting his head open. This would've kept a normal man down, but he got back up, almost as if he was being dragged to his feet, and continued on.

When he got to the boat, he appeared to fall over the side and went out of view. After that, the boat moved slowly away from the dock and disappeared out of sight. Ledger rewound the tape and turned the brightness on the screen. He played it in slow motion and watched for any signs which might explain what'd happened. Leo told him to pause it and pointed to the screen.

"See there? The lighting isn't right. You're past the overhead light and it should be shining a light on your back, but it isn't. It's like there is a shadow between you and the light," Leo explained.

Ledger peered closer and could see it. It was as if a giant was standing between him and the light, blocking it. He started the tape again and they continued to see what seemed to be a shadow behind him. Not a defined shadow they could pinpoint, but rather like a disruption of light. When he fell, they noted again how it looked like he was almost being picked up by something. After he disappeared on the boat, his mother gasped and hit the pause button.

"The boat couldn't have just pulled off. It was tied to the dock. Go back a couple of frames and look at the ropes."

They moved back a couple of frames and watched frame by frame, focusing on the tied-off ropes. That's when they saw it and Ledger felt his blood run cold. A hand reached out and untied the rope. It wasn't his, nor was it human. It was almost as if the ink-black night had formed into long, creature-like fingers and set the boat free. Leo whistled low.

"I don't know what to say. The police watched the footage and laughed it off. I suppose they saw what they were expecting to see. That was something else entirely."

Ledger turned off the screen, not wanting to see what none of them could deny. He'd not been alone that night, that was clear. The doctor hadn't been there, though. It wasn't him. Something not of this world had gotten him to the boat and set Ledger adrift. He was trying to get to Iris and it made sure he didn't. He believed his father was the only reason he made it back.

Iris. They'd talked on the phone briefly, but she had a full house and Ledger didn't want to say something which might set anything off. He was aware he could no longer go to the Lodge as his presence was enough to trigger the battle. She was too busy to come to his house, now that the season was in full swing. He needed to find a way to see her and safely begin to let her know what they were facing. She wouldn't believe him. He hardly believed himself. He had a plan, but it would take him addressing one of his own fears.

Leo and his mother went for a walk and Ledger decided to call Iris to put his plan into action. She answered after a couple of rings but her voice sounded strange. Disconnected almost. He could hear guests in the background talking loudly and quite drunk.

"Hey, I was wondering if I could steal you away for a few hours for a picnic tomorrow or the next day?" he asked.

"Are you up for that? Shouldn't you be resting?" Her voice sounded almost irritated; Ledger sensed things were moving faster than he hoped. Whatever had a grip on her was taking over.

"No, the doctor said fresh air is good," he semi-lied. "I miss you and want to see you, Iris."

"I miss you, too. You want to come to the Lodge?"

"No!" He didn't mean to come out so forcefully and softened his voice. "Sorry, I just want some alone time with you. I can pick you up?"

"Alright, I guess. I'm free after lunch until the evening when we are having a poetry slam."

"A what?"

"Basically reading poetry but making it sound cooler. One of the guest's ideas," Iris replied with a verbal eye roll.

Ledger laughed and felt them connect through the phone. She needed him to keep the other at bay. The more they were together, the looser its grip on her became. "I can't wait to see you. It's been too long."

"Well, stop trying to kill yourself," Iris said and drew in her breath sharply. "That came out wrong. Sorry."

"I knew what you meant. Okay, so one tomorrow?"

"Sure. Are we taking your truck?"

"No, meet me at the dock. And bring Roar."

"Ledger! Your boat? Are you sure?" Iris chided.

"Have to get back on the horse."

Iris was quiet and Ledger tried to figure out if he'd said something wrong. Finally, she spoke and it sent chills down his spine.

"I'm glad you called. I didn't want to burden you because of everything that happened, but something is going on."

"What do you mean? What's going on?" The hair on his neck prickled and he knew it was serious.

"I can't say right now. Or maybe it doesn't matter. But I'm scared." She lowered her voice to a whisper.

"Iris, are you safe? Is there something I can do?"

"Ledger, I feel like I'm being watched. But it sounds crazy," Iris replied, then laughed uncomfortably.

"Crazy how?" Ledger asked, knowing nothing she could say would sound crazy to him anymore.

"Like I'm being watched from inside me."

CHAPTER TWENTY

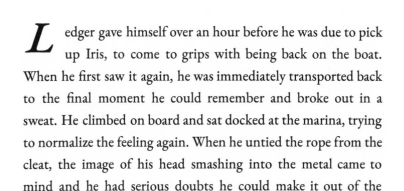

*L*edger gave himself over an hour before he was due to pick up Iris, to come to grips with being back on the boat. When he first saw it again, he was immediately transported back to the final moment he could remember and broke out in a sweat. He climbed on board and sat docked at the marina, trying to normalize the feeling again. When he untied the rope from the cleat, the image of his head smashing into the metal came to mind and he had serious doubts he could make it out of the marina. Fear gripped him and he leaned over the railing, afraid he would lose the contents of his stomach. He caught an image of himself in the water and was taken aback.

He was thinner, gaunter. His wavy hair no longer had any semblance of being kempt and curled randomly around his head and shoulders like a mane. The gash was healing but left a dark red scar across his forehead. His normally amber eyes held a deeper hue to them, which made them seem slightly sunken into his face.

He stared, attempting to connect to the reflection. He appeared a bit demented and a little like a battered warrior from a romance novel cover. Setting his resolve, he finished untying the boat and slid the key in, half expecting it not to start. It fired right up. The keys, his phone, and his wallet were found in his truck parked outside the marina lot, which had been locked for the night when he disappeared. Try as he might, he could not draw up any memories past seeing the shadow pass in front of him on his way back to the Lodge. But clearly, he'd scaled the fence into the marina down to the dock. Something had been controlling him to go to the boat.

He drove the boat out, feeling like all eyes were on him. The general consensus of the island was that he'd gotten three sheets to the wind, climbed into the marina, then took the boat. He'd wasted everyone's time and resources in their mind. Like his father, he was treated with a level of discomfort and disregard. There was no point in trying to convince anyone otherwise. His story was too out there, too unbelievable. He wondered if Iris would even entertain it. He needed to try. The time to leave her out of all of this had passed and for them to face what was happening, they needed to do it together. This time he brought proof.

Iris was standing on the deck, holding a basket as he came down the channel. The smile on her face gave him the courage to push on and she waved ecstatically. He eased next to the dock and she climbed on board. A soft meowing was coming from the basket and she put her hand in to settle the confused cat. Ledger drove away from the dock, trying not to look at the Lodge, however, his eyes drifted upwards to see a man standing on the porch, watching them.

"Who's that?" he asked and kissed Iris.

"Oh, my new handyman. After Bertie died, I put the word out I needed some help around the place and this guy showed up. He's a little odd but seems to know what he's doing," Iris replied. She pulled Roar out of the basket and the cat peered around, scared by all the water.

Ledger scooped Roar into his arms and placed her on his shoulders. Instantly she began purring and settled into his hair. Her purring seemed to vibrate with whatever was inside of him. She was aware of the change within him. He stroked her head, keeping one hand on the steering wheel.

"I've missed you both so much," he whispered and drew Iris toward him. "Thanks for coming today, I know you are busy."

She smiled, sliding her hand around his waist. "Are you kidding? I've been beside myself with worry every day about you. Did your mother tell you she and I talked every night you were missing?"

"She didn't. I'm glad you had each other to lean on. I'm sorry about all of this. I'm sorry I worried you."

"I'm guessing there is a lot more to the story?"

Ledger sighed. He wanted to have his feet on solid ground before he opened that can of worms. He bobbed his head. "There is. I have a little island earmarked for us to stop at. I can build a fire and we can talk, okay?"

Iris eyed him, feeling the tension in his body. "Is there a reason you wanted me to bring Roar?"

"Yes and no. I missed her, for one. Two, I think she has a sixth sense about things."

"What kind of things?"

"People, events, things like that," Ledger explained, not wanting to point out anything specific.

Iris shrugged. "Well, she doesn't like the handyman, Doyle. She scratched the hell out of him the first time he tried to pick her up to put her outside. I didn't think he'd come back. He said it was no big deal, but his eyes said otherwise. He glares at her every time he sees her, now."

"Doyle, huh? He's not a local. Do you know where he came from?" The man's demeanor made Ledger feel strange. Learning Roar didn't like him either, made him worry the man was up to no good.

"He doesn't talk much but did say he was hired by the hotel and when he got there they didn't need him. Said he needed work. He told me his last name when we met, but to be honest I don't remember it."

Ledger knew the hotel could be like that. They'd overhire for the season and then ditch people if the demand wasn't there. It was a shitty tactic, but they'd been doing it for years. It could be true, or Doyle could be using that as a cover since it was believable.

"Well, I guess lucky for you. Is he nice?"

"It's hard to say. He does his work but isn't overly chatty. He doesn't like Roar, that's for sure. I have to lock her up when he comes inside."

That made Ledger uncomfortable and he rubbed the cat's fuzzy head. She continued her loud purring and nestled in closer to him. "It seems unfair she gets booted in her own home because of him."

"Probably, but he acts like she is going to maul him if I don't."

Ledger laughed, trying to picture a grown man being afraid of the little puffball around his neck. Iris reached up and touched his face.

"You look like you've been through hell. We were really worried," she murmured.

"I feel like I've been through hell. Regaining my strength fast, though, which is surprising. Must be all my mother's doting and making me eat."

"You're lucky to have her. She loves you and Duff so much. Is it true what the people are saying? I mean, let me rephrase that. People are saying you got drunk and broke into the marina. It doesn't sound like you, so I didn't believe it. Why are they saying that?"

Ledger gritted his teeth and stared out at the water. He'd almost died out here and people were gossiping about his character. Had he not been revived, they would still have gossiped but less openly. Openly they would've shared stories of him when he was a kid and pretended they cared. He could see the island he was heading for in the distance and shrugged.

"People are full of shit. I was on my way back to the Lodge."

"Why?"

"I needed to talk to you. The truck wouldn't start after I'd pulled off on the side of the road to talk on the phone. This guy came by and gave me a jump, then I was heading back to the Lodge."

"But you never made it. Did something happen?" Iris asked, her eyes dark with concern.

"I don't know. I have no memory after that. The weird thing, too, is the guy who stopped to jump me, is the doctor who talked to my mother in the hospital and offered his services, so I could be moved home."

"Oh wow! It is strange but I guess with such a small island, people's paths cross a lot?"

"Sometimes. Still strange," Ledger agreed.

They fell silent as they neared the island, and Ledger got as close as he could to make it easier to haul things in the dinghy. He brought Iris and Roar over on the first trip with Roar clinging painfully to his shoulders with her nails. Iris had to pry her loose once they hit land. After a couple of trips, they were set and built a fire. Roar, familiar with that, explored a little and curled up near the fire.

Ledger sat near Iris and wrapped his arms around her. She wound her fingers in his hair, sighing. Once they were away from the Lodge and the island, things felt easier. They made small talk for a bit when Ledger knew he needed to come clean with her. To tell her what he knew. It could destroy everything between them but at least being here, they'd have to deal with it.

He stoked the fire and sat down facing her. He took her hand and squeezed it. "We need to talk."

She nodded with her brows furrowed and waited. Ledger gazed out over the ocean, then laughed nervously. "Jesus, I don't know where to start."

Iris watched him, her blue eyes fixed on his face. She rubbed his leg. "Start with why you were coming back to the Lodge that night."

"Maybe I should begin before then. Let me start with Bertie since that's when it honestly began going all to shit." He told her what Bertie had told him about the girl hanging in the room and what Leo had said about the girl going missing. How girls were shuttled back and forth. Iris listened stone-faced and scoffed at that.

"Ledger, you know people here. They like a little drama. Who's to say any of it's even true?"

"Iris, I don't want to admit this and just recently found out, but my father was one of the fishermen bringing the girls over. He didn't know what was going on but knew enough he should've stopped it. Or at least stayed away."

"Okay, so girls were being brought over, and supposedly one went missing. Is there any proof? Bertie had probably just spooked himself into seeing things."

"I saw a girl that night on the dock. I thought it was you but it wasn't. But she was there, plain as day."

Iris shook her head. "Come on, Ledger, this all sounds way too out there. Ghost girls and what next? Demons?"

Ledger stared hard at her, the image of the demonic face breathing into his own. "Maybe? I need to show you something about the girl. A picture my mother took the night we came to dinner."

Iris watched as he fished the photos out of his bag and handed them to her. She sifted through him and stared back with a question on her face. "The pictures are a little out of focus, but I don't get what you are getting at?"

"See this photo?" Ledger pointed out the one with the reflection. "Look at the mirror."

Iris moved the photo closer and leaned in to peer at it. He could visibly see her realize what she was looking at. She put her hand to her chest and recoiled, pushing the photo away from her.

"What the actual fuck, Ledger?"

"I know, I felt the same when I saw it. After finding out the history of the Lodge and talking to Bertie to find out my father had been unintentionally involved, I knew there was something darker at play."

"Something darker? That sounds awfully ominous and a little fantastical, don't you think?" Iris tried to reason, her voice giving her fear away.

"Looking at that picture, do you think it is?" Ledger met her eyes without blinking.

Iris stared at him, her eyes large and scared. "I don't like any of this. It's horrible. Maybe we just need to leave it alone. Bad things happened in the past. Maybe they should just stay there."

"Iris, listen to me. It's not just about a ghost girl. That's part of the history but the history *is* what the problem is. Something was opened there. Ignoring it won't make it go away. I know this is going to sound crazy, but part of me thinks I was born to stop it. Maybe my father was dragged in back then to stop me, maybe it was a coincidence."

"Wait. You think you were born to close some kind of portal in the Lodge. You know how crazy that sounds, right?"

Ledger nodded. "I know. But there is more."

"Okay?"

"It's not like a portal. I mean, it is but it's more than that. It's a battleground, as well. There are living entities on either side. Some are us, some are attached to us, some are on their own."

"So, they are the redcoats and we are the patriots?" Iris asked, laughing but serious.

"I don't really know. I know there is a side that wants to gain ground and we need to fight it. If we don't, it will take over the Lodge, the island... who knows what else?"

"Alright, in theory, say you're right. How would we even know how to fight something like that?"

"I think it needs you to be at the Lodge. I think the Lodge is part of it, but you are the catalyst," Ledger answered.

"You think if I packed up and left, it would just stop?"

"Well, not exactly. It brought you here and I imagine it'd find a way to bring you back."

"What do you mean it brought me here? My grandmother left me the place and I wanted to reopen it. This was my idea," Iris reasoned.

Ledger knew he was beginning to tread on dangerous ground. Iris was being told a lot of things with very little substantial evidence. He knew to push further he was going to have to show he'd betrayed her trust and gone behind her back. He looked at the woman he loved more with every passing day, knowing the next thing he said might be the thing that would push her away forever. If he didn't though, it would end them all.

"I spoke to your doctor. The one who did your surgeries and sterilized you."

CHAPTER TWENTY-ONE

*T*he look on Iris's face shook Ledger to the core. It was a mixture of shock, horror, and mistrust. He wanted to reach out and tell her he was sorry, that it was for her own good, however, he knew she needed a moment to process what he'd said. When her tears began to fall, he felt like he'd fractured anything between them and wanted to hold her. She drew her knees to her chest and rested her head on them. Roar, sensing something was wrong, came over and rubbed under her knees. Iris's hand petted the cat, but she didn't look at Ledger. She sat quietly for some time, stroking Roar in silence. When she finally spoke, Ledger wasn't sure if it was a statement or a question by her tone.

"And he said."

"Iris, can you look at me?" Ledger pleaded, his heart pounding in his chest.

She raised her head and glared at him. "What did he say?"

"He said what you told me. That you died on the table. Twice. He said the second time, the surgery room filled with a smell."

"A smell? What does that even mean?"

"Like a gas. A sulfuric gas. They couldn't breathe and it made their eyes water. He closed you up and hoped he'd done enough to help you survive." Ledger knew that wasn't exactly what Arbuckle told him but didn't want Iris to know he'd pretty much written her off that day. Let her fend for herself, yet again.

"Where was it coming from?"

"I mean, who knows? He said it happened when they revived you the second time."

"So, it was coming from me," her voice was flat and quiet.

"Iris, he thinks that when you died, something may have attached itself to you and come back with you. From the other side."

Iris laughed bitterly. "What, like a demon?"

Ledger sat quietly, the words stuck in his throat. Nothing he could say would make this any better. Iris met his eyes hard and her face went pale.

"Like a demon? Is that what he said, Ledger?"

"He said after that, he kept having dreams or visions of a demonic type spirit, showing him it was using you as a life force to get what it needed. He thinks you survived because it needed you to."

"It's the south, everyone thinks there are demons around. The whole get saved or demons will move in. Come on, that sounds crazy!" Iris spat, waving her hand dismissively.

"Your grandmother kind of agreed with him."

"She what? No, she was not into all of that fire and brimstone shit in the south. We didn't even go to church. Did he tell you that? He was caught up in his own religion. What was the context?" Iris had stopped crying and was now behind a wall he couldn't reach.

"Uh, I don't know how to say this, Iris," he sputtered.

"Spit it out, Ledger. You got this far, so how bad can it be?"

"He told your grandmother about the visions and she told him about the Lodge. About what they did there. She was worried for you." Ledger measured his words to protect Iris's image of her grandmother.

"I'm not following." Iris stared at him, her eyes dark and confused.

"She asked him to sterilize you. To give you a tubal ligation. It isn't scar tissue, it was intentional."

The horror on her face matched the horror he felt when he'd found out. She jumped up and shook her head. "That's not possible. She would've never done that to me. She took me in and protected me. He's lying!"

"Iris, he knew things about your family he had to have found out from your grandmother. Plus, she signed off on it, the paperwork for the surgery, I mean. I think she *was* trying to protect you, to stop all of this. Nothing about this makes sense because nothing about this makes sense. You and I are being used by forces our brains can't comprehend."

"You and I?"

Ledger watched her, unsure of how to reach her. She was shaking. He put his hand out, relieved when she took it. He pulled her down next to him and drew her close. "I have things about me to tell you, as well. Things about when I died and came back."

"Oh, did you also bring the gates of hell back with you?" Iris asked sarcastically.

"Not exactly, but I didn't come back alone."

Iris sat back, watching him. "What do you mean?"

Ledger sighed and tried to form something without description into words. "When I died, the moment between then and when I came back, I was shown things. Things about me, about both of us. Like why we exist, our purpose, what we're supposed to do."

"Why do we exist?"

"This is hard, Iris, so bear with me. When your aunt built the Lodge, it was more than walls and a roof. It was built either in a place or with an intent to become a living entity. Through the ceremonies, it basically was giving birth to these things. Demons, whatever. So, did it open a door, or create the door? I don't know but it seems like it. What I do know, is it has been lying dormant for years, waiting for this all to play out."

"For me to come back?" Iris chewed her lip as she narrowed her eyes.

"Sort of, but it's bigger than you. It has to do with me, as well. I was born to stop whatever this all is. To close the door." Ledger reached out and brushed a strand of hair off her face.

"You were shown that?"

"Yeah. I was shown that this is bigger than our timeframe, but that I was brought into this world to fight this particular battle."

"Wait, so there are other battles?" Iris asked, pressing her fingers into her temples.

"Between good and evil? I imagine. Maybe not this big. This one is the monstrosity. It's because of your great-great-aunt and those ceremonies. They were feeding it, so to say. Making it stronger and more pervasive. It was still hungry and wanting to grow. It just needed something, or someone, to come along and give it new life."

"Which is why I'm here." Iris was beginning to understand.

Ledger wanted to comfort her and assure her everything would be okay. But if he loved her, she needed to understand her part in all of this. "Yes. I was born to fight this. You were born to keep it strong. Maybe even to stop me."

"I'd never hurt you, Ledger," Iris said adamantly. He knew she meant it. It wasn't her he was worried about.

He hugged her tightly and kissed the side of her head. "I know that, Iris. I'd never hurt you either. Maybe that's how it planned to stop me. Through my love for you."

Iris shuddered, then sighed. "Now what? It tried to kill you when you came for me. Why didn't it this time?"

"I don't know. When I was out to sea, my father came to me. We talked and he saved me, I believe that. He regretted any part he had in all of this; maybe in a way, the boat is a safe zone now. I can't go back to the Lodge unless I know I may not make it out. I haven't ruled it out."

"Ledger! You can't! If it will cost you your life, then you need to stay away. You said something came back with you? To help?"

"Maybe... I hope so. It definitely is making me stronger. Iris, the only way to fight this thing will be at the Lodge. I'm trying to figure it all out. I can't tell you anything because I feel like it can read you. It knows I'm after it. It's going to try and take me down. I mean it already has, but I feel like I'm being watched on the island."

"Like me?"

"Yeah. I can only see you on the boat and out here away from the island. It's why I had you bring Roar. I wanted to get her used to riding on the boat. I need to see you, Iris, I need you in my life."

Iris turned her big azure eyes on him and nodded, her eyes filled with hurt. "Do you think I was born just to be used like this? That I was meant to die just to carry this shit back with me? That's all I am?"

Ledger shook his head. "No. You were born to come to me, so I could be complete."

Iris leaned against him and Ledger saw a tear slip down her cheek. "I hate them all."

Ledger knew what she meant. From her first breath, she'd been a pawn and abused. Her mother should've left sooner, her father should've never had the chance to hurt her. Her grandmother sacrificed her future to try and stop this, her doctor took away a vital part of her. Her great-great-aunt conjured up evil. In all of this, Iris had been a victim of others' shortcomings or demented plans. Now, she was being manipulated by the Lodge. Ledger was her only chance out and she was his. She'd been a vessel to everyone but him. To him she was life. She needed to believe that.

"Iris, when this is all said and done, I want you to be my wife. I want to take the boat far away from here. You, me, and Roar. I want to cook dinner for you and make love to you. I was dead before you came. You brought true breath into me and I cannot imagine life without you in it. Fuck all of them. I don't care why we were born, I care why we're here now. I'm here for you. Body and soul."

Iris sat up and moved to face him. She tucked her legs between his and held his hands. "No one has ever made me feel the way you do. Can we just run away now?"

Ledger shook his head. "I don't think so. From what I've seen, it can get into our heads and control us. I think the only way out is to take it down. We're going to need all the help we can get. I need a plan to face this. I think I'll need my family to help."

"Aren't you worried something will happen to them?" Iris asked, lines forming around her mouth.

"I am. I've kept them out of it so far. But if I can't take it down, I have a feeling no one on the island will be safe. Whatever had started in the Lodge has spread its borders and wants to grow. The water stops it from leaving the island I think, but it can move freely outside of the Lodge."

"Do you think the doctor, the one who helped jump your truck, is involved?"

"I think anyone who I don't recognize as a local could be. I mean, even a local could be if they walk a certain line. Are open to it, so to speak."

"What about guests at the Lodge?"

"I don't think all but maybe some. That one guy last year was clearly off."

Iris frowned and shook her head. She didn't remember. "Do you think it's somehow controlling my thoughts when I'm there?"

"I do."

"Oh. So, if you come to the Lodge to fight it, will I try to fight you?"

"Honestly, Iris, I don't know. Pay attention to how Roar reacts to things... like people, unseen things. She saw something that night by the piano. She doesn't like Doyle. Those things matter. Don't speak to anyone about any of this. Try to act like you always have. If I ask you to take a ride on the boat, please do everything you can to go with me. If I show up at the actual Lodge, then it's time, though I'll try to come by boat for safety. You may start to feel strange things, see things. Do you understand?"

Iris nodded and clutched Roar close. He knew she was terrified but now that she'd started to sense things, it meant the Lodge was growing stronger. Too much longer and they wouldn't be able to stop it. "What if I ask you to come there?"

Ledger considered that. He chewed his lip. "If you ask me to come by boat and are willing to come on board, then yes. If you ask me to come to the Lodge, I may not know if it's you asking me. I may still come, but I'll come to fight."

Iris bobbed her head. "I understand. I feel like the snails."

"The snails?"

"The ones down by the beach with the fragile shells. I feel like them. Just trying to live my life and be left alone. But I am exposed out here, and so many things are trying to crush the thin veneer that protects my soul. I feel like I'm out of place and vulnerable."

Ledger could relate. He pushed the hair off of her shoulder and leaned in. "You are stronger than you think, Iris. You're a survivor. Those snails are just in the wrong place. Their environment is what is causing them to be vulnerable. If they were in a different place, maybe they wouldn't be so fragile. Change their environment, change the outcome."

"But they can't. Something is keeping them there, keeping them fragile."

"Maybe so, or maybe they can but aren't," Ledger countered.

"Perhaps it's their destiny to be there and nothing can be done," Iris reasoned.

"Fair enough. We can't explain why certain things are the way they are. But, Iris, you aren't those snails. You are you. You have aspects to your life which make you different from them."

"Like what?" Iris rested her head on his shoulder and ran her fingers across his back.

Ledger drew her in close to him, sighing. "You've already survived someone trying to crush you. You didn't just lay there and accept your fate, you fought for your life, for your existence. That says a lot about who you are and your drive to survive. Those snails continue to live there day in and day out, not moving to a better place. Maybe they don't know what's over the horizon, or perhaps it's just the way it's always been, so they don't know anything different from that reality. I can't really say, nor do I understand their plight. You know you have a choice now, you aren't stuck. You just need to find your path out of there. It may be hidden but it exists. Besides, Iris, there is another thing, too."

Iris watched his face and cocked her head, waiting for him to go on.

Ledger squeezed her hand and smiled, knowing the words to be the difference for both of them. He didn't know how this would all end, but he knew Iris had someone on her side.

"You have me and I'll protect you with my life."

CHAPTER TWENTY-TWO

*T*hey made love on the beach and stayed as long as they could before Iris knew she needed to get back to the Lodge. Neither wanted to leave the other and now that she knew, Ledger feared for both of their lives. Time was running out. Roar being with Ledger gave him some small comfort, the little lookout. He was glad Iris had the small cat to sense things at the Lodge. He took his time getting his boat to the island and held her as close as possible.

Once they pulled up to the dock, he felt it. The energy coming off the place was palpable. For the first time, he could see Iris felt it, too. She stared at him wide-eyed, shaking her head as fear radiated off of her. Ledger hugged her close and rubbed her back.

"Just stay strong. Remember it *needs* you. You have the upper hand. Unless you turn on it, you should be safe. It's me it's after for now. Can you move your bedroom?"

"My bedroom?"

"Remember what Bertie said? And how Roar won't go up to the loft?"

"Oh. I can use one of the cabins. Roar can sleep with me out there."

"Alright, that might be better. Do they lock?"

"Yeah, I had new locks installed on everything. I can move my things down tomorrow. I'll just sleep out there tonight. Me and Roar."

"Call me in the morning, okay?" Ledger whispered, twisting a tendril of her hair around his finger.

"Are you kidding? I'll probably end up calling you multiple times before then. I'm spooked as hell," Iris said, chuckling softly.

"Do you want to come home with me?"

"Yes, but no. I think it's best if I keep things as they were, so to not to make anything obvious. As you said, act like I have been, so nothing gets wind of the change."

"Call me as much as you need," Ledger said and kissed her firmly, feeling her melt against him.

"I will. Get home safely," Iris murmured into his chest.

"Will do my best. At least now, I feel like something is guarding me."

"I hope so."

Iris scooped Roar up and her basket. She glanced back at him and he could see she was afraid. He felt like shit not being able to go up with her, however, knew she was right. Keep things as normal as possible. He waited until he saw her climb the path and disappear to the cabins. He'd left the boat idling to make sure he didn't get stuck there and turned it around in the channel.

The drive home by moonlight was peaceful and reminded him how sometimes his father would take him and Duff out for a midnight ride. That was before they put fencing up and locked the marina up at night. The gates could be opened from the inside of the marina, but not the outside. His father would pack snacks and take them on a ride around the island, telling them folklore and history.

The water had always seemed so sacred, a moat that protected the island from the outside world. But now it seemed it was protecting the outside world from the island. Whatever was growing at the Lodge didn't cross the water. It was why he was safe on the boat and the outer islands. It was contained. Whatever came back with Iris had been a messenger, a guide to get her there. Something inside of her had not closed when she came back. It needed that.

How could he close that without killing her? The Lodge wasn't the portal, she was. The Lodge was the beast. Whatever came back with her was bringing her to the Lodge. The ceremonies had been the portal before but it'd closed once the people performing them left. The Lodge needed it reopened to channel through its power. That now existed in Iris. Ledger racked his brain, attempting to figure out how to stop this without harming Iris. He may have been sent to stop this, but he hadn't been given a handbook. He was just a guy with no clue. He docked the boat and walked up the plank. He didn't even know where to begin. He couldn't just show up at the Lodge with nothing to fight with. How did one fight evil?

He sighed with relief when the truck engine turned over and he drove home, feeling like he was between two worlds. He could see the island he grew up on but it seemed different.

Unfamiliar. When he got home, he saw the light on in Duff's room and drew some small comfort from it. He needed to tell his family everything, but knew they'd push back on some of what he had to say. He slipped in quietly and headed for Duff's bedroom.

"Hey," he said at the door.

Duff rolled over from reading. "Was wondering when you'd be home. Can't sleep now until you are. Got me all up and worrying now, like a dad."

"Sorry, I took Iris out on the boat."

"That a smart decision?"

"Because of Iris or the boat?" Ledger asked without humor.

Duff sat up. "Both."

Ledger rubbed his head, then shrugged. "I think it's okay."

"You take too many chances, Ledge. Why can't you just let it go? Let her go."

"You know I can't. She isn't just some girl. I want to marry her."

Duff winced and cocked their head. "You just can't take the easy way, can you?"

"It gets worse."

Duff watched him, their eyes fixed on his face. "Are you in danger?"

"I don't know. I may be. We all may be. I need to talk to you and Mom tomorrow about all of this. First, I need to do some research."

"On what?"

"The occult."

Duff whistled, then bit their nails. "That's some shit you should *not* get into, Ledger. I've heard things can attach to you if you get in too deep."

Ledger looked at his sibling and sighed. "Too little too late. Regardless of what I find out in my research, I think I'm already in this."

"How?"

"I can't get into this tonight, but I'll talk to you and Mom tomorrow. Get some sleep."

"Sure, come in and tell me we could be in danger and you might be involved in the occult. Then tell me to go to sleep," Duff replied dryly.

Ledger leaned in and kissed Duff on the forehead. "I won't let anything happen to you. You and mom are all the family I have left."

Ledger went to his room and lay in bed. He messaged Iris to let her know he was home and she messaged back a picture of Roar, sleeping on her chest. It made him feel better. He surprised himself by falling asleep and while his dreams were chaotic and stressful, there were no messages in them. When he woke up, the sun was up and he could hear his mother in the kitchen. He went in to hug her, grateful for her steady presence in his life. She turned, grinning.

"Ledger! What time did you get in?"

"Around ten."

"How is Iris?" she asked with a twinkle in her eyes.

"Good, she says hello," Ledger replied, his ears turning pink.

"Are you hungry? I made pancakes and eggs."

"Always."

She handed him a plate and he sat at the table. He watched her and felt an overwhelming desire to protect her. She'd been through so much already. "Hey, will you be around this afternoon? I'm going over to the mainland to the library. I was hoping to talk to you and Duff after."

"I am. Leo is coming for dinner tonight. Why are you going there?" his mother asked as she gathered dishes into the sink.

"Research. The library here doesn't have what I'm looking for."

"You should be taking it easy."

"I feel fine, great actually," Ledger replied honestly. He'd never felt stronger.

"You worry me. What are you researching?"

"I'll tell you later. I'm glad Leo will be here, too. He might have some insights."

"I think Duff was planning to head over to the mainland, as well. You should go together," she suggested as she rinsed a plate and set it in the rack. They'd never had a dishwasher and she preferred that way.

"That right? I'll ask them if they want to. I'm taking the ferry."

"Ask me what?" Duff asked from the door and grabbed a pancake from the plate.

"I'm going to the mainland. You want to go with me?" Ledger offered.

"Oh, yeah, for your research? Sure. I'll skip the library though, I get enough books with school. I need to run some errands anyhow," Duff said while shoving the pancake into their mouth.

"Alright, we can rent a car and you can drop me off at the library."

"Sounds like a plan. Will you be ready in about thirty?" Duff asked, scarfing down another pancake. They were a bottomless pit when it came to food.

"I can be."

Ledger quickly finished breakfast and went to get ready. Iris had called. He called back but got her voicemail. He left a message.

"Damn. Sorry, I missed you. I'm about to go to the mainland for a bit. I should be back by this afternoon. My mother is making dinner if you want to join us. I'll call you when I'm back. I love you."

Duff was waiting by the truck when he came out and waved at him to hurry up, tapping an imaginary watch on their wrist. Ledger laughed and shook his head. "You're an impatient little fuck, aren't you?"

Duff snorted. "You know for a dude, you take a long time to get ready."

"I guess we can't all be as put together as you," Ledger replied sarcastically.

"At least you are aware of your shortcomings," Duff said and climbed in the truck.

The ferry was full, so Ledger and Duff squeezed their way to where Leo was. He was explaining to a tourist that the boat ran on a schedule, and they couldn't make him come and go as they pleased. They huffed as they walked away and Ledger patted him on the back.

"Hey, Leo. Mean to tell me you aren't at their beck and call?"

"Fucking tourists," Leo muttered, scowling at their retreating backs. "Are you two headed in?"

"We are. Mom said you're coming for dinner?" Ledger replied.

"I sure am. Your mother is a diamond, you know? Hard to believe she's been alone all this time."

"She truly loved my dad. Losing him broke her heart. She seems to have taken a shine to you, though."

"Ah, we're just good friends. I think she's real pretty, too, if you don't mind me saying. I don't think she'd be interested in an old coot like me."

Ledger stared at Leo. He was only about five years older than his mother and had the ruggedness of a sea captain with his graying hair, light brown eyes, and crinkles that showed he laughed more than frowned. Ledger saw the way his mother looked at Leo and knew she more than did. Duff laughed from behind them.

"Can we talk about something other than old people love, please?"

"Duff! Don't be an ass," Ledger hissed.

"Am I an ass or a fuck? You can't have it both ways," Duff teased.

"You are most definitely both."

Duff grinned with pride and opened a book to read for the trip. Ledger turned back to Leo apologetically. "Don't mind Duff, they're full of themselves. They don't know when to keep their mouth shut."

Leo laughed. "Oh, I've known you both from birth. I'm well aware. That one had a mouth from the moment they started to speak."

Ledger took a seat next to Duff and closed his eyes. Even as a kid, he liked being a passenger on a boat. It allowed him to feel the waves, to become part of the motion. He imagined it was like what it felt like to be in the womb. Not a care in the world.

He must have dozed off at some point because when he awoke the ferry was on the other side. He stood up and peered around. He could see Leo on the dock smoking a cigar and jumped off the boat, heading toward him. Duff was nowhere to be seen.

"Did Duff leave?"

"Just to get a car rented for the day. Said you needed the rest and would be back. I'm waiting on my next load of passengers, so figured it best to leave you be. You alright?" Leo asked as he blew out smoke in small circles.

"Enough, I guess. I have a lot on my mind."

"I can see that. You want to share?"

"I'll tell you more later, but it has to do with the Lodge," Ledger said.

"I figured as much. Ever since we talked about it that first time, I've seen a change in you. A drive."

"I don't want to put you in any danger, Leo, but where do you stand about that place? I mean, how do you feel about the Lodge?"

Leo watched him, rubbing his mouth in thought. "They should've burned it to the ground after that girl went missing."

"Why do you say that?"

"Because nothing ended when they closed it up. Dark shit has been part of this island ever since. I grew up here. It was different then. When they opened that place and started doing those ceremonies, things began happening more here. Neighbors turning on one another, men beating up their wives that never had. It just changed. Then with the fishermen bringing them girls over, it got even worse. It got a little better when they closed it down, but there has always been this underlying potential for bad things since. It changed people here. The innocence was gone."

"I saw my dad when I was out to sea. When I almost died," Ledger said, hoping Leo didn't think he was off his rocker.

Leo nodded, his face revealing he knew more than he'd let on. "I know you did, you crossed over. Did he tell you?"

"Tell me what?"

"That you came here to change things."

CHAPTER TWENTY-THREE

*L*edger thought about what Leo said, on his way to the library. He'd asked Leo to hold the thought until they could all sit down for dinner and they were able to dig into what Leo meant. Ledger had a feeling what Leo had to say was important and wanted everyone to be there, so they could hash things out. About the time Leo said those words, Duff came back with the rental car and Ledger was anxious to get moving. Leo read the energy and winked.

"I'll see you tonight and we can talk more. It's more than we can go over here, anyhow. What time do you think you'll be done?"

"Not sure. Duff is running errands and I'm going to dig up what I can at the library. Maybe a few hours?"

"That will work. It's busy today, so I'm running back and forth extra. I have a kid I'm training on my next run. He's taking over the evening shifts, so I can come to eat."

"Oh yeah, who's that?" Ledger inquired.

"Dan Sauter's son, Caleb. You know him?"

"Of him, I think Duff went to school with him. Hey, Duff, you remember Caleb Sauter?" Ledger called back to Duff.

Duff laughed, nodding. "Who doesn't? Class clown. Why?"

"He's training with Leo to run the ferry."

Duff eyed Leo, then shook their head. "Damn, Leo, you're a brave man to trust Caleb with the boat. He's a bit of a partier."

"Yeah, well, so are you," Ledger teased.

"True, but I'm not driving a boat full of people," Duff retorted.

"Noted," Leo said. "I'll keep my eye on him."

Duff and Ledger headed into town, grabbing a bite to eat first. Growing up on an island, it was always a bit like letting loose to come to the mainland. Drive-through restaurants, chain stores, and all kinds of different people. The island was stuck in time for the most part. It didn't even have a stoplight. Duff dropped Ledger off at the library and continued on. Ledger found an empty computer to search up books and even seeing titles about occult books made him uncomfortable. He wanted to gain knowledge, however, he didn't want to open anything else up by accident. He went to the section and pulled out a few books, which seemed the most legitimate. The covers were disturbing but the books themselves were steeped in facts and did not glamorize the practices.

After a couple of hours, his eyes hurt and while he gathered a lot of information on the occult and black magic, he was still at a loss on what he was supposed to do. He wasn't willing to try any sort of magic himself, aware it could backfire and didn't know exactly how he was supposed to defeat this thing. He copied some pages and went out to meet Duff. Maybe Leo would have some insight since he remembered some of what happened there previously. Duff wasn't in the lot yet when Ledger went out, so he sat on a bench and rifled through the pages. He got the impression he wasn't alone and peered up to see the doctor who'd treated him walking toward him.

"Hello, Ledger. Fancy seeing you over here!" His blue eyes were intense and he seemed to be reading Ledger's mind. His smile seemed genuine, but Ledge still felt there was something he didn't know about the good doctor.

Ledger rolled up the papers in a flash, then nodded. "It's good to get off the island sometimes."

"Indeed it is. Doing some research?"

Ledger felt his throat tighten and even though the words on the papers weren't visible, he felt like he'd been caught doing something wrong. Luckily, at this point Duff pulled up and laid on the horn, making both the doctor and Ledger jump. Ledger got up and gave a quick wave. "Sorry, my ride is here. Nice seeing you, doc."

The doctor watched him walk away and called out, "I'll be coming by."

Ledger paused and turned back, his brow knitted. "Sorry?"

"To give you a final check-up. I need to sign off on your care for the insurance."

"Oh. Sure. Tomorrow?"

"Tomorrow then. Have a nice day, son."

Ledger got in the car and shook off the feeling of being admonished. Duff laughed and gunned the car, skidding out of the parking lot. "That dude is freaking weird. I wouldn't be surprised to see his picture on the news that he had people chained up in his basement."

Ledger stared out the window but didn't reply. The truth was, he wouldn't be all that surprised either. They dropped off the car and walked down toward the dock. Leo had his trainee, Caleb, with him and was trying to explain the schedule.

"You have to stick to it. Even if no one shows up, you wait at least fifteen minutes to make sure. You don't make special trips and no matter how hard people push back, you leave on time, no sooner, no later. Understand?"

Caleb nodded. "I think so."

Leo waved at them and did a quick introduction. Caleb grinned at Duff. "Hey, I remember you from school. Smartass, right?"

"One and the same," Duff replied. "Jokester, right?"

Caleb gave a small bow. "That's me."

"I thought you went to school in, like, Ohio or something?" Duff asked.

"I did. Pennsylvania actually. Didn't work out so much."

"Oh, why's that?"

"I guess 'cause I didn't go to class," Caleb replied, shrugging without a care in the world.

"Yep, that'll do it. You back for good?"

"God, I hope not. But probably. Leo's training me on the ferry runs now and I'm helping my dad out with his fishing boat."

"Nice. Anyway, it's good to see some young blood around. Not that I plan on staying forever," Duff said with a grin.

"Good plan. Alright, Leo's giving me the eye, so better get back to work. It was good seeing you again, Duff."

He skirted up to the front of the boat where Leo was impatiently waiting. The boat started to fill up, so Duff and Ledger grabbed seats at the back of the boat for the fresh air. Ledger noticed the doctor getting on board and groaned. He couldn't seem to shake him. The doctor didn't notice them, or if he did, he ignored them. Ledger closed his eyes and turned his face to the sun. At this moment, he could forget everything and just be a guy from the island with nothing to worry about. He knew it wouldn't last, but it was a fun game to play for the time being.

When they deboarded the ferry, the doctor was nowhere to be seen, which was just fine by Ledger. His mother was out when they got home and Ledger slipped to his room to grab a nap before the evening festivities. His room was cool and dark; exactly where he wanted to be. His eyes closed almost immediately, drawing him down into layers of sleep. Images flashed through his head like a television being fast-forwarded. Information coming to him at high speed, yet comprehensible. It was as if something had been put in him to absorb concepts on a level beyond a supercomputer. When he awoke, he lay in bed staring at the ceiling, his waking self not grasping what his sleeping self could. It was data he didn't know how to access.

He could hear his mother laughing and cooking in the kitchen, Leo's low voice talking to her. Ledger washed his face and wet down his hair, which resembled a bird's nest. He headed to the kitchen and grabbed a beer out of the fridge. He wasn't ready for the conversation they were about to have and needed a little added courage. Duff came in, plopping down at the table.

"Hey, when are we getting this show on the road? Kelsey is picking me up tonight, so we can go fuck some shit up at the dump."

"Duff, don't cause trouble. Why can't you just do something which doesn't border on illegal?" their mother asked, exasperated.

"Because, Mom, we live on a fucking island with nothing else to do. Besides, she was pretty excited to hear Caleb is back and his shift doesn't end until everything else is closed."

"Just stay out of trouble, huh? I don't feel like coming to get you."

Duff nodded and took a bite of a roll from a basket on the table. "Fine, Mother. So?"

"So, what?"

"What time are we doing this thing?"

"Patience. I'm pulling the casserole out here in a minute and it needs to cool. Iris hasn't arrived yet, either. If Kelsey shows up early, she's welcome to eat here," their mother offered.

"I don't think my friends want to sit around with a bunch of old people tonight," Duff replied dramatically and snickered.

"In all fairness, Duff, none of us want to sit around with your friends," Ledger replied, his voice tinged with boredom and irritation.

A knock came at the door and Ledger got up to answer it. Iris was standing outside with a bottle of wine. She waved it in the air and grinned.

"I remembered Duff's favorite food," she joked.

Ledger pulled her in and kissed her. "You're a sight for sore eyes. Are you ready for this?"

"Of course. Beats being at the Lodge with grumpy, demanding guests."

They headed back to the kitchen and exchanged pleasantries. Ledger's mom set the casserole at the table and grabbed a stack of plates. "Ledge, can you grab silverware? Duff, if it won't trouble your highness, can you grab lemonade and glasses?"

Duff groaned and got up. "Fine, but I'm drinking that wine Iris brought."

"We *all* are drinking that wine Iris brought, so don't get any ideas," Ledger said firmly.

They sat down and dished out the food. Leo sat next to their mother and from the way they were with each other, Ledger assumed they were getting more serious. He frowned and thought about his father. He was long gone but it was still hard seeing his mother with anyone else. He wanted her to be happy, however, actually observing her interacting with Leo was weird, to say the least. After the small talk died down, Ledger cleared his throat to get everyone's attention. All eyes turned to him and Leo gave him a little nod for support. Ledger thought about his words and realized there was no way for this to not all sound bonkers.

"We all know weird stuff has happened recently. Really since the Lodge reopened. First, with me seeing things out of the ordinary there. Then with Bertie telling me things about the place, and about Dad. From there it has spiraled, and I think it's time we address what needs to happen."

"What needs to happen? What do you mean?" his mother asked and set her fork down. "I mean, what can happen?"

Leo sighed. "Let me jump in here because it's only going to get crazier. Bertie was right about the place. Bad things happened there. Intentionally. Even after that girl went missing, it still seemed to have a bad energy. No disrespect to your family, Iris, but your great-great-aunt was not a good woman. Outside of just being caustic and belligerent, she seemed to gain some satisfaction when other people suffered. I don't know how Bertie did it, helping out all of those years. She spoke to him like he was a junkyard dog. After the Lodge closed, I'd sometimes run deliveries out to her from the ferry. God, I hated that woman. Nothing was ever right. But she paid well, and being from here it was how I was raised to help a neighbor."

"Do you think she was still involved in black magic?" Ledger asked.

"I know she was. She was always ordering things the average person doesn't order. Besides, she talked about it. Cursing people and casting spells. She said she was wronged, and she was going to unleash something to reclaim what was hers."

"Did she say how or what?" Iris's soft voice spoke up from the end of the table.

"Not specifically. She talked about the day of reckoning, though. That it was coming. How her blood would set things right," Leo answered.

"Her blood as in her blood in her body, or her family?" Duff asked.

"She never said. She'd go on tangents and I'd keep my head down and stay out of it. All I know is, she was determined to get revenge. Anyone who crossed them would pay. I was just trying to drop stuff off and get out of there. The place gave me the creeps."

"Did she ever say anything specific about what they'd done there?" Ledger inquired, gripping Iris's hand under the table.

"Not in those terms, but she'd say how a war was coming and they'd kill all who interfered. That a change was coming. She was specific about one thing, though. Like, dead set on it."

"What's that?" Ledger asked.

"You. She said a male child had been born to stop them and he'd need to be exterminated," Leo replied, meeting Ledger's eyes.

"But why do you think that's me?"

"Because she told me so. She said she even tried to go into the hospital when you were born and kill you. She took you from the bassinet in the room."

"What? That never happened," Ledger said, attempting to make sense of the story. "Right, Mom?"

His mother's eyes were huge and horrified. She shook her head. Her voice was small and far away when she spoke. "You were only missing for about ten minutes. I'd gone to the bathroom and when I came out, you were gone from your bassinet. They found you in the bushes and no one was around. They didn't have cameras or anything like that back then, to tell what happened. You weren't out of my sight after that, at all."

"Whoa," Duff whispered from the other side of the table. "That seems like something maybe we should've known before now."

"So, why didn't she kill me then?" Ledger asked, feeling the energy strengthen inside him. If someone had taken him as a baby, they could've killed him easily. He'd been completely defenseless.

Leo cleared his throat. "She said you burned her hands. She'd smuggled you out of the hospital and was going to perform a sacrifice on you. All of a sudden, you became so hot she couldn't hold you any longer. She dropped you, then fled."

CHAPTER TWENTY-FOUR

N o one moved or spoke around the table. Ledger stared at his mother for confirmation. She shook her head, her eyes wide. She didn't know much, only that he'd disappeared from the room and was found minutes later in the bushes outside. Even Duff was silent, which was unheard of. Ledger shifted his eyes back to Leo and frowned.

"It sounds like the ramblings of a crazy old woman," he said and grasped Iris's hand under the table.

Leo met his eyes, unblinking. "I'd be inclined to agree and chalked it up to as much until you told me what you did. What happened out there when you up and disappeared. Now, I don't think so."

"What did you tell him?" his mother inquired.

Ledger sighed. Now, he was going to sound like the crazy one. "When I was out on the boat, I saw Dad. He told me things and when I died, I was shown everything. Like, past, present, future. Why I'm here."

"Why you're here?" his mother asked and bit her lip. "You're here because we wanted children. You and Duff. Your father and I wanted a family. We wanted you in our lives."

"Maybe my body is, but my soul came to undo some things. Things that began with the Lodge. I was sent here to stop whatever was started there," Ledger explained.

"And apparently I'm here to keep things going," Iris whispered.

Duff stared back and forth at each of them. "So, what you are saying is that there is something supernatural at the Lodge, and Ledge you are supposed to stop it, and Iris in essence is supposed to stop you? You are supposed to fight against each other?"

"No, she isn't against me. In a way, Iris is just a catalyst. Or was. Her presence brought power to whatever was there. Lying dormant. The Lodge needed her to open something."

"Okay, so why don't you just leave?" Duff asked Iris, glaring at her.

Ledger tightened his fingers around Iris's hand and cleared his throat. "It wouldn't matter anymore. Things are in motion. Besides, I need Iris by my side. Whatever has tried to keep me from stopping this sooner succeeded. Now, the only way out is to stay and fight. Together."

"Fight how?" his mother asked, her voice low and stressed.

"I don't know yet. I've been reading up on the occult and black magic, but it isn't totally clear on how to take something like this down. I honestly don't know what we're fighting. What form it takes. I think we need to destroy the Lodge, though."

"Destroy it like burn it to the ground?" Duff questioned, a little too eagerly.

Ledger nodded. "Something like that."

"Well, hell, I can go do that tonight," Duff insisted and laughed.

"It's not that easy. Once it knows you are aware and mean it harm, you'll have a hard time getting close. I tried twice and almost died twice. Actually died once. It's not a simple solution. Not to mention, I'm not sure who there, or anywhere really, can be trusted or is part of this."

"Like real people?" Duff asked.

"Yeah. Like the doctor, like guests of the Lodge. Even Doyle, the handyman out there. Anyone we don't know could be part of this. I feel like there's a battle brewing and each side is bringing in their own army."

Leo shook his head. "Tough season to try and sort that out. There are more strangers on the island right now than locals."

"Exactly. I think that's why it has gotten stronger and whatever is going to happen will happen sooner than later. We are off our guard because so many people are unfamiliar," Ledger agreed.

"Happen like what?" his mother asked. She rubbed her face, and Ledger noticed for the first time she was showing her age.

"Mom, I'm not sure, to be honest. What I gather is that either it affects people or calls to people who are already aligning in that way."

"Aligning? Like bad people?" she said, her face already understanding the truth.

"Yeah. Either way, it puts the residents here on the island in danger. I think the water around the island acts like a moat, keeping it from spreading but once flesh and blood people are involved, I think it'll use that to spread off the island en masse. Use people to carry whatever power it has across the water."

"This is way too much!" Duff exclaimed and got up. "This sounds like some made-up bullshit, Ledge. Maybe you got some brain damage from being out on the boat. You're just fucked up from all that happened... and her."

"Then explain what Leo told us, about Bertie, and even how I ended up on the boat in the first place?" Ledger replied, his voice gentle and slow. "Duff, I wanted it to not be true, but if I keep denying it, we all could end up dead. Stop blaming Iris, she's as much a victim in this as we are."

"Fuck this," Duff hissed and left the room.

Duff had just been eight when their father died. A little girl who'd run to greet her daddy when he came home and wrap her small arms around his neck as he scooped her up. Ledger remembered Duffey crying night after night until one day she just shut down. They'd been shut down ever since. He got up from the table and went to find Duff. They were on the front porch and Ledge could see they'd been crying. He sat beside them and let out a heavy breath.

"Duff-"

"Don't. You can't come and tell me some ghost shit is after you and expect me to just believe it. I don't know what's going on, but leave me out of it. I'm tired of this family and all our constant drama."

Ledger watched Duff and wanted nothing more than to wrap his arms around them and assure them it'd be alright. But he knew the truth and whether or not Duff wanted to hear it, it wasn't something he could just let go of. "I'm sorry, but it's the truth, Duff."

"Yeah? Whatever, Ledge. Tell Mom I called Kelsey and she's coming to pick me up, now. I'm going to stay with her tonight."

Duff stepped off the porch and into the night, heading toward the driveway. Ledger watched them go and shook his head, sighing. He headed back inside and paused at the door to the kitchen. Leo was comforting his mother, who was beside herself with worry. Iris seemed to have shrunk in her chair, knowing her presence was what brought this all on. Ledger sat next to her and put his arm over her shoulders, drawing her close. She rested her hand on his thigh which sent heat up his leg. His mother peered at them.

"What do we do?" she asked.

"I think first, we need the Lodge to be empty. Iris, can you clear the schedule of guests?"

"I think so. I have a big group this week, but it drops off after that. I can call the guests coming in after this week and let them know we'll have to cancel their reservations. I'll call tomorrow."

"I don't trust Doyle. I think he may have been brought by the Lodge. Can you get rid of him, too? If even for that time?" Ledger inquired.

Iris nodded. She frowned and tipped her head to the side. "You don't think he'll try to hurt me, do you?"

"I don't think so, but keep Roar away from him. Where's Roar now?"

"Locked in my cabin."

"Okay, good. Just don't let her wander. I may need to move to stay on the boat for now."

"Ledger, do you think that's smart? With what already happened?" his mother questioned.

"No less safe than being here. Probably more so. Remember in the video where I was on the boat and something untied it from the dock? It didn't leave with me. It stayed behind, so I do think my best bet is out on the water. It might make you all safer, too, not having me around. I'm the threat, more or less."

"I can run you supplies, as well," Leo offered. "Stay and have a beer now and then."

Ledger laughed, nodding. "That'd be good, Leo. Oh, Mom, Kelsey is picking Duff up and they're going to stay the night over there. I think this is all too much for them to absorb at once."

"Duff will come around, honey. It's a lot to take in. I'm not sure I totally get all of it, but I trust you, Ledger. You were always such a serious child. Very matter-of-fact. I believe that what you experienced was real," his mother said and covered his hand with hers. "I just can't lose you, do you understand? You're still my baby boy."

"Mom, I'm doing my best to keep that from happening," Ledger responded, meeting her eyes.

"So, what's the plan?" Leo asked.

"Once the Lodge is empty, I'm going to go near there and see what happens. I can't know how to fight if I don't know what I'm fighting. If it were easy, I'd just go and burn it down. However, I think it's going to be a bit more complicated than that. Even setting foot on the property may put my life in danger."

"I want to help," his mother said softly. "Your fight is my fight."

Ledger stared at his mother, understanding how deep her love for him went. She didn't want to live without her child and there was no way he could stop her. She was fighting alongside him either way. "Thanks, Mom."

"Where your mother goes, I go. Count me in," Leo replied.

Iris squeezed his hand. "You know I'm in."

Ledger stared around the table at the ragtag group and felt tears well up in his eyes. Not only did they believe him, they wouldn't let him face this alone. Iris met his eyes with her beautiful, vibrant, blue eyes and smiled. She knew the risks and wanted to be by his side. They were in this together. She reached up and traced her fingers along the bone beneath his eye.

"There would be no life without those amber eyes gazing at me, you know? I love you, Ledger. You are my life, now. It's time to fight."

Ledger leaned in and kissed her, feeling a tear slip down his cheek. He whispered in her ear, "After this will you marry me?"

Iris laughed and let her lips brush against his. "Of course."

Ledger felt her breath against his face and prayed they'd both make it out alive. He sat back and met his mother's eyes. She'd heard. What would normally be a joyous occasion, was tainted by the reality they didn't know what the future held. She smiled slightly and sighed. No matter what happened, they were all family now. Iris and Leo included. She nodded at Ledger and he smiled back.

"Let's let this ride for tonight," Ledger said. "We can figure out a plan in the next few days. I'm going to do some more reading to see if there are any protections we can put in place. In the meantime, pay attention to strangers and situations which are out of the ordinary. If anyone seems suspicious write it down. Even if they don't but you get a gut feeling, make a note of it. Not all of them will be rude or obvious. I don't know the army we're facing."

They cleared the table and put food away. Leo and his mother went for a walk, leaving Iris and Ledger alone. Ledger turned to her. "You want to stay over?"

"I can't. Now, I'm especially worried about Roar. She's like my baby," Iris replied, then laughed.

"Fair enough. Maybe some nights you and Roar can sleep on the boat with me?" Ledger offered. He didn't want her all alone at the Lodge, and he didn't want to be alone without her.

"I think so. I do think I need to be at the Lodge to keep an eye on things. Especially if you think there are people around who want it to become what it was. Make sure no one is doing ceremonies or anything."

"I hate that you're alone out there."

"I'm not too thrilled by it either, but I have this sense I need to be there. To let it think I'm still at its beck and call," Iris explained.

"You rode your bike out here?"

"I did."

"You want a ride home?"

I don't think it's safe for you to come out now," Iris responded with worry.

"We can take the boat. I'll drop you off at the dock. I, uh, wouldn't mind some time alone with you," Ledger said, then blushed.

Iris met his eyes, getting his meaning. "Oh. Yeah, that would be nice."

They put her bike in the back of the truck and drove to the marina. Ledger texted his mother to let her know. The marina was locked but Leo had made him a spare key. They slipped in and boarded the boat. The night was clear, the stars blinking above them. Ledger took his time easing the boat out onto open water to head toward the channel. He cut the engine and dropped the anchor. They spread blankets on the floor of the boat and took off all their clothes.

Ledger's breath was taken by Iris standing naked in front of him and he ran his hands down her body. She responded and moved close to him, letting her fingers drift down his back, resting on his buttocks. He pressed her against him and moaned when she slid her hand around the front to grasp him. He was more than ready when she pulled him down to the blankets and welcomed him in. Their motions matched the shift of the waves and Ledger knew no matter what, he was home when he was with Iris. He kissed her breasts and took her mouth as he released inside of her. She arched to meet him, clinging to him as she let herself go and cried out. Ledger wanted to stay like this forever. He lay down next to her and watched the stars.

His cell phone was going off and he realized they'd fallen asleep. He sat up and fished it out of his pants. It was Duff. He clicked it on, answering the call.

"Hey Duff, why are you calling so late? Are you alright?" he asked sleepily.

The phone crackled and he could hear crying. He knew that kind of crying. It was like after their father had died and Duff would cry themselves to sleep. He could barely hear the other end but heard sniffling and what sounded like running through the woods. Duff's voice was terrified and frantic when they spoke.

"Ledger, help me! Something is after me!"

CHAPTER TWENTY-FIVE

*T*he line went dead. Ledger redialed Duff's number and it rang until it went to voicemail. He stared at the phone as dread filled him. He kept redialing the phone and cussing when it went to voicemail. Iris woke up and looked at him. She slipped on her clothes and put her hand on his shoulder. He was shaking so badly, he almost dropped the phone. He was on the verge of tears when he heard the phone pick up. Duff didn't say anything but Ledger could hear them in the background running. From something.

"Duff! Can you hear me?" he yelled frantically into the phone.

The phone sounded like it was dropped and picked up. Duff came on the line. "Ledger!"

"Where are you?"

"I went to the Lodge. Can you come get me, please?" their voice begged.

"Can you get to the dock?"

The line went dead again.

Ledger jumped up and threw his clothes on. He dragged up the anchor and fired up the engine. He handed Iris the phone as he guided the boat to the channel.

"If Duff calls again, tell them to get to the dock. They're in trouble."

Iris nodded and clutched the phone, staring at it. Ledger kicked the boat into full gear, but being a fishing boat full gear still wasn't fast enough. He headed through the channel and prayed Duff would be at the dock when they got there. They weren't. Ledger drew up alongside the dock and peered up the hill. Duff hadn't called again and the phone just went to voicemail when he tried to call. Ledger considered getting off the boat but knew he couldn't. They'd both be in danger if he did. Iris grabbed her bike and set it on the dock, understanding the predicament.

"Let me go look."

Ledger nodded and kissed her quickly. "Are you sure? Duff said something was after them."

"I'm sure. I live here and nothing has ever tried to mess with me. Yet, anyway."

She climbed out onto the dock. She pushed the bike by the handlebars up the hill and stopped when she got to the top, glancing around. The Lodge was quiet and except for a light left on in the main room, it was dark. She disappeared out of sight. Ledger checked his phone which was almost out of battery and chewed his inner lip. He saw something moving along the beach and fear knotted his stomach. Something was moving very fast toward him, however, he couldn't make out what it was by the shadow.

As it approached, he glanced around the boat for a weapon and snagged a spear he used for grabbing rope out of the water. There was no sign of Iris or Duff, and he considered moving the boat out onto the water. He made it to the steering wheel and was about to shift the boat into gear when he heard the scream coming from the beach. He paused, peering down the shore. The scream was erupting from the figure moving toward him. Just as he was about to leave the dock, he saw it was Duff as they hit the dock and jumped on the boat.

"Go! Go! Go!" Duff yelled, collapsing on the boat's bottom.

Ledger forced the engines as hard as he could and made it away from the dock when he saw something move along the tree line of the beach. As they pulled away, it disappeared into the trees. It was large. Bigger than a person. Ledger called Iris as quickly as possible. When she answered, he practically yelled in her ear.

"Get to your cabin and lock yourself in! I have Duff and we're out on the water!"

"What's going on?" Iris asked frantically.

"Please, Iris. Run to your cabin. Let me know when you are in there and that you and Roar are safe. Something is in the woods."

"Okay, hold on."

Ledger could hear Iris running toward her cabin and heard the key in the lock. Roar meowed as he heard the door slam shut and the lock slide. He sighed with relief. Iris came back on.

"Ledger, I'm in. Our girl is fine, maybe a little hungry. What's going on? Are you and Duffey okay?"

"I don't know, but I saw it. Duff made it to the boat and I saw it disappear into the trees as we got out into the channel. We're safe, for now."

"What was it?"

"I don't know. Not a human, though. It was big."

"Now, I'm scared," Iris's voice cracked.

"It doesn't want you. I don't think so, anyway. I'm not sure why it wanted Duff, but I intend to find out. Just stay locked in tonight with Roar. Whatever is there doesn't like being around her. Feed Roar and I'll let you know when I know more. I love you, Iris." Ledger's heart was pounding in his chest as he spoke.

"Call me when you know. I don't think I'll be sleeping anytime soon. I love you, too."

Ledger clicked the phone off and drove the boat out of the channel. Duff was huddled in a heap at the back of the boat, shaking uncontrollably. Ledger made sure they were nowhere near land and dropped the anchor. He went back to Duff and sat on the bench next to where they were wound into a ball with their legs pulled up to their chest. He placed his hand on their head and sighed.

"You want to tell me what that was? How you ended up there?"

Duff lifted their face which was streaked with dirt and tears. They had fallen and their hands were bloody and torn. "I didn't believe you."

"Okay?" Ledger got up and grabbed the first aid kit to clean Duff's wounds. "You do now?"

Duff stuck their hands out and winced when Ledger poured alcohol over the cuts. "You saw it, right?"

Ledger nodded. "I did. How did you end up there? At the Lodge? On the beach?"

"It was stupid. I was angry at you when I left," Duff answered.

"Angry at me? Why?"

"I don't know. The whole thing seemed like a ploy for attention, I guess. It just seemed so far-fetched, I felt like it was you trying to make something dramatic for effect. I mean, Christ, Ledger, you'd already almost died twice, so it seemed like you being the center of attention again. Ledger, here to save the world."

Ledger shook his head. "Geeze, Duff, not like I want to die, you know? I hate all of this. How it's tearing everything apart. And I'm not here to save the world, but I *am* going to do what I can to stop whatever this is. You need to know the reason I wanted everyone there tonight was because I can't do it alone. I need you, Mom, and Leo on my side."

"And Iris," Duff replied bitterly.

"Yeah and Iris. I don't know what your issue is with her. Iris likes you a lot. She loves me and our family."

Duff sighed. "Because I'm an asshole. It's nothing against Iris. It's just that since Dad died it's been just you, me, and Mom. You've never been serious about anyone. And the first person you are comes with demons. Literally. How fucked is that? Ledger, I think that was what was chasing me. Some kind of demon."

Ledger didn't doubt it.

He pulled Duff up to sit next to him and wrapped his arm around them. "You are and always will be my family, no matter who I love. I want to see you every day of my life, you get that? It's why I never left. I need you in my life, okay?"

Duff nodded and leaned against Ledger, suddenly seeming like the small child again, who'd climb up next to him when they were scared. "Okay."

"Now, tell me how you got there. Last I saw, you were leaving with Kelsey."

"Like I said, it was stupid. She came to pick me up and had Caleb along for the ride. We went to the beach and got pretty drunk. They were making out and I felt like a third wheel, so I convinced them to go for a drive. Caleb was the soberest, which isn't saying much, so he drove. I wanted to prove you wrong and convinced him to drive over to the Lodge. We parked on the main road and hiked in. We were passing a bottle of whiskey around and could see the light from the Lodge through the trees. We kept stumbling and falling which was funny, but also kind of scary. All of sudden, we heard a woman screaming. I told them it was foxes. But Ledger it wasn't."

Ledger hugged Duff tight and sighed. He shuddered with the memory. "I know."

"You do? Anyway, it scared the shit out of all of us and they said they were going back to the car. I didn't want to chicken out and begged them to keep going with me. They refused and went back the way we came. I almost went with them. I should've but my pride wouldn't let me. I told myself it was just foxes and kept walking to the Lodge. As I got closer, I was relieved to see the light and the outline of the building. Then I saw this woman standing there, maybe a girl. She had her back to me and I thought it was Iris. I was so glad to see her because I was scared out of my wits. I called out to her and she turned but it wasn't Iris. Ledger, her eyes were hollow and her mouth was twisted in a cross between fear and rage. I'm not exaggerating. She reached out to me and started screaming. I ran as fast as I could past her toward the Lodge, but could feel her breath on my neck."

Duff began sobbing at this point and put their face in their hands. Ledger rubbed their back and felt the fear oozing off of them. "Duff, I'm so sorry, you don't have to tell me anything else."

Duff shuddered and choked back a sob. "No, I do. You were honest with all of us and I mocked you. I didn't believe you. Now I do. I kept running and tripped and fell into an old pool. Except it wasn't a pool anymore. It was weird. There were tables and chairs at the bottom. And plants. I was confused and thought I had fallen through an alternate reality."

"Iris put those down there. She wanted to make a secret hideaway," Ledger explained.

"Oh. Well, it was definitely a secret. I stood up and tried to get my bearings but couldn't understand where I was. I ran my hands along the wall until I felt the ladder and realized I had fallen into a pool. The plants broke my fall. I hid in there, hoping to wait it out. I crouched down and listened out. It was completely silent. I figured by then Iris would've made it home and if I could just get from the pool to the Lodge, I could get to her and be safe. But I was too scared to move. I was just about to call you from down there and have you send Iris to me when I felt it."

"Felt what?" Ledger asked, not sure he wanted to know.

"I can't explain. If fear and darkness had a form and a temperature, it would be like that. I felt like I wasn't alone down there. It was pitch black, so I couldn't see anything except the stars above. But it was in there with me. This thing. But it wasn't just in *there*. It was trying to get inside of me. Like, absorb me. Every shitty thought I've ever had and every fear came to the surface. I felt like I was drowning in my own nightmares. I tried to scream but my throat was tight, so I couldn't. I moved to the wall and ran my hands along the side until I got to the ladder and tried to climb out. It was dragging me back."

"But you got out."

"I did. I was crying and all of a sudden it was like when I was little and Dad would scoop me into the air. It was like he was there and pulling me out. As soon as my feet hit the ground, I went toward the Lodge but it was in front of me, blocking me. I ran around the side and down the path. I tried calling you but the line went dead right after you answered. I ran into the woods toward the beach and could feel it coming after me. When I got to the water, I was alone. I saw you calling and answered. I heard you talking and then saw it at the tree line. It was huge. Indescribable. Like a monster but also like a human. A demon. I was so scared, I dropped my phone in the water. As I went to grab the phone, I realized the thing couldn't get to me in the water. It was hesitating as I was in the water. I saw you drive up to the dock but knew I needed to use the beach to get to you. I was afraid if I swam it would take too long and you'd leave. I ran up the shore, keeping my feet in the water. That slowed me down and the thing followed along the beach near the trees. I saw you start to pull away and screamed, knowing if you left, it would get me."

Ledger felt goosebumps rise on his arms and brushed the hair off of Duff's face. He'd almost left Duff behind. He hugged them to remind himself they were there and safe. For now. He had seen the thing in the tree line. Bigger than a human but not like the demons in folklore. No horns and tail. As if a shadow of something like that came to life. Jagged and dark. Eyes hollow and evil. Long clawed arms and a gaping mouth. He'd seen it before, he knew. When he'd been told about what happened to Iris. About her coming back from the dead. He'd imagined that creature clawing its way out of the woods, instead of her. Bringing itself to life to use her for survival. This was Iris's demon. The one who forced breath back into her, so it could force breath into itself and thus the Lodge. It wouldn't harm her because it was the guardian demon, meant to keep Ledger away. And now Duff. Anyone who knew the secret was now marked. It only survived because Iris did.

The question was how to destroy it, without killing Iris?

CHAPTER TWENTY-SIX

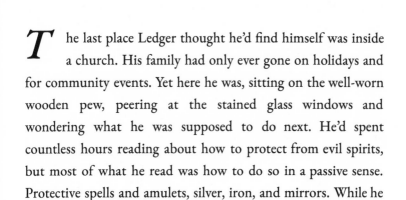

*T*he last place Ledger thought he'd find himself was inside a church. His family had only ever gone on holidays and for community events. Yet here he was, sitting on the well-worn wooden pew, peering at the stained glass windows and wondering what he was supposed to do next. He'd spent countless hours reading about how to protect from evil spirits, but most of what he read was how to do so in a passive sense. Protective spells and amulets, silver, iron, and mirrors. While he did like how some fishermen would paint big eyes on their boats for protection, nothing he read told him how to fight when he came face to face with a being who wanted to harm him. He leaned his head forward on the back of the pew in front of him and took a deep breath.

"You alright there?" a gentle voice said from the aisle.

Ledger glanced up and saw the minister smiling at him. She was young, maybe mid-thirties, and he remembered how some of the older people on the island balked at the idea of a young, female church leader. If it wasn't some old, male curmudgeon with bushy eyebrows, they didn't trust them. The idea made Ledger chuckle and he nodded.

"Yeah, just trying to figure some things out."

"Can I help?"

Ledger stared at her and wondered how she'd take him trying to explain what he believed was going on. He shook his head, considering how to start. "I don't know. Can I ask you something?"

"Sure." She sat down on the pew in front of him and rested her arm on the back to face him. Her face was round and freckled, giving her the look of someone much younger than she was.

"Do you believe there is truly good and evil? Like demons and stuff like that?"

She laughed softly and rubbed her short dark hair. "Well, I might be in the wrong line of work if I didn't. Can you elaborate on what you are asking?"

Ledger let out a long sigh and stared at the front of the church, attempting to put it into words. "Like, do you believe they can be in the physical realm? Not just spiritual."

"Spiritual can be physical. But I get what you're saying. The thing is, our understanding is limited to what we've been shown. Some people are committed to what they can't see, but most of us want some sort of proof, you know? More than wisps and vapors."

Ledger chuckled at this. Wisps and vapors would be easier to swallow than what he was facing. The minister had kind eyes and Ledger felt he could tell her a little more. "I'm Ledger, by the way."

"Ledger? Nice to meet you. I'm Sandy. I don't think I've seen you here before?" she replied without any kind of condemnation.

"Not in years, not since my father died, I suppose. We used to come for special occasions when I was a kid, but you weren't here yet. Just the old guy who coughed a lot."

Sandy smiled. "Ah, Reverend Bancroft. Nice fellow, though very set in the old ways. What brings you here today?"

"If I told you, you wouldn't believe me," Ledger whispered, feeling his face get hot.

"Try me."

"I need to know how to fight demons."

Sandy stared at him unblinking, then bobbed her head. "Internal or external?"

Ledger met her eyes and appreciated her openness. "External, the internal ones will have to wait for another day."

Sandy grinned. "Indeed. Those are the harder ones, anyhow. So, external. You're seeing demons?"

"I'm not crazy or delusional, so you know. I know all of this sounds completely off the wall, but yeah. The first time I saw one was last year. I had a feeling my girlfriend was in danger and was going to go to her when my head started pounding. I barely made it in my home when I collapsed and saw this demonic face hovering over me."

"Did it say or do anything?"

"It told me she killed him and was coming after me."

"She? Your girlfriend?"

"I don't know what it meant. I guess I should backtrack some. The reason I was worried about my girlfriend was because she'd reopened the Lodge and some bad things happened back in the day there. I was trying to let her know what I'd found out. I think the demon was trying to stop me."

"I see." Sandy glided her fingers back and forth across the smooth wood of the top of the pew. "What happened after that?"

"I passed out. The doctor said I had meningitis but the tests came back negative. I was down for weeks. I found out more about the Lodge and how they would bring girls back and forth there. How they did things to them and how one went missing and they shut it down."

"Why were they bringing girls there?"

"Hell if I know." Ledger blushed when he realized he'd cussed but Sandy waved it off. He cleared his throat. "They were doing ceremonies there. Occult-type stuff from what I understand. I think the girls were used as part of that. And...uh, like sex stuff."

"Oh, I think I saw notes about that in Bancroft's journals. The Crowley place?"

"One and the same. I saw things when I was there. A girl standing on the dock, who wasn't really there. Iris, my girlfriend, never did. The Lodge was left to her when her grandmother died and her great-great-aunt was the one who started it all. Iris wanted to reopen it as a hotel of sorts. But everything is just off there. Even the people who stay seem weird."

"Do you think they are strange to begin with or the place makes them so?" Sandy watched him with genuine curiosity.

Ledger shrugged. "Your guess is as good as mine. It gets worse. Bertie, the handyman, died the same night I saw the demonic face, and he'd told me things right before it happened.

Something he saw there one time when he was doing some work there alone. A girl was hanging from the ceiling in one of the rooms. But she wasn't there when they went back to check. Like the girl on the dock."

Sandy nodded, knowing they were getting in deep. "Could be a coincidence but go on."

"My girlfriend, Iris, has a backstory. Her father tried to murder her when she was a kid, but she came back from the dead. I found the doctor who saved her and he told me things. How when they saved her, the room filled up with a sulfur smell, and he'd had visions she brought a demon back with her. That it attached itself to her. I think to get her here and reopen whatever the Lodge is."

"Has anything else happened since?" Sandy asked, taking it all in.

"The night I talked to the doctor, I was going to the Lodge to tell her but never made it. I woke up out in the middle of the ocean on my boat with no way to get back to shore. No keys, no phone. No recollection of how I got there. Stranded and alone."

"Oh! I heard about that. People said you got drunk and took your boat out," Sandy said without accusation.

"People say things. That's not what happened. I was sober, driving my truck, and the next thing I knew I was out on the boat. I died out there."

"You died? Wait, so how are you here?"

Ledger shook his head. "I guess I had some beings on my side, as well. It's too crazy to explain but I didn't come back alone."

"Like Iris?"

"Sort of. Except whatever came back with me became part of me, in a good way. To help stop whatever is going on there."

"Was that the last time you saw anything?" Sandy asked, her voice confident in what he was saying.

"No. A couple of days ago a demon chased my sibling, Duff, through the woods and down the beach. They, er, Duff didn't believe me and went to the Lodge to prove me wrong. Instead, they proved me right. They saw a girl in the woods but when they got to her, the girl's face was twisted and hollow, and they realized it wasn't a real girl. Not on this plane of existence anyway."

"They? Duff?"

"Yeah, Duff is non-binary and identifies as they," Ledger explained.

"I see. Go on."

"So, Duff ran and hid, thinking they were safe from whatever it was, but then a demon came behind them and began chasing them. They called me and I was out on my boat. I made it to the dock to see the thing, the demon, chasing them down the beach. Duff jumped on the boat and we got out onto the water."

"It didn't follow you?"

"I don't think it can. I think unless it's attached to a person, it can't cross the water."

Sandy rubbed her chin and sighed. "That's a lot to take in. I don't doubt you, I want you to know that. As a child, I saw things, good and bad. It's what drove me to the church. My family has a history of visions, or so they call them. It terrified me as a child. Sometimes it was just people who'd passed on, other times it was I guess demons or dark spirits when I closed my eyes. Anyway, I knew from a young age I wanted to learn to control and block them. Church did it for me. I understand it was my path and am not saying it's everyone's. We all find our connection somewhere. In nature, old churches, music, whatever."

"Did those things you saw ever come after you or harm you?"

"No, but like Iris, I think they wanted to use me. I was a sensitive child and they seek out those who are vulnerable in some way. Iris because of what she went through, me because I was already opened to the spirit world and too delicate to know how to fight it. I gained my strength and confidence here." Sandy waved her hand around at the church.

Ledger glanced around. It was never a place he'd felt connected to. He felt more connected to things unseen when he was out on the boat. When the wind blew in his face and he smelled the salt water, he felt like he understood the divine. He looked back at Sandy and she placed her hand over his.

"Ledger, I can see in you a higher calling. Not the church, I'm not trying to recruit you. This was my place to find my path, you need to find yours. But you *are* something special. You were brought here to make things better, to set things right. Do you understand?"

Ledger bobbed his head. "That's why I came here today. I don't know what else to do."

"I'm here to help. What do you need from me?"

"I need to know how to fight demons. Literally. Not through prayer or wishful thinking. I need to know what to do when I come face to face with them."

Sandy chewed her lip and thought. She stood up, putting her hands on her hips, and stared at the altar. "Okay, so how do you fight in the physical realm? I mean, there are things like holy water and crucifixes."

"Don't be offended but I think that's child play to these monsters," Ledger replied dryly.

"Not offended at all. It does seem like parlor tricks when you get down to it. However, they serve a purpose, even if it just slows it down. Is this thing, like, in physical form? Like you can reach out and touch it."

"I can't say, I haven't tried."

"Fair enough. But physically enough you can see it and it can chase you?"

"That much I know," Ledger agreed.

"Where there are demons, there are angels. Have you come across any?" Sandy asked, running her hand across her chin.

Ledger shrugged. "Like winged beings with halos? No. Haven't seen any."

Sandy chuckled, then tapped her finger against the pew. "They present in many forms. Even human forms."

"I'm not sure. There are a lot of new people around but that's pretty common during tourist season every year. How could I tell?"

"What is it Mr. Rogers said? Oh yeah. *When I was a boy and I would see scary things in the news, my mother would say to me, 'Look for the helpers. You will always find people who are helping.'*"

"Mr. Rogers? Like the guy on television from when I was a kid?"

"That's the one. Wise man. Point being, you need to look for those who show up to help. Angels are like that. They'll be around, keeping an eye on things, ready to jump in when push comes to shove."

"So, angels, holy water, crucifixes. Got it. Anything tangible?"

Sandy smiled. "I don't think there is a store where you can buy demon-killing swords or bazookas."

"Would be nice if there were," Ledger replied, running his hand through his hair

"Indeed it would. Ledger, you're not taking into account your best weapon," Sandy whispered as if she knew a great secret.

"What's that?"

"Yourself."

CHAPTER TWENTY-SEVEN

O n the ride to the marina, Ledger considered what Sandy
told him. What would happen if he turned and faced the
monster? Would something come out of him to even the playing
field? Would he summon the strength needed to fight back? Or
would he simply be tossed aside like a piece of tissue paper? He
didn't feel any more prepared for what needed to be done than
before, but he also knew he was running out of time. He'd sent
Duff to the mainland to be safe and was sleeping on his boat. Leo
had been staying with his mother, which made him feel uneasy
but also understood she needed to not be alone. The Lodge
would be empty the following week and whatever needed to be
done, needed to be done then.

The marina was quiet and he crept through the gate to
his boat. He dropped the anchor in case something untied the
boat from the dock, then slipped into the cabin. He made a light
dinner and read through the documents he'd gotten from the
library. Ultimately, what they all said was to do *something*. To

come prepared, whether that was with religious items, spells, or other trinkets meant to repel evil. Sandy gave him a couple of crucifixes and holy water, but he had a feeling they were more of a placebo than anything with power. However, he was in no position to discount anything available to him.

He checked his phone and saw he'd received a message from Iris.

"I miss you, Ledger. Can you imagine a time when we could just be together wherever we want?"

"Every day. One day this will all be over and I'll hold you forever," he texted back.

"I'm holding you to that."

"Please do. Can you get away tomorrow for a bit? Maybe take a ride?"

"I think so. I have a full house right now, but I do have the chef for dinner. I should be able to escape for a bit," Iris said.

"Bring Roar."

"Is that the real reason? You miss our cat?"

Ledger chuckled. "Roar is the bonus. I miss you."

"I wish you were here," she replied.

"Maybe not there, but I wish I was with you. Can you get away for the night?" he asked.

"As long as I'm back in the morning, sure. I'm in charge of breakfast."

"Leave them milk and cereal. I can't wait to see you, Iris. Dock at three?"

"See you then."

He turned the phone off and bedded down. He imagined holding Iris, her cool slender arms wrapped around him. He sighed and held onto that thought. Everything was so fractured now. They were all in different places but still together. He imagined all of the people he loved in their respective places. Connected through time and space. Waiting on the call. He dozed off as the sun disappeared in the sky, trying to keep the image of Iris with him.

He was running up the trail. He wasn't alone and could feel something pushing him on. As he approached the Lodge, he could feel its presence. It was waiting on him. He ran inside and was immediately lost in a series of mazes. Each ended in a dead-end with a mirror at the end. No matter how many ways he went, he'd always end up back at the mirror. He could hear a woman crying but couldn't find her. Just the reflection of himself over and over again. Exhausted, he stopped before the mirror and stared at himself. It was him, but not totally. It was like a part of him was missing. When he reached up to touch his image, his hand was not reflected back. He wasn't strong enough, he was fading away. He punched the mirror and it shattered into hundreds of pieces, revealing a hallway behind. He followed the hallway, hearing the crying getting louder. It ended at a door and he could tell the woman was behind it. He pushed the door open and saw his mother lying lifeless on the floor. Iris was standing over her, holding a bloody knife. She turned, her eyes begging his forgiveness.

He ran to his mother and crouched down beside her. "Why?" he cried at Iris.

She shook her head and kneeled down, clutching the knife to her chest. "Because I am not alive," she whispered and started to crumble into dust.

Ledger reached out to her and felt her slip through his fingers. As she disappeared, she was replaced with the demon, its eyes boring into his as it leaped forward and drove the knife into his skull.

Ledger woke with a jolt and tried to shake the dream off. He was jumpy; even the normally soothing waves rocking the boat were making him feel insecure. He went out to sit in the moonlight and opened a beer. His hands were shaking as he replayed the dream in his head. The demon lived because of Iris and because it lived, his family was in danger. Iris was everything to him and he needed to protect her, but had to separate her from the monster. He couldn't let her know his intent because if he did, it would know. He needed to take Iris out of the picture.

The rest of the night he was too amped to sleep. He made a plan and if it failed, it could cost all of them their lives. It would take Duff and his mother's help. Leo too. In theory, the demon couldn't cross water, except with Iris. Even then, it didn't want to. He knew this because when she came on the boat, she was alone. He needed to figure out a way to isolate it away from the Lodge and Iris was the only way. If it thought she was at risk of dying, it would be forced to try and keep her alive. If she died, so did it. She was its vessel, its life force. Once it was across water, it couldn't get back without her. The Lodge had its own life, but the demon was guarding it.

The next day, Ledger met Iris at the dock and waited until they were out to sea before saying anything. He had to guard what he said because whatever she thought could be read by the demon. He dropped the anchor and went to sit next to her at the back of the boat.

"Do you trust me?"

Iris frowned, staring at him. "Of course I do, Ledger. What's going on?"

"I can't tell you specifically because I think your thoughts are being read. Do you trust me, no matter what?"

"Ledger, with my life. But you are scaring me."

"I'm scared, too. When this all goes down, no matter what I do, you need to believe I'm doing it to save us. To save you. Do you understand?"

"I think so. Can you elaborate at all?"

"Only that I may have to do something which will scare you, and might remind you of what happened when you were a girl with your father. But I swear to you with every ounce of my being, I won't let anything happen to you," Ledger promised, though his words felt empty even to him.

Iris stared at him and went white. She clasped his hands. "Ledger, I love you, but are you sure?"

"No. I'm not. But I think I know a way to end this all. You may not understand when the time comes but if it works, you will then."

"And if it doesn't?"

"Then we're all dead, anyway."

Iris started shaking and stood up. "I don't know if I can do this. I don't know if I'm strong enough."

"Me either," Ledger whispered. Iris came and knelt down and rested her head on his knees. He rubbed her head and ran his fingers through her long chestnut hair. "I won't do it unless you give me permission, Iris. I don't know another way, but I'd rather die than destroy your trust. You have to believe me."

Iris peered up, her blue eyes dark and wet. "Okay. I trust you and give you permission. I don't understand for what, but I know you love me and wouldn't harm me."

Ledger nodded, then told the first small lie. "I wouldn't."

Roar made her way over to them and jumped up next to Ledger. She eyed him like she could see through him. He tried to send her a mental message to make her understand. She sniffed him indifferently and climbed on Iris's shoulders. Iris pulled her off and held her close. The cat watched Ledger and he could sense she no longer totally trusted him. She sensed his intent. It made him feel horrible and judged by the small fluffball.

They made dinner and watched the sunset, neither having much to say. When it was time to bed down, Ledger drew Iris close and kissed her head. She snuggled in next to him, resting her head against his chest. He wished for the moment to last forever, to not break the bond between them. When he felt her breathing settle into the pattern of sleep, he rubbed her back and placed his cheek on the top of her head. To save them, he needed to betray her.

"I'm sorry, Iris. I promise you, I'll do everything in my power to end this all. To save us both. To save us all." The words were hollow.

She didn't stir and Roar lay on her other side, careful not to touch Ledger. It broke his heart to betray them both like he'd have to. He didn't have to kill Iris, but he needed to make her believe he was going to. It was the only way to draw the beast away from the Lodge, out onto the water. From there, he'd have to fight it. He reached out to pet Roar and she growled at him. She didn't want him to touch her. He drew his hand back and grimaced. There was no going back. He hoped he knew only how far to go. That he'd know when to stop; not risk going too far and killing Iris.

His sleep was restless and by morning he felt so anxious, every little sound or motion shot a sharp, white buzzing through his head. He was relieved when the sun came up and he could commit to dealing with the day. Iris was curled in next to him and he wanted her badly. He pushed away the feeling, knowing it would be unfair to be intimate with what he needed to do. They had coffee together and he dropped her at the dock. She turned and smiled as she stepped on the weathered boards.

"You want to get together later?" she asked.

She was so beautiful standing there, the breeze blowing her wavy hair back off of her face. He wanted to grab her and run as far away from there as they could, but he knew in time it would call her back or follow them. There was only one way to ensure they'd have a future together. He forced a smile and nodded.

"I have some things to do first, but maybe. I'll call you later, okay?"

"You'd better. I love you."

"I love you, too. See you soon," Ledger replied, hoping he covered his thoughts well enough.

She blew him a kiss and headed up the hill. Roar glanced back and stared at him, her eyes cutting through the make-believe. Ledger watched the small cat and recognized a lion could not be more protective of Iris than that tiny, orange ball of hair, nails, and teeth. He watched them traverse the hill and guided the boat out. He knew he wouldn't see Iris that night or the next. He wouldn't see her again until the time came. She paused at the top of the hill and waved at him. He raised his hand in a wave just as he saw Doyle come around the side of the Lodge toward Iris. He was frowning and talking to her when he spotted Ledger. His mouth twisted in a creepy smile which made Ledger's skin crawl.

Ledger headed home to pick up some supplies and was relieved to see his mother was home. She was folding laundry in the living room; for a moment he felt like he did when he was a kid and would come home in the afternoon. His mother was usually there, adjusting her shifts to be home with them, and would always ask about his day. When he was a teen, he'd roll his eyes and sigh at the question but was secretly happy she cared enough to ask. He paused and watched her, grateful she'd always been there for him.

She glanced up from the laundry, then smiled. "You look more and more like your father every day."

"I guess it could be worse," Ledger joked.

"Your father was the most handsome man I'd ever laid eyes on. The moment I saw him, I knew he was it for me. The love of my life," she said without a doubt as she tried to find matching socks.

"What about Leo?"

"Oh, Leo. He is the kindest man I've ever met. He doesn't make my blood hot like your father did, but he makes me happy. Then again, we're older now, and finding someone who makes you feel safe and special is just as important as making your blood all hot."

"I don't know if I should be grossed out or happy for you," Ledger teased.

"You can be both. No one wants to know their mother is a real woman," she replied with a twinkle in her eye. "You know, with desires and all."

"Okay, going with grossed out, now."

"So, what's the plan, Ledger? Are you just here for a bit today?"

"I am. I need to stock up for the next few days. I won't be back for a bit. Going to stay out on the boat until it's time."

"How will you know when that is?" She set down the laundry and met his eyes.

"Not really sure. I'm guessing it'll be more than obvious. Regardless, once the guests are gone from the Lodge I'll need to go there, even if it's not," Ledger replied.

"And what about us?"

"Mom, I need you. You and Duff. The only way we can take this down is by doing it together. I mean, if you're willing and able."

"The family that fights together, stays together. Am I right?"

CHAPTER TWENTY-EIGHT

*O*nce the last guest checked out, Iris called Ledger to let him know. Her voice sounded weird and he pressed to make sure everything was alright. She assured him it was but mentioned Doyle had been hanging around more than usual, and she'd found him watching her when she was locking up the cabins. He'd offered to help her, but in a way that made Iris feel she didn't have an option. She let him know she was fine and couldn't afford to pay him if she didn't have guests. She said he snorted and walked away, shaking his head. Ledger asked if he'd left the property, and she said as far as she knew he had. Ledger didn't trust him, even though they'd never met or spoken face to face. Doyle always seemed to be watching and his appearance at the Lodge didn't seem like a coincidence. Besides, there was just something about him that made Ledger's gut tense.

Ledger met Duff on the mainland and laid out his plan. It was rudimentary at best, not knowing what they were walking into. Ledger needed to get Iris onto the boat and hopefully lure the monster out there. Once that happened, the Lodge would be left vulnerable, allowing Duff and his mother to take it down. It all had to happen in sync or they risked the plan failing... or worse.

Leo would come for Duff and their mother in his own boat. In destroying the Lodge, Ledger was unsure if it would release anything, so he wanted his family as far away from the island as possible. They'd just need to make it safely from the Lodge to Leo's boat after.

Ledger met with Sandy at the church the morning of when he was planning to put everything into action. He felt safe talking to her in the church, even though he hardly believed in the religion. He told her what they were planning to do and she listened quietly. Once he finished, she watched him and placed her hand over his.

"You know there are risks with this, right? You're opening Pandora's Box and have no idea what might come out," she reminded him.

"I know. I can't see another way around this. I think Pandora's Box is going to be opened whether or not I intercede. I'm just speeding up the process." Ledger chewed his lip, coming to grips with the reality of the situation.

"Fair enough. But what if the Lodge is containing this and you are just spreading it out around the island? You need to consider all possibilities."

"I don't know. Is there anything you can do?" Ledger asked miserably.

Sandy laughed softly and shook her head. "I'm not sure. I tend to think of myself more as a guide than a warrior. Don't get me wrong, I believe in what I'm here for, but I think

Hollywood has given the clergy more credit than is due. So, can I pray? Sure. But can I fight off the hounds of hell? I doubt it. I will say this, though. You're not alone. I don't just mean in the spiritual sense. There are beings all around us who are watching and protecting. Hopefully, they'll come forward. I'll also do what I can. I'm not afraid of a little spiritual battle. Or in this case, a lot."

Ledger thought about this, then nodded. "I'll take your prayer if you got it. We're going in tonight."

"Why at night?'

"I have this feeling that's when I can lure things out. It seems like during the day, all is quiet. I don't really know. I've never fought off demons before," Ledger joked without humor. "Well, except my own."

Sandy chuckled. "As I said, those can be the hardest ones anyway, so you may be more prepared than you think. What time?"

"I think around ten. Cover of darkness and all that," Ledger answered.

"Okay. I'll be praying then. I'll put out a call for a prayer chain. You never know, just might help." Sandy shifted in her seat and watched Ledger carefully.

"I'll take any help I can get at this point." Ledger stood up to leave. He glanced around the church and still felt nothing toward it. He definitely believed in good and evil now but wasn't sure it was fought behind these walls. It was an internal battle of soul and mind. He also believed Sandy was one of the good ones and was putting up a fight, whether she was aware of it or not.

Sandy gave him a quick hug, then bobbed her head. "Be safe, Ledger. Let me know what happens."

"I will. Thanks, Sandy, for hearing me out."

He headed out into the bright sun, almost convincing himself this wasn't real. He walked to his truck and slid in. Whatever happened, he was going to have to tap into a much darker side of himself. He glanced in the mirror and was met with a scared boy. The boy who stood frozen, hearing his father was never coming home. He ran his hand through his golden curls and sighed. He'd always be that boy. Forced to be a man way too young and determined to take care of his family. Except now, he needed them to fight with him. He drove from the church through the small village.

He was either going to save them or condemn them all to hell.

At a four-way stop, he glanced around, seeing the doctor in the car across from him. Their paths hadn't crossed in weeks and he shuddered. Why was he seeing him today? The doctor wasn't alone. His companion was a young man about Ledger's age with dark red hair and startling, jade eyes that stood out against his deep tan, freckled skin. Ledger had never seen anyone who looked like the doctor's companion before. Like he was a mix of multiple races. The doctor raised his hand in a wave as he passed, his eyes fastened on Ledger's face, reading his mind. Ledger jerked his eyes away and cursed himself for allowing the connection. He couldn't trust anyone except his family right now.

He eased his truck into the driveway and sat for a few minutes before going in. Duff was coming in on the last ferry, but Leo was giving them a ride. Ledger would head out on the boat in the evening to get separation between himself and the island to clear his mind. Iris was to meet him at the dock at ten.

It would all start there. He prayed for forgiveness, sensing something was trying to get into his thoughts. He could feel it like a scratching inside his skull. He wore the crucifix Sandy had blessed and given him, not being able to deny he felt it was offering him some sort of mental shield.

The house was quiet and he wandered around, not sure what to do with himself. He took an old photo album out and began flipping through it. His parents on their wedding day, then his mother pregnant with him. His father, holding Ledger the day he was born. His father was young in the photo, but his eyes were haunted even then. He was smiling but only with his mouth. The pictures went on as Ledger grew and then Duff joined the family. There was one on the fishing boat, his father standing behind Ledger and Duff, a hand on each of their shoulders. Same smile with sad eyes. His mother must have taken the picture. She took a lot of them. They didn't have too many family pictures.

Ledger searched through the album, trying to find one and the best he could do was a photo of the four of them at some sort of town picnic. His father had his hand on his mother's back and was whispering to her, to which she was laughing in response. Ledger was half-turned from the camera, looking off, and Duff was waving a bubble wand in the air, causing clumps of bubbles to float briefly before gravity dragged them to the ground. Ledger followed his picture eyes to see what he was looking at and frowned. The picture wasn't clear but he could see a shadow in the treeline where he was gazing in the picture. He squinted and tried to make it out but it could've been just the sun casting a shadow from the trees. He was trying too hard to read into things. He slipped the picture into his pocket and closed the album.

He didn't need to add any more fuel to the fire.

He messaged Iris to see how she was and made something to eat. She texted back she was just deep cleaning and packing some things away. He felt like he should tell her not to waste her time, but he couldn't tell her anything. She couldn't be told any part of the plan or it would know. He didn't tell her that tonight was the night. She couldn't know. Just that he wanted to see her and take her for a night boat ride. He didn't know if she suspected or if she did, she didn't mention it. He called her to hear her voice.

"Hey! Everything okay?" she asked when she answered.

"Yeah, I was just missing you. I wanted to hear your voice."

"Aw, that's sweet. We're still on for tonight, right?"

"We are. Any more Doyle sightings?"

"No, he never came back. Just me out here, which is super weird. I kind of like it, though, because I've been blasting music and washing everything. Oh, except I had a guest show up and said he never got my message about not being able to host him. I let him know I couldn't host him, so he went on to the hotel. He wasn't too happy and was kind of pushy about it."

"Was he alone?"

"No, it looked like he had his wife with him. He railed at me for a while about being a bad business owner but finally left. He was a dick." Iris sighed, exasperated.

"What did he look like?" Ledger asked, thinking about the doctor's companion.

"Mmm, maybe mid-forties. Slightly balding, brown hair. Nothing of note. Why?"

"No reason, just wondering in case he causes you any more issues."

"I think it's fine. Just another self-entitled, middle-aged jerk. He huffed and puffed but then he left. Told me he was going to give me a bad review." Iris laughed, breathing out heavily. "I can't wait to see you. I need a break from all this work."

Ledger felt guilty, knowing that she didn't have a clue what he was planning to do. He needed to get off the line before she sensed the truth and gave the Lodge a head's up. "Iris, I love you. I'm so glad I met you. I want to see the world with you. Go exploring."

She was quiet and fear rose in him. Did she know? He could hear her breathing on the other end. He almost broke and said something to her. To confess and risk everything they were fighting for. He bit his tongue hard to stop himself, tasting blood. When she spoke, it was so soft he almost couldn't hear her.

"I trust you with my life, Ledger. I'd go with you anywhere."

Ledger fought back tears and leaned his head against the window he was standing in front of. How could he do this? How could he betray her trust, even if to save her? He breathed out and cleared his throat. "I'll see you tonight, alright?"

She agreed and they hung up. The ball was rolling. Everyone knew their part and everything was ready to go. Ledger lay in his bed and closed his eyes, attempting to summon courage. He'd never really been a fighter. Even as a kid, he'd try to talk his way out of confrontation and stayed back, observing rather than running his mouth. Duff got in more physical fights than he did. Then again, Duff was hot-headed and started a lot of shit. He chuckled, remembering how often his mother had to pick Duff up from the ferry because they were sent home for fighting. He prayed some of that fight would come out tonight.

By late afternoon, Ledger packed up and left to go to the boat. It was better if his brain wasn't ticking away on the island. His mother was due home from work shortly and she already knew what needed to be done. Leo would bring Duff to the house and the three of them had their jobs to do. Duff and their mother would come by beach, staying as close to the water as they could until Ledger got Iris out onto the water.

Ledger had gas cans on the boat to leave on the dock for them since they were too heavy to carry up the beach. They each had a pack by the door they'd wear. Leo was taking them by boat to the beach, as close as he could without being seen. They'd have to hike the rest of the way in. From there, Ledger hoped they could get the gas cans and move up to the Lodge with no problem, even though his instinct told him it wouldn't be that easy.

Nothing about this was going to be easy.

He headed out, leaving his mother and Duff a note, telling them how much he loved them. How glad he was they were his family. He cried when he wrote it, hoping it wouldn't be the last time they connected. He saw Leo when he got to the marina, leaving for the last ferry run. Duff would be coming back on the return trip. Leo waved and nodded, Ledger did the same. It was best if they all acted like it was any other day.

He eased the boat out and went out to the ocean. He'd stay out there until it was time to meet with Iris. He drew her to mind, letting his thoughts gently run over her image. Her long wavy brown hair, her blue eyes; sometimes covered by her small glasses. Her genuine smile and the way her eyes slightly crinkled when she did. Her slender wrists and petite frame. The way she cocked her head and furrowed her brows when he confused her. How she chewed her nails when she was deep in thought. Her lilting laugh and the way she'd let her head rest against his chest. So trusting and happy.

How could he do this to her?

Once the sun disappeared, he checked the time. It was getting closer and he worried he couldn't go through with it. He felt the weight of the gun in his pack and began to shake. He reminded himself this was the only way to save her. To save them all. He began to feel dizzy and vomited over the side of the boat. At first, he thought it was just from nerves but he began to sense it was more once his head started pounding.

It knew.

It was going to try and stop him. He shook his head and drew up the anchor. It was a race against time now, and even one mistake would take them all down. He turned the key, half expecting the engine to not turn over but it fired right up. He turned the boat back toward the island and headed for the channel. No matter what, it was time. Despite his lack of spiritual beliefs, he said a little prayer and wrapped his hand around the crucifix.

As he made his way into the channel, he reached out to the only being he knew was watching over him. He slid the picture of his family out of his pocket and stared at it. This was his army, the ones who had his back. Tears fell down his cheeks as he looked at them together, not knowing they wouldn't always be. Tonight he needed all of them. For them to be a whole family again. He held the picture of this family to his chest and closed his eyes.

"Dad, I need you now more than ever. Please come back to me."

CHAPTER TWENTY-NINE

*T*he dock was empty when he slid the boat up next to it. He loosely tied the rope to the cleat and set the gas cans in the shadows. The air felt thicker, almost claustrophobic, and crackled with static. The Lodge sensed something and was preparing itself for battle. Ledger watched cautiously, anticipating something to jump out of the shadows at him. He almost expected Doyle to be standing guard. It was too quiet. He checked his phone and waited. He thought he heard Leo's boat in the distance, but at this point, he wasn't sure what was real or what his brain was creating. They'd agreed not to communicate with each other, not knowing what could be transmitted from them to the Lodge or the beast.

Ledger saw Iris come out of the door and shut it carefully behind her. She started down the path and Ledger doubted himself. She trusted him, she had no idea what was coming. She waved and smiled as she neared the dock. Ledger tried to stop his hands from shaking and smiled back. He waited for her on the dock, hoping his face wouldn't give away his thoughts.

They climbed on board and Ledger made sure the rope was able to be pulled loose from the dock. Everything was down to just moments and the smallest error could put them in grave danger. Iris set her bag down and hugged Ledger, sensing his tenseness.

"Hey. Everything okay?" she asked nervously.

He nodded and watched her quietly. "You look really pretty tonight. Are you ready to head out?"

Even he knew his voice didn't sound like him. Iris frowned, then bobbed her head. She stepped back and stared at him, the realization dawning on her. He was running out of time. As soon as she understood, so would the demon. He grabbed his bag and drew the gun out, holding it carefully at his side. He shook his head as he met her eyes and fear flashed across her face as he raised the gun toward her. He set his face with determination, in an attempt to hide his true feelings. Her eyes darted to the side of the boat and she moved in that direction.

"Iris, don't. There is no other way. You're the reason the Lodge has power and the only way to stop it, is to stop you. I'm sorry, I didn't want it to be this way." His voice sounded cruel and cold; he prayed he could get through this. To hold on. It only would take long enough to convince her that her life was in danger.

Iris froze and her eyes pleaded with him. "Ledger, I love you. Why are you doing this? I thought you said we could fight this together?"

"I don't have a choice. It's you, or the world. You brought this monster with you and as long as you're alive, it is too. It's protecting and feeding the Lodge. The Lodge can kill us all and it needs you alive to do it."

Iris began to cry and Ledger fought the urge to drop the gun and go to her. He felt a shift coming from the Lodge and glanced up the hill. Something was moving toward them at a high rate of speed. He needed to hold out until it got there. Iris crouched on the floor of the boat sobbing, terrified for her life. Ledger knew she may never forgive him. If they made it out alive. He cocked the hammer and held his breath. Iris gazed up at him, her eyes accepting her fate. He suddenly saw her as the young girl whose father had taken her life and understood in her mind, he was no different. He stepped toward the rope and wrapped his foot around it.

As it drew closer, he felt his guts clench and swallowed the vomit that had risen in his throat. It was larger than he anticipated, both formed and formless. He had no idea how to fight it once it was on the boat. First, he needed to trap it on the boat. It hit the dock and Ledger instinctively took a step back. It was coming after him to protect Iris. His head was pounding and his vision started to blur. It could easily kill him. As it crossed the rail of the boat Ledger jerked his foot back releasing the rope and ran for the wheel. He gunned the engine, drawing the boat away from the dock. He could see the creature waver as it realized what was happening, so Ledger fixed the gun on Iris. He adjusted the gun slightly to the right of her and fired, grazing her shoulder with the bullet.

Iris screamed and clutched her arm. The demon, needing to protect her, bolted at Ledger. The separation was made. They were now on the water and it was trapped on the boat with them. Ledger fired the gun in the air to alert Leo and his family. Iris covered her ears, screaming. The creature paused and looked back at her, its form dripping with rage. Ledger realized Iris couldn't see it. In her mind, it was just her and Ledger on the boat and he was going to murder her.

"Iris." His voice was hoarse.

She wouldn't look at him. He needed to get to her but somehow had to get past the demon who was bearing down on him. Something told him to drop the gun and raise his hands. He threw the gun into the hull and put his hands out toward the creature. At that moment, he felt heat rise in him and the lights, which had joined him on the other side, came to his hands. The demon stopped in its tracks, realizing its prey came with weapons. The lights released from Ledger's body and went into the creature, causing it to buck and twist to get free. Ledger took this chance to get back to Iris, who was formed in a ball on the floor. He grabbed her and shook her.

"Iris, listen to me. I was never going to hurt you. I had to do this to draw it away from the Lodge. Iris, please look at me."

She glanced up at him, her eyes red-rimmed and terrified. That thirteen-year-old girl again. She shook her head and jerked away from him. "Leave me alone."

"Iris look! Can't you see it?"

She cast her eyes to where he was pointing but from the expression on her face, he could tell she wasn't seeing anything. She shrunk away from him. "You're crazy. I wish we'd never met. I hate you. You're just like *him*."

Her words cut through him, and he knew from her vantage point he deserved it. He sighed and stood up. The lights had deterred the monster but not stopped it. It had turned and was eyeing Iris. Ledger realized it was going to try to get back inside Iris to protect itself. She was its sanctuary. He couldn't let that happen. He moved between it and Iris and held his ground. It might kill him, but he couldn't let it get to her again. Weakened it came toward Ledger, the lights still visible inside of it.

It reached out its appendage toward him, placing it through his chest. Ledger could feel the cold tendrils wrapping around his heart, the beat becoming slower. The lights were trying to drag the demon back but it had a grip on Ledger and he was fading rapidly. He glanced at Iris as he went to his knees. He reached out to her but his hand dropped as he fell to the floor. Iris shifted her eyes from him and she squinted as if she was seeing something in the distance. Her eyes widened as something deep in her saw and recognized the beast. She rose and climbed onto the back of the boat. She teetered on the rail and leaned toward the water.

"Stop!" she yelled. "I'll jump in the water and drown myself."

Her words were like ice. The creature paused. If she died, it died. It drew away and motioned toward her to come to it. Ledger faded in and out as he watched Iris shake her head and beckon for the demon to come to her. It moved past Ledger and came face to face with Iris. She was going to sacrifice herself for Ledger.

"Iris, don't. Please." His words were weak and pleading.

She didn't look at Ledger or acknowledge him. She opened her arms as if to embrace the creature and it crept toward her like a child waking up from a nightmare. Just as it was inches away she smiled and sighed. It reached out for her like she was its mother, waiting to comfort it. Iris welcomed it in and as it went to join with her, the lights inside of it shot into Iris. In that moment, she began to glow from head to toe, brighter than the lights themselves. The light enveloped the demon and it realized its mistake, trying to yank away.

Ledger faded out to black as he saw the creature fighting in the light like a fly caught in a spider's web. It writhed and made a sound between nails on a chalkboard and tires squealing. Iris had never been so beautiful, her arms outspread and her head tipped back, laughing with her own power. The demon didn't stand a chance. She was the spider coming for its prey. Ledger would gladly let her sink her fangs into him to be part of her forever. The last thing he saw was Iris destroying the monster which had once brought her back to life, as her own light disappeared and she crumpled into a lifeless heap.

There was no tunnel of light, no visits from dead relatives. Just blackness. Pain radiated through Ledger and he knew he wasn't dead. He pried his eyes open and felt the boat gently rocking in the water. He crawled over and vomited over the side of the boat. He turned and leaned against the side to steady himself. The demon was gone. The boat was dark and quiet. Iris's body lay on the bench where she'd been standing, lifeless. Ledger moved slowly back toward her, every ounce of his body screaming in pain. He rested his hand on her head and brushed the hair away from her face. She looked so vulnerable and small. He began to cry.

"Iris, please don't leave me. If you are there and can hear me, I need you to come back. Come back for me. Come back for you. It can't end this way."

She didn't stir and he rested his head against her shoulder. In the distance, he could see shadows moving up the beach. His family. The demon was gone but the Lodge still remained. He took a flashlight off of his belt and clicked it on and off a couple of times to let them know the demon was gone. He shifted his focus back to Iris. He placed his hands on her chest and closed his eyes. At least if they'd died together, they'd still be with each other. He thought about the gun and how easy it would be to just end it. Then he thought about Duff and his mother, knowing they'd suffered enough. If they were forced to go through this life, then so was he.

The lights moved from Iris to his hands. He felt the tingling of their presence within him. He kept his hands on Iris and watched the lights grow at his fingertips. The glow spread to her and he leaned in to kiss her lips. As their lips touched, he felt hers go from cold to warm and he jerked back. The light had grown to cover her whole chest and his hands were hot from them. Iris drew in a breath and her eyes fluttered open. She met his eyes.

"Hey," she whispered. "Is it over?"

"You destroyed the demon. Duff, my mom, and Leo are going for the Lodge now."

Iris nodded and tried to sit up, her body giving out. Ledger pulled her to a sitting position and put his arm around her. She leaned in against him and held on for balance. They used each other for stability and gazed toward the Lodge. He could see what his family couldn't. As they were making their way up the hill toward the Lodge, Doyle and two other people were waiting for them at the top. Iris sucked her breath in and pointed at them.

"That's the last guest who came by. The guy and his wife."

If they were, they didn't look like she'd described. Like Doyle, they seemed larger, more physically built. More like creatures than humans. The couple had some type of weapons, medieval in nature, and were standing guard between the hill and the Lodge. Ledger had to warn his family but didn't know how. They weren't using phones, to stay in the cover of silence. He remembered when they were kids, he and Duff made up a secret language using flashlights. Sort of their own Morse code. He grabbed the flashlight and clicked out a message. He didn't know if Duff would remember the language or if they'd even see him sending it. He did something he rarely did and sent out a prayer for help.

He got up and moved to the front of the boat, considering if they should go back to shore to assist. Iris could barely move and he didn't know what kind of power the Lodge, or its protectors, might have over her. He wasn't much better off, his own body almost too weak to stand. All of a sudden, he saw a quick series of flashes of light. If he remembered the language correctly it meant *got it*.

He wasn't the only one to notice the light messages and saw Doyle and the other two move toward the hill. They were going after his family. Panic rose in him and he fired up the engine, turning the boat back to the shore. He couldn't leave them to fight this alone. He drove the boat toward the dock and racked his brain to think of a plan. He had the gun but somehow doubted it would stop them. These weren't humans they were dealing with. He could see Doyle and crew rapidly descending the hill toward his family and fear froze him. They were going to get to his family before he could.

He was out of time.

Just as they were about to meet, an ember of light floating through the woods near them caught his eyes. The ember grew bright and as it came upon Doyle and the other two it formed into two shapes. The shapes headed off the group and Ledger blinked when he realized what he was watching. The two shapes took form and like Doyle and the other two, they weren't necessarily human. But still, he recognized them.

It was the doctor and his companion from the car. They too appeared larger and stronger than they had before. The doctor glanced back at Ledger and nodded, his eyes boring into Ledger's soul. He was on his side. The doctor had been there to protect and keep an eye on Ledger. Ledger stared and nodded back, his mind reeling from what he was seeing. His mind tried to convince him his eyes were playing tricks on him.

It wasn't so much that he was seeing the doctor and his red-haired companion. No, it was what made them different from before. What told him Sandy was right. Where there were demons, there were angels. What was spinning his mind was not their presence.

It was that they had what appeared to be hawk wings sprouting from their backs.

CHAPTER THIRTY

*W*hat happened next took on a life of its own. The doctor and his companion... angels? Was that what they were? They weren't human, that much was apparent. Ledger shook his head and watched in a state of both disbelief and understanding. Angels, or whatever they were with their mottled bird wings, quickly faced off with Doyle and the other two. Ledger squinted to make out Doyle and see if anything about him was different. When Doyle turned to clash with the doctor, Ledger could see he too had wings. Not unlike the doctors but small, less formed. As if they were mutated. Neither held weapons yet what seemed like streams of energy were coming out of them as they fought. It was violent and majestic. Doyle was obviously the strongest of his crew and the doctor's companion was fighting the other two while the white-haired, old man showed his power over Doyle. He might have appeared like an aging doctor, but clearly was something not of this world.

He fought like ten men.

Ledger shifted his eyes to see where his family was now. They'd seen the battle and had diverted their path around, continuing up the hill toward the Lodge. Ledger could see his mother was getting tired and slowing down, but Leo took anything she was carrying to lighten her load. She paused and caught her breath, then followed closely behind Leo. They were almost to the top of the hill when one of Doyle's crew, the female, broke free and went after them. Ledger tried to call out to warn them but his voice was lost over the water. The female went after his mother and fear gripped him as he helplessly watched as his mother was about to be attacked. In an instant, a streak of light went from across the water toward them and Ledger just knew.

The light took a sort of form as it approached and moved between his mother and the female. It blocked her from getting close to Ledger's mother and pushed back, creating an impenetrable barrier. The female tried to go around without success, then focused her attention on Duff and Leo. The form again moved between them. By this time, the red-headed angel had defeated the male being of Doyle's crew and was moving at a rapid pace toward Ledger's family. As he approached, the female turned to face him and they went at each other. They clashed together which such force, the trees around them trembled.

Ledger's attention turned back to his mother and the form had moved over to her. It enveloped her in its light and he could see tears streaming down her cheeks. She reached out and placed her hands on the form, sobbing. He'd known what it was when it passed him over the water and now, she did too. His father had failed them in life but protected them in death. Protected them *from* death. The form moved toward Duff and circled them. Duff's eyes were wide and suddenly they were the small child whose father never came home. The small child who cried themselves to sleep every night, wanting their Daddy. Duff fell to their knees and covered their face with their hands. The form wrapped around them and then as quick as it came, it disappeared back across the water. He'd done what he'd failed to do before. He saved his family.

"Thanks, Dad. I love you," Ledger whispered as it dissipated into the night.

Duff and his mother were on the move again, pouring gas around the Lodge. Leo was following directly behind, lighting the trail of gas. As the flames began to light up the night and lick the edges of the Lodge, Doyle broke free of the doctor and half flew, half ran up the hill. He tried desperately to beat out the flames to no avail. His distraction allowed the doctor to come up behind him and drive an energy bolt through his back. Doyle screamed and turned, his eyes blazing a purplish glow. He raised his fists to the doctor, energy forming around them. He drove his fists toward the doctor, releasing the balls around his fists which struck the doctor full force. Both the doctor and Doyle collapsed onto the ground. Neither moved.

The red-headed man had defeated the female being who was turning into mist, or smoke, Ledger couldn't tell. The doctor's companion was now by his side, his head bowed in grief. Doyle's body was now also becoming the mist-like substance. He had lost. The doctor's body was lying immobile, now just in the form of a man. The redhead gathered him in his arms and took flight with him. He moved across the water and past Ledger's boat. Their eyes met and he nodded at Ledger. The doctor was still in form, he wasn't gone yet. Ledger watched as they faded into the night and shifted his eyes back to the Lodge. It was up in flames, a cloud of acrid smoke rising into the air as it was engulfed.

His family was watching as it burned, their backs to Ledger. He'd never felt so close to them in his life. As the fire crept up the walls of the Lodge, Ledger swore he heard screams coming from inside. Wails. The hair stood up on his arms and he shuddered. It wasn't one or two, but hundreds. He glanced at Iris who was staring wide-eyed at the Lodge. She'd heard it, too. She began to weep and he went to her, gathering her in his arms. She shook her head.

"I'm sorry I didn't believe you," she whispered.

"You were being prevented from seeing, it's not your fault," Ledger assured her.

Something caught his eye from the Lodge driveway and he peered closer. It was the minister. She was watching the Lodge burn. Sensing his eyes on her, she turned toward him and raised a hand. He raised his hand back to her and she nodded, giving him a thumbs up. She'd seen, she knew the truth. He touched his heart and nodded back. She'd believed him from the beginning. She turned and left back down the driveway. His family was moving back down the hill to the beach. His cell phone lit up with Duff's name. He grinned and answered it.

"Hey Duff, good show."

"Wasn't it though? Hope there isn't a sequel," Duff joked, but their words were tired and lacked the normal bite.

"Your lips to God's ears," Ledger agreed.

"We're going to Leo's boat. Want to get the hell out of here," Duff replied, laughing bitterly.

"Get the hell out of there. There's a play on words."

"Right? Fuck, my mind is blown. May have to be locked in the looney bin after this. Oh, hey, Mom wants to talk to you."

The phone crackled with shifting hands and his mother came on the line. "Ledger! Are you and Iris okay?"

"Yeah, Mom. I think so. Weak but alive. I love you so much."

"I love you too, honey. Did you see that light that protected me?"

"Dad? Yeah."

"You knew?" his mother asked, surprised.

"Yeah."

"Oh. It was the most beautiful thing. He's not a tortured soul anymore," she replied, her voice lighter than it'd been in years. His burden had been hers as well. Ledger understood... when you love someone, you carry their pain also.

"He's free, Mom. It's over."

"Ledger, I'm so proud of you. You and Duff. I never doubted your beautiful hearts, but I'm honored to be your mother. I hope you know that."

"I know, Mom. I feel the same. Leo too. He proved he's family." Ledger meant it. Leo had always been part of their lives, but now he was part of their family.

"What are you going to do?"

"I think Iris and I are going out to one of the outer islands for a bit to regroup. You?"

"Leo has a place upstate. We're going there to decide what to do next. I'm tired. Exhausted, truly. First, I'm going to sleep for like three days."

Ledger laughed, understanding. "I feel that. As soon as I can, I'll call you, okay? I love you, Mom."

"I love you, my sweet boy. Hold on. Duff wants to say goodbye to you." His mother shifted the phone in the background.

Duff came back on the line. "You still there, Ledge?"

"I am."

"Hey, you know this was epic, right?"

"I do." Ledger could think of no better word to describe what just happened.

"I'm glad you're my big brother. I'm glad you have Iris. Let her know that, okay?" Duff whispered, their voice hiding their emotion.

"I will. I love you, Duff," Ledger said, saying the words which came hard for Duff. "I'm glad you're my little pain in the ass, too."

Duff chuckled. "Love you too, Ledge."

They hung up and Ledger sighed. He'd see them soon. The one thing he knew, though, was that their life on the island was coming to an end. He felt it in his soul. Iris had gotten up and moved to the front of the boat. She was shaky and holding onto a bar to keep herself steady. Ledger went behind her and wrapped his arms around her. She leaned back against him.

"We did it. You are free," Ledger murmured into her hair.

Iris turned and watched the Lodge burn. It was now gutted in the middle and only the chimney and adjacent wall still stood. Leo had saturated the ground around the Lodge with the hose and they could hear sirens in the distance. The island only had a small volunteer fire department, so they wouldn't be able to do more than just prevent the fire from spreading to the nearby trees. The Lodge was gone. As one of the fire trucks came down the drive, Ledger started the boat engine. It turned over easily and he called the fire department on his phone.

"Hey, this is Ledger Elliot. I'm at the Crowley Lodge. I have the owner Iris safely on my boat. We were out on a night ride when it went up. There was no one inside. Take down my number in case you need to reach her."

He hung up and glanced around. He'd been so caught up in everything he had spaced an important detail. Panic rose in his chest.

"Roar?" he asked, his voice tight with worry.

Iris chuckled and shook her head. "She's fine. I'd never leave her. I didn't have a chance to let her out before... well. Let's not go there."

She went over to the corner of the boat where she'd put her bag and unzipped it. A very pissed-off, small, orange being peered its head out and hissed. Ledger laughed and pulled her out. She stared at him angrily, then sensed the change in him. Her fur settled and she watched up from her large, golden eyes. She began to purr loudly and he wrapped her around his neck. She burrowed into his hair. They were at peace with each other again. All was forgiven.

"There now, little one. It's all okay. Onto the next adventure, right?" Ledger mumbled into her fur.

Iris slid her arm around Ledger's waist. "I hope not. I could live a life with no adventure. Maybe a little place on an island with just the three of us."

"That's fair. Maybe a dog or two."

"Maybe. Right now, I need to rest and convince myself I'm not crazy."

"If you are, then we are together."

"Is your family okay?" Iris asked, peering at the beach where they'd last seen them.

"Iris, they're your family now, too. They're alright. Safe. Leo is taking them by boat upstate to a place of his. Once we're ready, we can meet them there. Figure out where to go from there. Mom says she thinks she's done with the island."

"What about you?"

"I've been done. I just needed to bring you with me. If Mom sells the house, she'll have enough to retire. Duff only came back because of us. Leo trained a replacement and he often talked about moving upstate. All the pieces just needed to fall into place. Admittedly, not how I imagined but here we are," Ledger replied, staring at the plume of black smoke rising in the air.

He'd heard once that the odor of a burning house smelled terrible because of all of the plastic and chemicals humans use in their everyday lives. But this fire smelled like the earth taking back what was its own. Almost a freshness, a cleansing. The Lodge was nothing but the bones of which it had been built. The evil and power behind it diminished to ash. Eventually, even that would be reclaimed by the ground beneath it.

They eased the boat out of the channel onto open water, once they confirmed nothing was left of the Lodge except the chimney. The smoldering pile of rubble of what it had once been was oddly satisfying and it no longer held any control over Iris. She was finally released. The police called shortly after daybreak to talk to Iris. She confirmed she had left with Ledger for a night boat ride. Yes, they were dating. No, no one was in the home.

Did she suspect foul play or think anyone had anything against her?

She mentioned a handyman she'd hired, who she'd refused romantically, and how he wasn't happy about it. Threatened her and stormed off. Oh, and a guest who'd shown up unannounced after the reservation had been canceled and yelled at her about it. She'd sent them to the hotel, maybe they could check there? She hadn't seen the handyman since he left the day she turned him down. Doyle something or other. She'd paid him in cash and spaced his name. He'd always made her uncomfortable. Didn't like her cat.

So, it gave the police some things to work with, but nothing they could actually track down. They asked if she was okay, did she need anything? They could call the Red Cross, do a donation drive. Small towns are like that. People will come out of the woodwork to help a neighbor in need. Iris assured them she was alright and didn't need anything at the time. Ledger's family would take care of her in the meantime. The Elliot family? Yep, good folks. Old island family. The police told her to reach out for anything and they'd try to track down the handyman and guests. They were glad she was safe.

Once the sun was in the sky, they got out to open water and dropped the anchor. Both were exhausted and needed to sleep. They climbed down into the cabin and lay in the small bed. Despite every bone in their body aching, they held each other and made love. It was different this time. Fragile and delicate. Ledger rested his elbows on either side of her and they kept their eyes locked as if to remind themselves, and each other, they were one. They moved slowly together and as they let go, their eyes allowed their souls to combine into each other.

They slept for hours, through the day and into the next. Roar joined them, a little orange puff of fur between them. The waves rocked gently, soothing them like a baby in the womb. Neither moved except to shift in their sleep or reach out to confirm the other was still there. The sleep was dreamless and heavy. A thick quilt of protection covering them, allowing them to heal and recover.

They'd each died and come back to life. Brought back by external powers intended to pit one against the other, but they found resilience in fighting together. Though Ledger had to convince Iris he was against her, deep down in her soul she'd still known it couldn't be true. Just true enough to convince anything outside of them she was in danger. All the forces against them stood no chance against the one thing it had not bargained for. Their undying love and need for each other.

They were one.

CHAPTER THIRTY-ONE

*L*edger was woken up by Roar's insistent meows. She was tired of sleeping and was hungry. It was dark out. They'd been sleeping for two days. He checked on Iris who was still asleep. She was so beautiful curled up in the blankets. Her hair was a tangled mess around her and she was breathing lightly with her mouth slightly open. He brushed her cheek with his fingers and she smiled in her sleep. Roar made biscuits on his leg to remind him she was waiting. He watched Iris for a moment, not wanting to leave her side but Roar's nails were starting to dig in deeper. If he ignored it for too long, she'd draw blood. He detached her claws from his leg and sighed.

"Alright, alright, you little beast."

He scooped her up and took her out of the cabin. He'd loaded the boat with supplies, knowing if they succeeded at their task they wouldn't be going back anytime soon. He dug through bags and found the cat food. He poured Roar some fresh water and filled her bowl until it was overflowing. She purred loudly and set to devouring the food, no longer interested in his presence. Ledger glanced around at the expanse of ocean and yawned. It had always been home. He didn't know where they'd go but the sea was home, it would be somewhere there. The water was a barrier between them and the other world. A breeze kicked up and he felt something on it. Something heavy. He headed toward the cabin when he heard the voice. Soft, sad. He was afraid to turn around when he heard it again.

"Help me, please."

The hair rose on his neck and he turned slowly to where he heard it from. On the back of the boat, sitting on the bench was a girl no older than fourteen or fifteen. Her clothes suggested she was from a different time than the one they were in. She was wearing a flowered dress that fell below her knees. Her deep brown hair was pinned up in the front but loose in the back. Her large, blue eyes met his and held there. She reminded him of Iris. She was the girl from the picture, the girl from the dock, the girl Duff had seen in the woods. She was the missing girl. The one brought to the island, who never left. He didn't know how to help her and he was afraid. He knew he needed to figure out a way to set her free.

"What's your name?" he asked, his voice gentle and protective.

"Bess. Do you know me?"

Ledger shook his head. "No. I mean, sort of. You were brought to the Lodge by someone, right? What happened to you there?"

Bess put her head down and began to sob. She shook her head. "They hurt me. The men. She, the lady there, had them take me to a room and they did things to me. They tortured me.

They left me for a while, but I knew they were coming back. I couldn't let them hurt me anymore. I found one of their belts and put it around my neck. I climbed to the edge of the bed and fastened it on the iron light fixture and stepped off. The next thing I remember, I was in the woods. I tried to find someone but no one could see or hear me. It's been like that for..."

She stopped and stared up at Ledger. She shook her head. She didn't know. She'd been wandering the woods for decades and no one could save her. Bess had said "she" had the men take her to the room. Iris's great-great-aunt. She really was evil. They'd raped Bess, tortured her, and were coming back for more. She'd done the only thing she could to save herself. They must have found her and buried her. Or dumped her body somewhere out in the woods. She was nothing to them, just a convenience.

Ledger felt rage flood through his body. Like Iris, she was disposable to them. All the girls they'd brought to that place had been. The sick people running the Lodge had used the girls' vulnerability against them. He wanted to help Bess but didn't know what to do.

"Bess, I'm sorry. I don't know how to help," Ledger replied, frustrated.

"I do."

Ledger turned and saw his father standing beside him. He was watching Bess with compassion and concern. His father moved over to Bess and sat next to her. She stared at him and her face wrinkled in recognition.

She drew back, not wanting to be near him.

"I know you. You brought me there. You ran the boat that brought us there."

Ledger's father nodded and hung his head. "I did. I didn't know what they were doing to you girls. I was wrong for my part in it and I'm sorry, Bess."

She watched him, confusion crossing her face. "How can you help me?"

"I can take you home, away from there."

"Home? I never truly had one. I was a runaway when they found me on the streets. My mother died and my father was not a good man. I ran away to be safe. I don't have a home to go back to."

"No, your true home. A place where all of your wounds will be healed and you won't ever suffer again. Do you understand? You died, Bess, and were trapped at the Lodge. You're free now. You can go home where you'll be loved and cherished. No one will ever hurt you again, I promise you that. Do you trust me?" He put his hand out to her. She stared at his hand and then at Ledger for reassurance.

Ledger nodded. "Bess, that is my father. He also killed himself when he realized what was going on, what happened there. By accepting his hand to go, you'll set both of you free and put the past to rest."

Bess frowned, then nodded. For whatever reason, she trusted Ledger. She turned to face Ledger's father. "I forgive you."

She took his hand and like dandelion seeds leaving the stem, they started to become part of the air around them. Ledger's father met his eyes and smiled.

"Ledger, you are the man I should've been. I'm so proud of you. And Duff. You are all I ever needed. I wish I had known that then. You are my legacy."

"Dad..." Ledger didn't have words to say. He was saying goodbye to his father again and his throat tightened.

"I know, Ledge. We'll be together again one day. Until then, love your life, your family. It's a gift. I wish I'd understood that. Please tell your children about me."

With that, they were gone. Ledger wanted to tell him that Iris couldn't have children but something in him knew that had changed. Iris could. *They* could. The wrongs had been righted and she was healed. At that moment, he knew they needed to go back to the island one last time. He pulled up the anchor and headed back toward the marina. Once he had service, he made a call. By the time they docked at the island, the sun was making its way into the sky and he gently woke Iris up.

"Hey," she murmured.

"Hey. Will you marry me?" Ledger asked, taking her hand firmly in his.

"Of course, I will."

"I mean, right now."

Iris sat up and pushed her hair out of her face. "Huh? How?"

"We're at the dock of the island. I called in a few favors. We just need to run by city hall and pick up our license, then go to the church. Sandy is waiting for us. Will you marry me today? Please, Iris?"

Iris nodded and rubbed her eyes. "Okay."

They gathered their things and put on their best clothes, which were what they had on the boat. Ledger wore jeans and a blue button-down shirt. Iris wore a light blue skirt and a white peasant blouse. They loaded Roar up and made sure they had what they needed for the license. City Hall wasn't open yet when they got there but Ledger had called ahead. Brenda pulled up and climbed out of her car, yawning.

"You owe me one, Ledger," she teased, fumbling with her keys.

"I know I do," Ledger replied, knowing in truth he'd saved the island from a dark fate they had no idea about and knew they were good. His debt had been paid. His family's generational slate was clean.

By the time they had the license in hand, they were both a bundle of nerves and headed for the church. Ledger made a quick stop in the pharmacy, which also served as a gift shop, and held a small bag in his hand when he came out. Iris cocked her head at him. He grinned and kissed her forcefully on her cheek.

"You'll see."

They made it to the church and the minister, Sandy, greeted them at the door. "You ready?"

"Yes!" they both replied at once, then laughed. The church was lit only by a few candles and an organ player was performing a song as they walked in. Sandy turned to them, smiling.

"I figured you need a witness and music is always nice for a wedding, so I called Jenny in."

Ledger recognized Jenny, the cashier from the general store, and waved at her. She smiled and nodded as she continued to play. They walked to the front of the church to take their places, facing each other as Sandy handed Iris a bundle of freshly picked flowers.

"You need a bouquet, right?"

Iris blushed, tipping her head in gratitude. "Thank you so much for thinking of us."

Sandy grinned and leaned forward to them. "It's the least I could do for the people who just may have saved humanity, and at least saved the island."

Ledger busted out laughing, shaking his head. "Well, when you say it like that..."

Sandy winked and took out her book. She started reading from it, talking about marriage and the sanctity of two souls becoming one. She read about love and commitment. She spoke about friendship and tough times. By the time she got to the vows, all three of them were teary. She asked Ledger if he promised to honor and protect Iris as long as he lived. He let tears roll down his cheeks as he met Iris's eyes.

"I do. And for eternity," he replied as he slipped the adjustable metal and sea glass ring he'd bought at the pharmacy onto Iris's finger.

Sandy asked Iris the same. Ledger handed her the other matching ring he'd bought and she smiled, meeting his eyes.

"I do. And for eternity," she replied and slipped the ring on his finger.

Sandy hardly announced them man and wife before they were clinging on to each other and kissing through salty tears. Jenny played an upbeat song as Sandy signed the certificate. Jenny signed as a witness and once the paperwork was finalized, Ledger barely was standing with relief and disbelief. The tiny girl he met that day on the docks, peering at him through her glasses with big blue eyes was his wife. And would one day be the mother of their children. It seemed all too unreal. Iris grasped his hand tightly, meeting his eyes, her own large and wet.

"I always knew, you know?"

"Knew what?" Ledger asked.

"This."

Ledger leaned down and kissed her. He had, too. Maybe not on the surface, but deep down he never doubted. He didn't know if he should tell her what his father said, and end up setting her up for disappointment. He drew back and stared at her. No matter what, they had each other... and Roar. Plus, Duff, Leo, and his mother. They were all family and needed no more secrets between them. He cleared his throat.

"I have something to tell you. It may not come to anything, but it might."

"Okay?"

"My father. I saw him again on the boat when you were sleeping. He came to right the last wrong. He told me you and I would have children." He watched her face to make sure what he told her wouldn't cause her any pain. She smiled and placed her hand on his cheek.

"Oh, we will. One way or another, Ledger. I know that. You were meant to be a father. I've always known that. For now, I have you. You have me. It's more than I ever thought could happen. Right now, all I want is to find a small island, build a fire, and begin my life with my husband. And our temperamental cat."

Ledger grinned and felt the tips of his ears get hot.

He now was someone's husband. No, not only someone's. He was Iris's husband. His purpose may have been to come to stop what was happening through the Lodge. To stop what Iris was bringing. To stop Iris. But it wasn't Iris he needed to stop, it was to protect her from what was holding her hostage. To set her free from the demons who were tormenting her.

To allow her to have a life where she wasn't a pawn in a sinister game. Where her existence was her own. Finally, he knew his purpose was to build a life with Iris. For them to save each other.

Now, they were both free.

EPILOGUE

*T*he new bridge onto the island was completed within three years of the Lodge burning to the ground. It crossed the channel and brought traffic in over where the Lodge had once reigned. Now, the Lodge was nothing but a shadow under the concrete. Its memory and power encased in cold, hard cement. Iris sold the land to the county for the bridge, making sure the area with snails became a protected area. A walking bridge parallelled the driving bridge and a garden was planted around the fragile snails to prevent their home from being destroyed. A plaque was placed there to explain their existence and plight, along with a dedication to Ledger's father and his family's history on the island.

With the new bridge came commerce, and Ledger's childhood home sold almost immediately. The ferry still ran daily, but more to outer islands and for tourists who wanted the experience, so Leo was able to retire to his home upstate. With Ledger's mother. They married in a quiet ceremony with just family and an orange cat. Ledger's mother got allergy shots, so she could hold her furry grandchild.

Duff graduated college and met a nice person to move in with. They were close in a way people who are not bound by societal rules can be, though Duff wasn't one to talk much about it. But Ledger saw and it made him happy to see Duff happy.

After the wedding, Ledger and Iris escaped to an uninhabited island until they ran out of supplies. On the final day, they sat by the fire and talked about the future. Where to go, what to do. The options were limitless. Iris still had money, so they went to the mainland, loaded up supplies, and took the boat down the coast to see something different. After a few months, they knew what they wanted.

Iris put the land from the Lodge on the market and they made an offer on a small island for sale. The county quickly made an offer on the Lodge land, having eyed it for years for a bridge. Ledger and Iris moved out to their island and started building. It was slow going since they could only haul out what fit on the fishing boat and spent the winter months with Leo. By the time the bridge was built, so was their small home. It all seemed to make sense. They brought out chickens and sheep, then planted a garden. Roar was joined by a very rambunctious mixed hound puppy, who she was happy to keep in line. They named him Howl.

He fit his name well.

Three years after the Lodge burned and the bridge was finalized, Ledger and Iris were standing on the shore of their tiny island, reflecting back on their life since they'd met. Howl was running through the waves, his long wet ears flopping back and forth. They laughed when he spooked himself and yelped as he jumped over a wave.

Ledger leaned in and kissed Iris's cheek. "Maybe another dog?"

"Maybe," she murmured. "I'm sure Howl would like a pal to play with. Then again if he can just wait another seven or so months, he'll have a lifelong pal."

Ledger frowned and stared at her. "How's that?"

"Well, I guess seven months and until it starts to crawl, right?" she replied cryptically.

"It? Iris, what on earth are you talking about?" Ledger asked, shaking his head.

"I mean, I don't know the gender yet. I'm talking about our baby."

Ledger stared at her and she smiled slyly. He tried to read her face. "Our baby? Seven months? Wait..."

As it dawned on him, Iris began to laugh and placed his hand over her lower stomach. Ledger felt warmth, almost an energy, coming from her and his eyes grew wide. She nodded. He grabbed her close and buried his face in her hair. Was it true?

"Our baby?"

"Yes, Ledge."

He pulled back just as Howl ran up to them and shook water droplets all over them. Ledger grabbed a stick and threw it into the surf and Howl bolted after it. Ledger pictured a child playing on the beach and grinned. By standing up and fighting against the Lodge and its sinister intent, he and Iris had ended up here and were now adding to their family. They both suffered as children and lost their childhoods to find each other as adults. They trusted each other and won. He couldn't have done it without Iris, without his family, without Leo. He'd no doubt this child would be special.

Any child that came into their lives would be powerful, a fighter. No, a warrior. None of them were normal, they all carried a power within them. They were called to this world to change it. He knew this meant they'd need to stay alert, to pay attention to when they were called. Shortly after leaving the island, a letter showed up in their post office box they checked when they went to the mainland. No return address. When they opened it, Ledger grinned at the two scrawled lines on the thick paper.

I am proud of you, son. We are glad to have you in our fight.

Doc

The doctor had survived. Relief washed over Ledger when he read those words. They weren't alone in the world. The side they were on had protectors, guides, and observers. His family would be okay no matter what came their way. Or what they sought out to set right.

Ledger wrapped his arms around Iris, drawing her tightly against him. His other half, his reason. He rested his head on hers and sighed. "You know this is just the beginning, right? We still have work to accomplish."

Iris leaned back and met his eyes.

"I do."

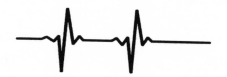

Acknowledgments:

To my mother who was the first to introduce me to true horror, not gore. She had me read Shirley Jackson's *The Lottery* at the tender age of eleven and it forever changed how I saw the world.

To all of the writers who know how to chill to the bone and don't fall to party tricks. I've had many a sleepless night trying to convince myself nothing was under my bed and the shadow in the corner was just my coat.

To all the teachers who encouraged my writing throughout the years. Your guidance and words of support helped me to believe I had something to say.

To Lizzy, Justin, Austin, and others who were willing to read and give me feedback on my first horror novel!

To Chebeague Island, Maine, and its residents. My summers there showed me a whole different world and the simplicity of life on the island has shaped my own desire for a simple life.

To my readers, your reviews, feedback, and encouragement is amazing and fuels my fire!

More from Juliet Rose:

Contemporary/Literary Fiction out now:

Do Over
We Don't Matter
Prick of the Needle

To be released:

Horror

Carrying the Dead - 2023

Literary Fiction:

Trigger Point - September 2022
Catch the Earth - 2023

Thank you so much for taking your time to read my novel!
Please feel free to leave a review for this and other books on
online retailers, Goodreads, and other review sites. You can
follow me on my website **authorjulietrose.com**, which has
links to my books, my social media, events, interviews, and
my email.

Made in the USA
Columbia, SC
21 March 2023

13899707R00186